BOY IN BLUE

BY

S R KAY

Boy in Blue

www.1889books.co.uk

ISBN: 978-1-915045-29-4

Author's Note

Boy in Blue is based on a true story. The latter events in the story can be read about in newspapers of the time. It remains, however, a work of fiction so the motivations and true characters of those involved, most of whom actually existed, can only be surmised. More background can be found at www.1889books.co.uk/boy-in-blue

Prologue

On a northward tramp for work in the woollen mills you may pause to take in the view of your destination and a draw or two on your clay pipe. As the stinging smoke rises in the cold air, your eyes may pick out through the winter's mists what you could be forgiven for thinking was Windsor Castle over on the hill. But you have not taken a wrong turn: the inhabitants of this citadel are of a different kind. Within the stone curtain walls are four huge halls radiating out; the whole forming the shape of a monstrous stone starfish with two lost limbs not yet re-grown. In this stronghold beneath imposing soot-blackened turrets the Diamond Queen secures at her pleasure those fruits of her Empire that are best left to rot, or, once plucked from the gallows-tree with its adder-bitten root, become no more than a stain wiped clean beneath the walls, in smouldering, unmarked, caustic graves. This is Armley gaol.

It is the time of chapel. Bodies have marched, three yards apart, through the iron city to receive their daily dose of spiritual consolation. No word can be spoken, no orders are barked, the whole machine moves to the clock and the bell, today as every day.

In a ground floor cell in Hall B a young man sits on his plank bed and rocks. He is not for chapel today.

It is hard to make him out in the gloom, the only light coming from the outer hall through a dirty ground glass window above the door, and, barely penetrating the barred window, dawn light from one of those December days which makes you wonder whether the sun ever really made it above the horizon.

His clothes are the same ones he had on four months ago except for his prison boots and socks – gifted by a warder with a residual grain of humanity, from a dead man – his own having fallen apart. He is cold. He shivers. He pulls his knees up and rocks.

'Mother…'

His brown hair has grown long and hangs in untidy snakes; his brow is furrowed.

'Mother?'

His nails are chewed and sore.

'Mother. Let me out please, Mother. It's dark in here and I'm scared, Mother. I didn't mean it.'

He gets up. Still six short steps from the iron clad door to the wall. He looks up, but this window was like the others: no sky to be seen, no connection with the world outside.

Six steps back across the hard stone floor, his toes sore from chilblains. He pauses. His penetrating blue eyes flash left and right behind long lashes. He puts his palms over his ears.

'Leave me alone. I am not that thing you say. Leave me alone. I've done nothing wrong. I didn't know I was doing wrong. Please don't hurt me again. Please.'

He squats on the floor and rocks himself again.

His body jerks upright. He reaches up and picks the bible off the solitary shelf. He turns to John chapter thirteen, stains from tears streaking the grime of his gentle face. He tears the page out and puts it in his mouth; chews and swallows, placing the book back where he found it.

He smooths down his hair with both hands.

'Mother, when will father be home? Will he ever come back to us? I'm sorry, Mother.'

A key turns in the lock and the door swings open admitting light into the gloom.

'Get up, you foul beast,' say the thick side whiskers under the peaked cap. 'Justice awaits,' he adds with a grin.

Kilroy struggles to his feet.

Chapter One

John

I thanked Father O'Sullivan as I stepped out into the bright clear light of a spring day; a shower of rice, wheat and barley bouncing off my shoulders the only precipitation of the day, my eyes straining after the sombreness inside St Patrick's. On my arm: Annie, in her simple ivory dress trimmed with white lace, holding a bouquet made of cherry blossom and primulas. Prettier than I'd ever seen her before, looking around her and smiling at the small gathering on the pavement. Everyone spilling out, cautious of their shoes, onto the compacted mud of Darley Street. She looked up at me then, with warmth in her eyes. I bent down and touched her soft cheek with my lips. Smelt her smell. She was indeed pretty and would make a most suitable wife for me. I was sure of it. There were prettier girls around, but I'd known Annie of old and it was the gentlemanly thing to do, to make up for my past mistakes. And she had behaved so properly and decently in agreeing to leave her family and life behind and come and share my life with me here in what they called the "Heavy Woollen District" of Yorkshire.

Our party headed off for refreshments at the Queen Hotel overlooking the green, breaking into small groups of friends or relatives.

'I wish we could have married in Sheffield so that more of our family could have been here,' Annie said.

'We've been over that – you know I couldn't get time off duty – the Inspector wouldn't allow it. Anyway your mother, and Mary and Virginia, made it.'

We walked a little further.

'John, do you think my father will be looking down on us and smiling?' she said.

I squeezed her hand, so tiny in mine, like a child's. 'I expect so.' I said.

'He would have loved so much to have given me away himself.'

I took out my silk handkerchief and wiped away her tears. A good job she didn't know how I'd come by that handkerchief. A packet had arrived at the office a few months back addressed simply "to the best looking single policeman in the force." When it was opened there was no accompanying note, just the silk handkerchief. It was nearing two o' clock, the time when the second relief came on, so the office was quite busy. Sergeant Hebron had waved the handkerchief around saying: 'this clearly wasn't meant for me.'

There had been much amusement. Love and Ashbourne, two other coppers on the relief, both tried to lay claim to it.

'You may well spout off about your prowess with the ladies, 182, but, the fact is, my terrier is better looking than you, and anyway you're hitched now; and, 174, even your mother would probably concede your only asset is height.'

I had laughed along, but when the sergeant said, 'No, give it to pretty boy over there,' nodding in my direction, I knew I'd gone bright red and was now the butt of the joke. I'd stuffed that handkerchief away in a drawer and only found it again when I was getting ready for the wedding that morning after I'd finished duty.

Annie stroked the ivory handkerchief. 'Thank you, John,' she said, squeezing my hand back. 'Where did you get it? It is beautiful?'

'Ah… that – it was a present.'

My mother and father walked in front of us. Thank God I'd got my looks from my mother. At nigh on six feet tall I towered over them both – something I'm sure my father resented from the moment I outgrew him – former Sergeant Martin Higgins of Sheffield City Police, surpassed by his useless son. That useless son: now walking tall next to his bride. I felt proud, I thought Annie must be feeling proud of me too, and feeling lucky – she had married a policeman on twenty-nine and tuppence a week, broad shoulders, golden slightly wavy hair, blue eyes, good teeth and a fine moustache.

Drinks, sandwiches and pork pie were followed by a few speeches in the lounge bar of The Queen. My father gave a toast. He was never one to let such an occasion to hear his own voice go begging. 'Having spent thirty-five years in the force myself and appreciating the value of up'olding law and order, I must say how proud I am that my prodigal son has returned, so to speak. I was concerned at his first choice of career, but he has now settled into that most honourable of professions.'

There was a cheer from those members of West Riding Constabulary present.

'I am also relieved that he has found himself a lovely wife to keep him on the straight and narrow and to look after him – I was starting to think that somehow the bachelor life suited him too well and that he would never settle down and give us grandchildren. Well done, Annie, for finally nailing him down. Your patience paid off.'

It was a short cab ride up Westgate and Frost Hill from Heckmondwike to Liversedge. Neither of us spoke much on the way. Annie sighed.

'What's the matter, Annie love?' I said.

'Nothing. It's just so much has happened so suddenly. And I shall miss mother and my sister terribly. I think I shall go to see them onto their train tomorrow.'

'I'm back on duty at six in the morning, so you'll have to go on your own.'

We fell into silence again, me worrying what Annie would make to my lodgings and its sparse furnishings. I also felt queasy about my responsibilities that night, and what I was expected to do and how a new bridegroom was expected to behave. How could it be gentlemanly? I'd no doubts that everything worked down there – if anything too well; I had battled with my sin.

I was now doing the right thing, though – taking control over my weakness. I looked at Annie. She was gazing at the passing street, looking thoughtful. I did not want to cause her any pain. She could so easily have said no to my offer of marriage after the way I'd behaved towards her.

Mrs Shaw was going to make the room tidy and put clean sheets on the bed. On night duty the week before I had been on my beat and heard a noise down an alley; I had crept down and shone my bullseye and illuminated a pair of white buttocks pinning a woman up against a wall. The couple had then scurried off after rearranging clothes – she was not a known prostitute so I didn't pursue them, not believing there to have been an offence. I had seen so much more of life in that last year than I had in the previous twenty-seven. Behind all those doors I imagined the crimes and sins that were being committed: gambling, drunkenness, assaults, larceny; I had seen them all being escorted to the station. I had washed their blood off my hands, blood from broken noses and wounds. The night ahead came back into my mind. I had heard there could be blood – I didn't want that. Couldn't bear the idea.

The cab driver deposited Annie's things onto the path leading up to the front door and pocketed the shilling I gave him. I wasn't sure if he'd expected more. He wasn't very personable. I stood before the door to the house then pushed it open. Annie held out her arms like a child wanting to be picked up. She wasn't particularly heavy. I felt her breath on my neck making the hairs stand on end as I carried her in, this life in my arms, the closest contact I had ever had with her – I had only held hands and kissed her gently before.

'I'd best not try to carry you up the stairs,' I said.

I opened the door to my room on the first floor, overlooking the street, and went in. Annie held back. She took a step forward as I held out my hand to her. Some primulas, like in her bouquet, a thoughtful touch of Mrs Shaw, stood out shockingly on the washstand. It was then I realised, for the first time, that there was nothing in my room that was not functional and drab. And it was dominated by the brutal cast iron bedstead. There was little that could be described as decorative – even the wash jug and basin were plain in colour and undecorated, and what pattern there had been on the oilcloth on the floor was almost indistinguishable.

'I'm sorry it's not grander,' I said.

'Oh, I'm not used to grand. It will do just fine – until we can find somewhere better.'

I felt I had made an awful mistake in bringing her here and not finding somewhere we could call our own; somewhere that wasn't just a bed with a room.

'Well, it's no longer mine but ours – so you must feel free to make whatever improvements you like. I'll get someone to help bring your box up.'

When I returned with the box I found her sat on the chair with her back to me, looking out of the window onto the field opposite. I stood beside her and placed my hand on her shoulder: she didn't respond – if anything she stiffened. The hawthorn bushes at the edge of the field were coming into bud.

'They'll have May blossom on them soon,' I said.

She didn't reply. I looked down and saw her cheeks were wet.

'Annie love, whatever is the matter?'

'Nothing. I am happy. It's just everything at once – a lot to take in – all the emotions of the day.'

I put my uniform on in the dark the next morning, and it was only when I came to shave that I lit a candle: the light woke Annie and she started, sitting up in bed, ghostlike in her white nightdress.

'I'm sorry, I didn't want to wake you.'

She rubbed her eyes. 'Can I see you in your tunic?'

'Let me shave first.' I didn't want to get shaving soap on it.

I put on my tunic and fastened the silver buttons.

'And your helmet.'

I stood to attention before her, like I was on parade.

'Very smart,' she said.

I crept out of the room, down the stairs, out of the front door and breathed the cool morning air. My first night sharing a bed. There had been no blood, so far as I could tell. Annie had been kind to me. 'It didn't hurt,' she said. It hadn't lasted long – not what I had expected – not the act I had heard spoken of in triumphal tones. If anything I had felt shame and disgust at using a woman that way. Perhaps things would be easier now. I needn't feel so self-conscious.

We had eaten shepherds' pie in the dining room with Mr and Mrs Shaw, their daughter, and one of the coarse, stout little miners. I felt that all eyes were on us, as if they were all thinking what would happen that night. Godfrey Shaw, the owner of the house let the attic room to fellow miners from Strawberry Bank colliery: three of them, little more than kids. They slept on two mattresses on the floor, their shifts always meaning they had a bed to themselves, unless there was a strike or a lockout.

On my way to the police office I met PC Love.

'Tha looks tired, Higgins. Kept thi up all night did she? Why she did – tha's gone all red! I'd have never had thi down for the marrying type.'

I didn't reply but ducked under Love's arm as the door was held open for me. The sergeant made a similar joke and said that in order to save me my energy I was being detailed to fixed point duty on the corner of Station Lane and Huddersfield Road.

'And try to stay awake, Higgins,' he barked.

I always hated point duty: staying alert, or rather looking as if you were alert, waiting for something to happen, rendering assistance to the public, keeping a lookout for criminals and keeping the traffic moving. At least on the beat you got to see the scenery change and always had the challenge of spotting a gambling ring or arresting a vagrant.

Nothing ever happened on fixed point duty: the runaway horses never seemed to go past when I was on duty. I longed to see one so I could run alongside and bring it under control before it careered into a mother and her children. That way I would get a silver merit badge and perhaps ten shillings off the chief constable. Stood there I wouldn't be able to improve my charge rate. It had been noted that I hadn't made any arrests lately. The most excitement I was likely to get was being taunted by the local ruffians on their way to school, and perhaps getting one of them back.

I listened to the drone of the carpet mills and watched one or two stragglers hurrying through the gates to avoid getting into trouble. Eight o'clock went by and the shop deliveries start to arrive. I ran through in my mind the report I would write if that grocer's cart collided with a runaway hansom.

'I beg to report that at…' I pulled my watch out of my pocket: precision is everything, '…eight thirty-five a.m. on Friday the ninth of April inst (I still don't know what "inst" means but it is what you always write) a collision occurred at the junction of Huddersfield Road and Wakefield Road. PC 188 Higgins brought the horse under control, then sent for a veterinary surgeon…'

'Excuse me, officer. May you direct a young lady to the railway station please?' a voice said.

It was Annie, in her straw hat, basket on her arm, beaming up at me.

'I'm going to catch the train back to Heckmondwike so that I can see mother and our Mary off. Then I said I'd do some shopping for Mrs Shaw on the way back. You look terribly fierce stood there.'

I felt a little annoyed at this unexpected incursion of domestic life into my duty. I tried to gather myself and speak in the right way.

'Of course, Madam – up this street here and to the left as soon as the road bends,' I said, and tried a smile. 'Say farewell to them from me as well. Don't let Mrs Shaw take advantage of you, will you.'

'Oh, it's all right. I'm pleased to help. It gives me something to do. I've cleaned the room and put some of my things out; it's not like I've much to do.'

'I'm sorry, Annie. I mustn't get caught chatting or I'll get put on a report.'

'Oh, John, surely not for passing a few pleasantries with your new wife.'

'You don't know what they're like, Annie love. Do take care. I'll be home before three o'clock.'

I watched as she bustled off up Station Lane, thinking how she was now mine! I smiled. I felt very lucky. She had behaved so normally, as if the night before hadn't happened – and to think I could do it again when the fancy took me. Perhaps that doctor had been right. Perhaps all that was behind me now.

Chapter Two

I had had various jobs since leaving school: working as a butcher's boy, and then as a telegraph boy. I was the oldest child and destined to follow in my father's bootsteps: maintaining the law and trying to get some order back into society. I had never questioned that – it was what boys did, follow their fathers to the steelworks or down the pit – until one day I had had an argument with my father.

I had been up in Ranmoor delivering a telegram up a long drive to a house where I had not received a tip. I had stood smiling at the woman but she just looked at me, cold-faced, and closed the door. It only seemed right, when seeing some apples over a wall, that I should scale it and reach out to take a few for my pockets. My father later discovered them, and, suspecting their means of acquisition, subjected me to one of his police interrogations. The apples were seized as evidence and later destroyed – such a stupid waste. He'd blustered and threatened to get the truth out of his suspect, but I insisted that they were a gift. He seethed because he had no evidence to the contrary. I was sixteen and already looked down on my father; though I was still only slightly built. I was sent to my room without my tea until I would tell the truth. The stand-off lasted for weeks, neither of us able to retreat from the position we had taken.

'I'll take my belt to that boy,' he'd shouted.

'Just try it and I'll use it on thi,' I muttered back, not quite sure of myself.

'What did you say!' he raised his hand but I grabbed it.

It was probably only the intervention of my mother that stopped me getting hurt – I was physically not yet a match for my father.

To spite Sergeant Higgins, I took a job as an under-gardener at a big house belonging to one of the city's steel barons and vowed *I* would never become such a snoop into other people's business.

I had no real desire to be a gardener, other than to get revenge on my father's hopes, but I soon found that I took to it. It was the physicality – of climbing and lopping branches, of keeping nature under control, of digging and planting and watching things grow – that gave me pleasure. I was outside and I more or less determined my own work rate. And I enjoyed mashing tea for myself and old Art, the gardener, my boss. We had a little spirit stove in the tool shed when it was time for our tea break. I grew with the seasons too – my shoulders and jaw broadened and I let my beard grow; my face and forearms bronzed in the sun.

At about the time I came of age, instead of inquiring about the police, I applied for a job at a mansion in Broomhill, newly acquired by a successful solicitor. The garden had been neglected and this solicitor chap only took one look at the physical specimen that was Sergeant Higgins' son and decided I was just the man he needed. Looking back, I suspect what he actually saw in front of him was a boy not yet at ease in his large frame and facial hair; blond hair that an attempt had been made to tame. I was not at all like Edward, his son: in his own image. Edward, self-assured, and already feeling the world owed him something – that he had a right to his stake in life. On the contrary, that man-boy in front of him, cap in hands, losing several inches in height because of his posture, had no such sense of worth – I was one of that class of people always looking down, seeing where they could fall rather than relishing the climb. But I am getting ahead of myself.

*

It was spring when I started my work in the garden. At the front of the house were trees leading up the drive, a terrace in front of the house with steps down to a croquet lawn that was more like a meadow. Then behind the house were dilapidated greenhouses and three quarters of an acre or so of grounds sloping gently upwards through what was intended to be different themes of garden: an ornate garden for the ladies, rockeries and a grassed area, ornamental beds, and beyond that a vegetable garden and a small orchard.

It was important for the self-respect of the family to start at the front, to gain a sense of order; so I spent days with my sickle, or cutting out dandelions, raking moss, forking and sanding. All the time the back was getting wilder as spring ran ahead unleashed, and paths became blocked and beds choked. I despaired at times at the magnitude of my task and the family wanted everything at once: to be able to walk along gravel paths in the long evenings, to have vegetables grown in their own garden, to be able to wander up and pick fruit in the late summer. I cursed the rapid growth of things that shouldn't grow, and the pathetic pace of those that I wanted most. Then, as I tamed one area, the others raced away, and the greenhouses, now repaired, stood frustratingly empty.

*

It wasn't until two whole seasons had passed that I felt I was master of the garden rather than its slave. The family were now happier with my work – they could enjoy their garden: entertain guests to drinks and home-grown strawberries, and play croquet on the lawn; and as a result I was rewarded by an extra sixpence a week. The girls and their mother could walk arm in arm on the limestone chippings and brush the lavender with a trailing hand and admire the Greek-style statue of a woman draped, decently, in a robe clasped at the shoulder. I didn't see much of them – I preferred to work away from their gaze. I sometimes noticed one of the girls observing me from a back window as I bent and weeded, and, not being able to bear it, I moved to another part of the garden. There were two girls in the house, to my knowledge; at least I had seen two together with their mother on a number of occasions but whether they were the same two each time I couldn't be sure: to me they looked so similar, dressed alike and spoke alike: telling me to fetch this or that bloom for them. There was also a young boy I saw, often in a sailor suit, who liked to ride his 'horsie' on the drive and who treated me as if I were just another garden ornament.

But I had my shed as an escape. This was my domain: so much so that even the solicitor himself would knock before entering. I had made it so much my own that perhaps it felt too alien to a man more accustomed to oak panelling at home and at work. That shed of mine smelt of grease, potting compost and creosote. I had a neat workbench next to the windows whose curtains I had made from sacking nailed to the lintel, with the pretence of keeping the frost out of the shed in winter, but which I would sometimes let fall so that no one walking past could see what I was up to inside. I had an old wooden chair that I had padded using sacking and hay, and which after a while of use uniquely fitted my shape. And I had a spirit stove for making thick black tea in a tin. The tools hung on nails on a wooden partition that created, behind it, a sort of depository for untidy looking stuff that every gardener needs or can't bear to throw out.

There was also another part of the garden that was my empire. Next to my shed was a brick outhouse for coal and logs; and both backed onto the boundary wall of an adjacent house. Here the boundary wall went into a dog leg around my shed and next door's outhouses. The effect was that when I climbed onto the roof there was a sheltered spot where I could sit with my back against warm roof slates, unseen from the houses and part overlooking next-door's garden. I sometimes used to sit up there and get out my snuff box, not wanting to give myself away with smoke. I enjoyed being unseen, watching servants from next-door's going out to empty their dustpans or to take vegetable peelings out to the compost.

It was August of my third summer and I had eaten my snap: bread and cheese it usually was, and had taken my mug of tea up onto the roof for a sit before starting work again. One of the next door's maids came out, her back slightly towards me, only a dozen or so yards away. She slowly uncurled her back as she stretched up towards the white clouds drifting across the blue and she rolled her neck from side to side. She was about my age, I thought, and had her hair tied up in a white headscarf. I kept very still.

'Been bending over all morning,' she said to herself. 'Scrubbing floors and wiping furniture. Ooh!' She stretched her arms out wide, still looking out over the garden.

'Well, aren't you going to introduce yourself?' she said as if to the garden itself.

Barking mad, I thought to myself with a smile.

'Well, cat got your tongue?' She turned her head and looked straight at me.

I felt my cheeks burning, and for a brief moment I wondered whether she hadn't really seen me but was just a mad-woman.

'Well, how rude you are, you great lummox. Spying on a girl and then not even answering a question.'

'Oh, sorry,' I said. 'I didn't think you'd seen me.'

'I know; often seen you up there.'

'Have you? I thought…'

'Well, are you going to introduce yourself now you know you're not as invisible as you thought you were?'

I felt really stupid, like when at school I was made to stand on my chair that time for making a rude noise. I hadn't meant to – it took me as much by surprise as the schoolmaster.

'Yes, I'm…' I then realised that I was sitting with my legs splayed and wanted to jump up to my feet, but that would look stupid, so I slowly tried to cross my legs coolly.

'You forgotten your name?'

'Yes… no, I'm mean I'm John Higgins. I'm the gardener here.'

'Well, John Higgins, pleased to meet you. I'm Annie – Annie Cross. I'm a servant, here,' she nodded behind, 'and I'd better be getting back to it. We're supposed to shake hands at this point but that would be a bit difficult with you up there like a cat on a roof.'

'Yes. Sorry. Nice to meet you.'

'See you then.'

'Yes.'

She smiled up at me and then almost marched back in. I cringed – what a fool I must have come across as. A big, lundy fool. I finished my tea quickly and climbed down.

I spent the afternoon replaying the encounter in my head – only this time I was more suave and wasn't sat in such an ungainly position but had one leg swinging nonchalantly and my voice and manner were calm, self-assured and unapologetic. She wasn't like most girls I had met – she had been very bold, not very ladylike; indeed there was something altogether quite tomboyish about her.

The garden continued to improve. The fruit trees and current bushes held more fruit that year; my potatoes filled several crates in the store and my tomatoes had been a reasonable success. I knew by this what to do next year: start my seeds off earlier in small batches and get some nettles to make tomato feed with: a big stinky gloop in a barrel, but nothing better.

I became friends with next door's maid; she would pop out to see me at lunch time when I was on my roof, and I would snatch a few minutes of her time before she had to get back to work. I brought her the occasional strawberry or tomato, or faller from the apple tree. Annie was a good catch and although she said, 'Don't you dare, John Higgins, I'll drop it!' she didn't. She was full of praise for my skill in making things grow and said that my garden was by far the nicest in the neighbourhood from what she could tell from looking out of the top windows. Our paths never crossed out of work for some reason: it might have been our differing hours of work or that Annie hurried away on her days off to spend time with her family who lived across town.

*

The following winter was long, cruel and drawn out. Snow covered the garden for weeks on end. I had not been able to work in the garden since before Christmas and I had feared being laid off like many others I knew. I was put to work in the kitchen, fetching and carrying for the bossy cook – the kitchen boy having, unfortunately for him, but fortunately for me, gone down with pneumonia. I thought a gardener should be the equal of a cook, but I was treated like the kitchen boy, if not worse, and given jobs like clearing out the cellar. I was also given the task of eking out the coal for the boiler and the range, and supplementing it with any wood I could find: coal being in short supply given the state of the frozen canals. I had not seen Annie since a fine autumn day in early November: my roof was not a spot for cold and wet days.

It was towards the end of January that I heard of events at the house next door. I was sitting with my snap in the kitchen as close to the range as cook would allow, it being well down in the twenties outside, listening to the women's gossip.

'Topped hissen apparently. Blood and gore everywhere apparently. It were young Lizzie Clark that found him lying there. They say he was out of his mind. Never got used to being on his own – not since his wife passed away.'

'When were that then?'

'What were it? A year last November I reckon.'

'Apparently, he used to walk around the house talking to her, even though she were dead and buried.'

'Ooh, that'd give me the creeps. Just imagine!'

'He also thought he was heading for the workhouse.'

'What him, with all his money?'

'Yeah, like he hadn't a brass farthing! Just one of them paintings he has hanging up would fetch more than I'll earn in my life I shouldn't wonder.'

'What are you two prattling on about?' I asked.

'That cutler fella what lives next door at Tapton Cliffe, Collishaw… I mean lived… Done away wi' hissen.'

'So what's happening to the servants there?'

'That depends on whether there's any family that want to take it on. They say not. So it'll be sold and everyone will be laid off, I should imagine. Might keep one or two on in the meantime to keep it dusted and to stop it freezing up.'

I might not get to see Annie again, I thought. No more little chats over the wall. Only then did I realise how much I had enjoyed those chats.

Spring came eventually and I got back out into the garden and nature managed to bounce back, the daffodils seeming to come out at the same time as the crocuses: as if, having been held back, they could not wait their turn. I went up on the roof for the first time and Annie did not appear. Nor did she the times after that – the house seemed empty – the shutters were all closed and I noticed no movement.

At Easter I headed along with many others to Weston Park with a couple of lads I knew from school who lived up on Crookes. The band was playing "When I Survey the Wondrous Cross" and the warm southerly air meant that people could sit around the bandstand on the grass for the first time that year. People were out in their best clothes. For me, gone was the neckcloth and blue striped shirts I favoured in the garden. Instead I wore my grey suit, white shirt, and a clean collar and tie. On my head a dapper-looking straw hat the same as my pals. Our demeanour as we had stepped out into the street had said: "We'll turn some heads."

We stood at the edge overlooking the crowd, pointing out girls, enjoying the sun on our backs.

'Lovely day ain't it, Mr Higgins?'

I turned round and there was Annie looking up at me, smiling, her face shaded by a blue straw hat which matched her skirt and jacket.

'Hello, Annie, what are you doing here?'

'I do get to go out occasionally you know. I'm here with two of the others who used to work at Tapton Cliffe.' She indicated to two girls sat on the grass, who waved when I looked their way.

'Yes, I heard. I'm sorry about what happened.'

'Well?' she said.

'Oh, these are my old chums, Stan and Harry.' They took her hand in turn and bowed ostentatiously whilst removing their hats.

'I fancied a little turn round the park but those two wanted to stay and watch the band play. You'll take me won't you?' she said, boldly placing her hand on my arm.

Stan and Harry winked as I set off with Annie.

'What are your friends' names?' Stan called after her.

'Marie and Ellen. And they're married,' she added with a chuckle.

'Sorry about those two,' I said when we were out of earshot.

I remember her hand was so light on my arm; such small dainty hands. In contrast mine were so rough they snagged on silk ties and handkerchiefs and never came really clean. It was the first time I had seen her up close and she was already touching me. Whether it was the melody, or the atmosphere in the park, or something else, but I felt short of breath: elated and almost a little dizzy.

'So, you lost your job?'

'Yes. The young master didn't want to keep the house on, not after what happened. So it's going to be up for sale soon, so I hear.'

'I heard it was suicide.'

Annie just nodded.

'Were you there?'

'Yes. It wasn't nice. I didn't really see, but poor Lizzie, it was her who was his chamber maid, saw everything: she found him dead in his water closet. He used a double barrelled gun on his head. We all heard a noise but didn't think it was anything like that… How could he?' She took out a handkerchief and sniffed into it.

'I'm sorry. I shouldn't have mentioned it.'

We walked quietly for a while, gravel crunching underfoot, down towards the lake and stood on the little wooden Japanese bridges, squinting at the glittering water and pretending not to notice the ducks misbehaving.

'It's nice to see everyone out enjoying a bit better weather after what we've had.' This was the best I could do to break the silence, I've never been much of a conversationalist, but it worked. She told me about what she had been doing since leaving her job: she had moved in with her mother. No, she hadn't found another position. She told me about her Easter church visit with her family and asked me about my family. It suited me that I didn't have to think of much to say. I would quite happily have walked round not speaking, and, now that she had recovered herself, every time there was a break in conversation of more than a few seconds, she would come in with another question: where did I go to school, how long had I been a gardener, what did I do in my spare time and so on, and before I knew it I had somehow arranged to meet her the following week also.

The weather that week was warm but wet, but I judged it a good time to get vegetable seeds in the cold frames and bedding plant seeds into pots. I took off my jacket and hung it on a peg in my shed, rolled up my sleeves, then got on with removing the glass frames and filling the brick base with the fresh compost I had prepared in the winter. The rain fell softly; not the bad sort of rain: it felt cool on my skin and, anyhow, I always had a spare shirt to change into to go home in. I would often change out of my muddy clothes in my shed. I was whistling "When I Survey the Wondrous Cross" as I worked. I like to whistle, it is one of my accomplishments. I was looking forward to Sunday – Annie was amusing and her complete lack of feminine reticence appealed to me. She was not great-looking but that didn't matter: she was good company. I heard footsteps approaching up the path; I thought it was the solicitor. I glanced up and saw a stranger in a dark suit, holding an umbrella.

'Good afternoon to you. Higgins, isn't it?'

'Yes, sir.'

'Nice tune that one – one of my favourites.'

'Yes, sir.'

'You must call me Edward – the Old Man owns this place. Been away at Cambridge and had a spell in Northern Italy – that's why you've not seen me around. I see you've been doing a fine job on the Old Man's garden.'

'I'm getting there – slowly bringing it under control.'

'It's looking jolly fine, I'd say. I believe it was a bit of a jungle to start with. Can't believe the Old Man made you do it all by yourself. You must have had to work like a Trojan.'

I felt awkward kneeling in front of the stranger; I got up and removed my cap. The young man was shorter than me and more slightly built, dark-haired with a well-trimmed moustache and clean-shaven chin. He wore a felt hat and carried himself rather stiffly.

'Cigarette?' he said, holding out a silver cigarette case. I took one and waited as Edward struck a match and lit his own cigarette; then held out the flame for me to light mine rather than passing me the match box. I had to lean forward under the umbrella, conscious of being watched by the other man.

'So, what are you planting?'

'Cabbage seeds, broccoli seeds, lettuce: that sort of thing. I'm taking a bit of a gamble, though – it could be a bit early but I could just steal an extra week if the weather picks up, and see there: weed seeds just starting to go, so I thought it worth giving it a try. I've still got a lot to learn, though: not like some of the old hands who just know what to do, and when, by signs of nature all round them.' I was prattling on like a fool.

'I wouldn't have the faintest idea where to start; they teach one a lot up at Cambridge but not much of it any use in life. Don't let me stop you, old sport.'

I returned to my work, conscious all the time of being under the gaze of the other man. The fine rain continued to fall, making little noise upon the ground or on the umbrella.

'Don't you mind getting wet?'

'No, not really – if I did mind I'd never get anything done. And this is nice rain – soft and not cold. And I've got a change of clothes in the shed.'

'Ah, I see. Mother never used to let me out when it was raining – believed a bit of rain would be enough to finish a young chap.'

I pressed a finger into the moist compost in each pot and shook a seed carefully into the dip.

'So, where do you get your seeds from?'

'For some things I just save them from the year before. Others I buy, or rather I tell your father what I want to order and from where and he writes a cheque. This lot came by post the other week: a dozen things – onions, carrots, sprouts, broccoli and what have you – all for about a shilling. I'll be able to keep cook supplied with fresh vegetables most of the year – and the young misses supplied with fresh flowers until October.'

'Fresh flowers, pooh! But, by George, all those vegetables for a shilling!'

'Pretty much. I'm chitting various seed potatoes ready for planting too. Some went in a week or so back, under straw: I'm hoping there won't be much of a frost now.'

'And if there was?'

'The new shoots could be nipped out.'

'And that's a bad thing, right?'

'I'd say so – could lose them all. Then you'd have no earlies.'

'Good God, that would never do. Mater and Pater going without their earlies!' He laughed out loud. 'I haven't the faintest idea what you're talking about, but it's all very fascinating, and better than those awful books I'm supposed to have my head in.'

I glanced up and smiled back. I felt I was caught between looking at what I was doing and being respectful: not appearing to ignore my employer's son. But, looking up at him, I relaxed. There was something in his roguish grin and his glinting dark eyes that said this was not a man who expected protocol, the opposite in fact; it was suggestive of someone who took delight in breaking rules and conventions.

'I sometimes envy fellows like you, Higgins. Dammit, I can't call you that. What's your Christian name?'

'John.'

'Good. Yes, I envy you, John: doing proper work – seeing things take shape – things you've done with your hands, things you've made. The Old Man wants me to follow in his footsteps into his law business.'

I laughed.

'What's so funny?'

'That's exactly what my father wanted me to do – follow his footsteps into the law!' I looked up. Edward's face – eyebrow raised, an astonished look, comical, made me burst out laughing again. I gathered some breath. 'He's a copper! But I told him to stuff it.'

Edward slapped himself on the knee. 'A policeman!'

Our guffaws had attracted attention. One of the girls shouted up the garden: 'Edward, mother says you are to come in at once!' Edward pulled a serious face, then smiled at me.

'Confound the woman,' he whispered. I went back to my work.

The next day started fine: I decided to work in the ornamental garden: pulling up weeds that were starting to push up through the limestone chippings – best to catch it early. This took the best part of the day. Then I scattered some new chippings over the areas I'd disturbed. It wasn't quite home time, so I made a start on the roses: removing suckers and pruning as old Arthur had taught me. I did one bush and then the rain started again, at first not too heavy, so I carried on clipping and sawing. The dark clouds then built and let loose. I stuck it out for a while, then retreated to my shed where I removed my soaking shirt. I was just rubbing the worst off my hair with a piece of cloth when I heard the door open. Edward stood inside the doorway, his folded umbrella dripping into a pool on the brick floor.

'Thought you might appreciate a drop of this,' he said pulling a whisky bottle from his coat pocket. 'Fend off the chill.'

I quickly fumbled for my spare shirt off a nail and pulled it over my head. I felt the colour rise in my cheeks. No one had ever come right into my shed before.

'Terribly sorry old chap, didn't mean to startle you. I'll go if you'd rather.'

'No, no, it's fine. It's kind of you. I, er… would you…? There's nowhere to sit really. Except that chair. A crate'll do me. Unless you…?' I looked at my chair, it suddenly looked very shabby indeed. In fact the only thing within view that wasn't shabby was Edward.

Edward sat down and smiled, like he had just sat on the plushest of plush chairs. 'I like it in here. It reminds me of dens I used to make as a kid, out in the woods, with branches and leaves and moss for seats. It's a proper little snug.'

He put the bottle on the bench and pulled a glass from his other pocket. 'I could only fit one in my pocket,' he said, 'if you don't mind sharing.'

'I could use my mug.' I picked it off the bench, shook the dregs of tea onto the floor and passed it to Edward who poured an inch of whisky in and handed it back.

Edward raised his glass. 'Your health, sir'

'Yours too,' I returned, and offered up my stained, chipped mug to the lead crystal.

'I like the curtains, very grand.'

'Oh they're just to keep the frost off from plants I have on the bench – like those seed potatoes there.'

'Ah, I see.' Edward sat back and surveyed the place like he owned it, somewhat to my irritation: so comfortable in the chair as he cast his eye round the shed. But then, at the same time, there was a thrill in seeing someone else's pleasure in sharing what was my private space. Edward got out his cigarette case, lit one and offered it to me, then lit one for himself.

Edward drew on the cigarette, half closing his eyes and blew the smoke out of the side of his mouth. 'Your father's in the police then?'

'Was. He's recently retired – a sergeant.'

'And he wanted you to sign up?'

'Yes, but I wanted to do my own thing.'

'That's how I feel. Not sure what to do yet – but not being stuck in an office for one thing, writing contracts, or whatever it is the Old Man does – profitable though it might be. Have to make my mind up soon though. I might go out to India – see life, that sort of thing.'

I swirled the whisky round the sides of my mug: multiple tidemarks from multiple cups of tea.

'So, what do you get up to when you're not slaving away for the Old Man and getting soaked to the skin?' he said.

'There's not much time for anything really. I do get to the odd match with my pals on a Saturday.'

'Match?'

'Yes, at Bramall Lane. Though it's been a bit cold to stand and watch recently. And the pitch has been frozen solid: like playing on a paved street.'

'I've only ever seen football up at Cambridge. Not really my sort of thing. I prefer boxing – seeing two fine fellows slug it out. Done a bit myself as well, though I wouldn't want her to know – mother, that is. Speaking of the old dragon, better be getting back to my blessed dissertation before she notices and bars me from the garden – frowned upon me chatting to you before, but said I was offering advice on 'crop rotation' – don't know what the bally thing is of course, but she's not to know that. Nice chatting to you.' He slipped the glass back in his pocket. He handed me the bottle and winked. 'Hide this will you. I'll not risk getting caught next time that way.'

I met Annie by Elliot's statue in the park. I leant against it, waiting, and saw her striding purposefully towards me through the fancy entrance gates. She brandished her folded parasol at me in greeting like some crazy bandmaster. Something about her just made me smile.

'I thought I would like to look round the museum,' she said.

'That sounds a good idea – I've never had call to go in.'

We went round the galleries, looking at the collection of insects and butterflies pinned out in their glass cases, Greek and Roman artefacts and stuffed animals staring wildly as if still startled at having been caught. Annie felt sorry for them stuck in their glass prisons and made me laugh by giving voice to what she thought they would be thinking.

'If only I could bend my head a bit further and get this nut,' she squeaked when confronted by a funny squirrel with fluffy ears and an earnest expression.

She attracted looks of disapproval from gentlemen who clearly believed that scientific study should be conducted with reverence and gravity. We left to avoid getting into further bother, stifling our giggles. We patted the stuffed lion and went through to the Mappin Art Gallery where, at the entrance, we were confronted by a statue. It was a plaster model of Vulcan – the same one as at the top of the new Town Hall, but this time starkly up close. Foot on an anvil, hammer in right hand, holding aloft two arrows. Strong jawbone, muscular frame. In all his glory. I saw Annie glance up and quickly glance away again, pretending not to have seen anything – that made me smile. She bustled over to look at a landscape.

I split away from her and looked at another picture of a mountain stream, then I stepped back to better take in the large scene. Checking over my shoulder to see if there was anyone around, I stole a glance up at Vulcan. The definition of his ribs; the way that the muscles looked real; across his belly; and his thighs seemed ready to move; the curve of his abdomen, and down. I looked back at the landscape, then back at the statue. Annie caught my eye.

'The waterfall looks ever so real on this one, don't you think?' I said.

She took my arm. I shivered.

'There were paintings like these in the house,' she said. 'He loved his paintings.'

We wandered round together. Many of the paintings were similar: rural landscapes occasionally livened up by an animal or two; portraits of the well-heeled. Annie stopped in front of one of a girl sat knitting in a cottage window and outside her suitor posed, looking up at her. She squeezed my arm. But I felt repulsed by it: it was cloyingly sweet, sickly even; they looked no more than kids, and neither old enough for true feelings.

'Where's Capri, John?' she said as she read the writing on a picture of some girls winnowing corn.

'I don't know – but it's not round here.'

We looked at the picture.

'Aren't they pretty John?'

'I suppose so.'

'I think it must be Italy.'

The picture showed the bare footed girls pouring grain out of baskets onto a sheet. Two nearby pigeons had other plans. A youth just wearing breeches was scooping a pile of corn off the sheet back into a basket and another elegant youth was bringing a full basket down some steps towards them. It looked warm and languid.

'Wouldn't you like to go to Italy?' I said. 'I was talking to someone who'd been.'

'Yes, wouldn't it be wonderful. Who were you talking to?'

'Oh, Mr Edward, from the house, the eldest son.'

'Only the likes of them gets to travel. I've only been here, and Lincolnshire.'

'And that's further than I've been.'

Near to it was a picture of a small boat alongside the shore of a lake – another scene that glowed with the warmth of the end of the day. A bare-chested man lay on his front on the boat and another stretched up to fold a sail. A figure on the shore was Jesus and on the boat were James and John.

'Shall we get some fresh air,' I said. 'I've had enough of being indoors.'

After we had strolled for a bit I told her my mother was expecting me back for tea.

'Thank you for a lovely afternoon, John.'

'It was nice. I've enjoyed myself.'

She seemed to linger after she had let go of my arm.

'I'll be seeing you then, Annie,' I said.

'Yes. Goodbye, John. And thanks again.' I turned right out of the gate and headed up towards Broomhill.

Chapter Three

Spring marched on into summer and the runner beans grew almost fast enough for you to watch them: I had planted one row of red, one row of white-flowered beans in what I thought to be a rather clever, striped pattern. I supplied cook with rhubarb, gooseberries, strawberries and raspberries. My forearms and face browned in the sun. I sat on my roof and looked on the empty garden beyond, which was getting out of control despite an occasional visit from a gardener – not like having someone full time.

I received a letter from Annie – it was handed to me by the housekeeper, addressed to me at the house. It had already been opened. It was written in a neat hand on one sheet of paper. It said that she was well and that she had secured a new position, working for a widow, looking after her house for her, she was the only servant so it was a bit lonely at times, but she had her own room. She inquired after me and hoped I was well and expressed her trust that the garden was looking nice. I put the letter in my jacket hanging up on a nail.

It was a blazing hot day, and snap time meant I could take cover from the sun in my shed. I started when I saw Edward sat in my chair smoking. I hadn't seen him since Easter, that time when he had come with the whisky.

'Hello, dear boy. Wondering when you'd show.'

'Hello, Mr Edward, sir. I was just coming for my snap.'

'I see you've not touched the whisky.'

'No.'

'Like a drop?'

'No, thanks, I was just going to mash some tea.'

'Already boiled, dear boy. Just waiting for you. And I've smuggled some milk in too.' Edward produced a small jug and another cup. 'One sugar please.'

I strained the tea through my makeshift muslin tea strainer. The cheek of the man – sitting there like he owned the place. And yet, there was something in his self-satisfied, boyish smile, and his bright eyes that made me happy to see him. He could in no way be described as threatening. It was strange, but I almost felt honoured. I sat on a crate and offered one of my butties to Edward, but was relieved when he declined.

'Well, I'm a free man, John – for now anyway. Finished my Tripos. That's me done with University. Now I've got the summer ahead of me before I have to knuckle down to work.'

'So, what are you going to do with yourself?'

'Not decided yet. I might stick around here for a bit or perhaps go abroad. What would you advise?'

'I'd definitely go travelling if I had the chance. I'd love to travel – never been anywhere – unless you count Hathersage.'

'Hathersage! Is that it? Good God, man!'

'I've seen pictures of foreign places though: Italy and where-have-you. I know I'd like it.' I laughed at the ridiculousness of my position. 'You know how it is – the only way I'd get to travel is if I joined the army or navy.'

'I suppose so – and get your bloody legs blown off in the process.'

'It was the warmth in the pictures that appealed – to be so warm that you never need a jacket.'

'…that you don't need a shirt, or breeches either – except to keep the sun off. The Mediterranean is so warm you can bathe in it for hours… here, you've got something in your hair.' Edward leaned forward and pulled a piece of goose-grass out of my hair, then casually brushed it back into place with his fingers, looking me straight in the eye.

I remember I flinched a little, but instantly wished I hadn't.

'You couldn't exactly walk around looking like that – makes you look an idiot. You'd love Italian girls, they're so friendly, not all straight-laced like here, and the boys too, it's so much more… relaxed. Not so many rules and conventions, especially when you get out of the big towns.' He breathed in slowly and closed his eyes. 'I think I'll do that – follow your advice.'

I looked down at the floor.

'Don't look so glum. Tell you what, I'll bring you something back. How about that? Shan't be going yet anyhow.'

I looked up. I felt humiliated. Very conscious of the gap between us.

'I love it here you know. It's a real man's place. No feminine touches anywhere – in fact I'll wager that this square of earth has never had a woman on it. Look, even your curtains totally lack any feminine guile – and there's not a single fancy thing in the whole place: even your mug is purely functional. When I get a place of my own, I'm going to recreate this shed exactly, just as it is. A place to get away from the women. Don't mind do you – me using this as a bolt-hole while I'm here?'

'Not at all. It gives me pleasure that someone appreciates it. And I like the company.' And I meant it. Sometimes I could go all day without speaking to a soul.

'Jolly good then.' Edward got up and slapped me on the shoulder. 'Better get back to it before you're missed, eh? – that mower calls!'

I spent the rest of the afternoon feeling very despondent. It was partly jealousy of Edward, resentment that he had come back, annoyance that he could go away again, just like that. And confusion. I didn't know what was going on. He behaved strangely, not at all like the other men I knew of my age – nothing like my other pals – could I even call him a friend? Was it even possible to have a friend like that? I had only ever seen people like him from a distance, to raise my cap to, to be spoken down at, to be told what to do. Never to have a conversation with: to be friendly towards. Was the way he behaved how it was amongst the Broomhill and Ranmoor set when they were amongst themselves – what was it they called it – in "society?" I didn't know how to behave back. Should I risk being over-familiar? But then again, I didn't want to come across as coarse or ignorant.

Over the next week or two I saw Edward most days; always in my shed either at noon when I broke off for my snap or in the evening just as I was packing up ready to head home. Edward would sit back, his feet up, smoking, while I sharpened my bill hook or wiped an oily rag over my tools and hung them up, then changed out of my gardening clothes into ones more fit to return home in. I felt more at ease with Edward by then. Happy to just have him around. Happy to leave most of the talking to him. He could be charming and funny one minute, pompous and cantankerous the next. He would tell tales of life in the house: the empty-headedness of his sisters – he wondered what the point of them was in this world – all they were being raised for was to grace the arm of some puffed-up industrialist, not to have opinions or a life of their own. His father just remained aloof from everything: when he wasn't working he was scanning the *Telegraph* looking to divine the next opportunity, leaving the running of the house to his mother. He told me of an incident that morning: he had risen very late and had gone into his closet. Upon emerging totally naked he had startled a chambermaid in his room about to start tidying, thinking he was down at breakfast. She had taken a sharp breath and left the room; trying to behave as if nothing had happened.

'I think she thought she'd be in trouble or something. That's given her something to dream about though, eh?'

I shook my head. 'The poor girl.'

'Poor girl indeed! Privileged I'd say.'

Edward didn't appear again that summer. I assumed he had taken off somewhere and I again felt annoyed when I thought of it, he had not even said he was off, or where to, and hadn't said goodbye. But then, why should I have been annoyed by that: what was it to me? It wasn't as if Edward was a proper friend as such. And it was not like I could ask anyone where he'd gone either. I had saved that amusing carrot for him as well. Now I wouldn't get to share the joke. Still, next time cook asked for carrots, I would put that one on top of the basket. Edward would appreciate that.

Things started to fade in the garden; Michaelmas daisies putting in the last hurrah of summer, the odd nasturtium snubbing its nose until its brazenness ended in dripping pulp, smitten by a cloudless night. I was kept busy managing Nature's retreat; hiding its decay, trying to extend its charm, if not its fresh-faced beauty of only a few weeks earlier. I raced to preserve crops; went up the hill to collect sackfuls of bracken to cover plants at night: what a triumph it was to be able to present fresh parsley into December. I left tomatoes in the hope of seeing them ripen before giving up and handing them to cook to add to pickle. Then the struggle ended with nothing left to do but clear the debris, and days of leaf picking until the trees too gave up their fight as they shed their mantle to the wind and hoar-frost. I did not despise the autumn; I could still achieve great things; and there was that calm atmosphere when a thin sun broke through still air, and my breath was like steam and my muscles glowed.

The solicitor's perusal of the trade pages was evidently paying off: he bought a horse and a dog-cart and the stable was brought back into use for its intended purpose. A stable-lad was hired but I was expected to keep an eye on him and to help out. Despite the affront, it suited me as it meant security for the winter when there was little to do outside except for laying of pathways and repairing walls and trellises – and the manure would be a welcome addition to my compost heap and rose beds.

I never did reply to Annie's letter, and it now seemed too late somehow. What excuse could I have; and anyway what would I say? I thought of her occasionally but when she wasn't there I didn't really miss her – she had been good company when she was around but it wasn't like she fulfilled a need in me at the time; she was just Annie; not the sort of girl to send a man crazy with desire.

One Friday in the run up to Christmas I had been sorting out the stable; scrubbing it out with the stable lad. Nothing had been properly planned: it would have made sense to get the stables cleaned out and ready before buying the horse and dog-cart; but the solicitor was not a practical man and his purchase had just turned up one day and everything else had to fit round that lack of arrangements. We also had to whitewash the walls at the same time as trying not to turn the brown mare dappled. Fortunately we had enough room to work around it.

'Get away home, lad,' I said from up the ladder. 'It's getting late and thi mother'll be mithering. I'll just finish this bit up here, and then tomorrow we can do the other half.'

The boy grabbed his jacket off a peg where the tackle hung and ran off down the drive.

I was whistling the tune to those words: "And His shelter was a stable, and His cradle was a stall, with the poor and meek and lowly," as I continued my painting – what more appropriate place to be working at Christmas than a stable? I smiled to myself. When I heard the stable door creak open, I said, not turning round: 'Tha left summat?'

'Only you, dear boy,' came the reply.

The brush fell from my hand to the floor; I looked round. There was Edward looking up, face lit by the lamp hanging from a beam, a big stupid grin on his face.

'Just had to get out of the house – far too hot in that drawing room – they think it fitting the season to keep throwing logs on – blazing away it is. And the company's dreadful. The old man's got some of his legal or business chums round, I don't know what, and their frightful wives! Bulging out of corsets, ugh! Don't they know it's the end of the century. And jibing me about the mistletoe. "Oh come over here Master Edward." Too bloody awful for words. Champagne?' He held out two bottles; one in each hand.

I came down off the ladder, laughing as Edward slumped onto a bale of straw.

'I'd shake your hand, only…' I said, holding up a whitewash-splattered hand.

Edward released a cork from a bottle and caught the foam in his mouth. 'Too good to waste. No glasses I'm afraid, best I could do was to smuggle these out.'

He held the bottle out to me and I took a swig then spluttered as the bubbles caught my nose. I'd never had fizzy wine before. Edward slapped me on the back, laughing; this obviously wasn't his first drink of the day.

'So, how you been, dear boy? It's good to see you again – I've missed our little chats. Often dreamt of that cozy shed of yours.'

'Just the usual. Nothing's happened here.'

'Not settled down, or got engaged, or anything daft like that yet then?'

'No, have you?'

'Impudent wretch, of course not!' He uncorked the other bottle, again catching the eruption. 'Here's to your health!' he said, clinking his bottle against the one I had in my hand. 'And to the life of a bachelor!'

'So where have you been then?'

'All sorts of places. Germany, Austria, Italy. You know: Milan, Florence, Rome. Then thought I'd better come back for Christmas and cadge a bit more money off the Old Man. Had a fine ol' time, me and Will.'

'Will?'

'Oh, he's a chum from Cambridge. Stinking rich. You'd like him.'

There he was in his waistcoat with a gold, double-albert draped between his pockets. I became conscious of my smock, paint-spattered hand and arm. 'Look, I'd better go and get some water to wash this off.'

'Yes, you do look a bit diseased. I'll wait here.'

I returned with a pail of water and a bar of soap.

'What's going on out there?'

'Oh, nothing, everyone in the kitchen, getting in a lather over dinner.' I pulled off the whitewash-splattered smock and knelt over the pail and started to scrub my forearms and hands with the soap. Steam rose from my warmth in the chill air of the stable, mixing with my breath. The champagne had already gone to my head: worse than cider.

I stood up to reach for a bit of rag to dry myself.

'You look better.' Edward had come across and stood in front of me holding out my shirt. That shirt, however, did not get put back on until some time later. He looked me in the eye and I looked back at him. He gripped my bicep, then rested his cheek upon my collar bone. This time I did not flinch. I paused on the brink of something; I did not know what. Then I put my hand on his hair, reassuring, and enclosed him in my arms.

Shortly after, the brown mare turned her head once more at the noise of an empty champagne bottle being kicked over; then she turned back to the wall.

Chapter Four

The stable was left half-painted and stayed that way until well into the New Year when a new gardener was appointed. I had arrived at work the next day only for the solicitor to appear almost immediately outside my shed. He opened the door and remained standing at the doorway as if in fear of stepping over the threshold.

'I don't know what has happened. And I don't want to know, but you cannot be kept on here. You will not see my son again. He is to be sent to London and will be dispatched to India as soon as possible.'

'But why?' I said with as much innocence as I could summon up.

'Damned insolence! All I know is he came in last night in a frightful state. Impudent, drunk, dishevelled and his suit ruined by whitewash.'

The image in my head would have amused me twelve hours earlier but now I knew I was in real danger.

'You will leave right away, and will keep his name out of this. Is that clear?'

'Here's ten pounds,' he removed a note from his pocket. 'There's no more, but you will leave us well alone. If you need to leave town altogether: so much the better. In fact I shall only give you a reference if you do leave town.' The solicitor held out the note at arm's length.

I took the money; that much money had never fallen my way before.

'You and your type disgust me,' he spluttered, a wine colour rising in his cheeks.

I realised my mistake in accepting it – as good as an admission. I'd fallen into his trap.

'Get out!'

I sat on a wall in the village, not sure what to do next. I now felt shame at what had happened, disgust even. I had been taken advantage of by Edward, but I hadn't cared, not one bit, I had let him. And now I had lost the job I loved.

I was drunk when I got back at teatime. I thought I was holding it together quite well until a plate of liver and onions was put in front of me and I had to rush out the back to be sick. My father then had a row with me about my lack of responsibility and ingratitude, and I left the house and went back to the South Sea Hotel.

My friend Stan was drinking at the bar when I arrived. I leaned forward trying to focus my eyes and my words, but the landlord refused to serve me. I banged my fist down and cursed, but Stan took me home with him to stay the night and sober up. I threw up the raw egg and whisky in the morning so Stan made me go out for a walk, it being Sunday, and we headed up to the countryside at Crosspool and beyond.

'It were a shite job anyway,' Stan said, 'for a fella like thi. We allus thought tha'd do better 'n us, what wi' thi reading and writing being what it were. Gardening? We thought tha'd at least get a nice office job. Nice an' steady. Why did he get rid on thi anyhow?'

'Caught me drinking on the job – just a little Christmas tipple, that were all.'

'Harsh that. Still tha's best out on it. Tha'll find summat better.'

I stayed with Stan a few days while I got sorted out; Stan doing his best to keep me clear of the drink.

One cold morning when Stan was at work I wandered down the hill and took a detour past where I lived as a child on Kenyon Street. I grew up believing all Sheffield spoke with an Irish accent; our neighbours all fled their homes to escape famine, or followed on after, seeking work. With them came the priests and teachers at my infant school. I glimpsed through doorways where plaster had fallen away from walls and looked into hollow eyes that viewed me as a stranger. I caught that smell wafting through archways from gloomy courts within: a smell both foul and yet which took me back to innocent days playing on the broken stone yards with all the other children. As I neared Scotland Street the temptation of the Old Turk's Head was too great. I knew it wasn't wise, but I knew I was weak, so why pretend.

My nerves steadied by Irish whiskey I climbed the hill on which St Vincent's perched and looked back over the smoke filled valley of the Don towards the moors. It was cold inside the building and my breath hung above me as I sighed into the quiet still space;, Christ on his cross looking down at me, exposed to the gaze of the Virgin and of saints. I sat alone looking up at the coloured light from the windows. I had never felt this way before about anyone – I had been completely swept away by my urges, abandoned myself to Edward, lost myself and the limits, the boundaries of my own body and those of another. What I had done, my sins of the flesh, could condemn me to prison, and that could mean death – and from there to hell itself. Eternal fire for a few moments of forbidden love and unbounded joy. I was shaking, perhaps not just from the cold.

'Is all well with you my son?'

I had not seen or heard him approach.

'Will you hear my confession? I am carrying such a burden.'

I followed him over to the wooden boxes down the side of the church.

I sat quietly at first. 'Is it really such a sin to have feelings for another man, Father?'

'Do you speak of love?' I could not find the words to reply. He filled the silence himself: 'Not if that love is pure and spiritual as the love for a brother. Christ loved his disciples and they loved him. But bodily love is a mortal sin. Of which do you speak?'

Again I could find no voice for all the things in my head. The father wanted more detail than I could bring myself to speak of.

I said no more and slunk out of the church. All I really wanted was to speak to Edward again, to talk it over with him; he would be sure to have answers, know where we stood, but he was beyond reach. I knew I would have to deal with this on my own. In the pub my friends told foul jokes about men who did things to other men, and said they deserved worse than prison. What could I do but join in with their expressions of disgust that such crimes could even take place?

On Christmas Eve I went home; I was broken, no longer sure of myself and my place in the world. There would at least be some warmth and comfort at home, and I would be let back in if I apologised for my behaviour. I took gifts for them all, bought with the ten pounds: for my brothers and sisters, as well as my mother and father. All of them would be gathering that evening, returning to the parental hearth. I explained that I had lost my job and that I now needed to put that behind me, move on. I was treated like the prodigal son. When alone with my father, he could see I regretted how I had behaved.

'Perhaps now would be a good time to think about joining the police? What with my contacts and a reference, I know the Sheffield force would take you on.'

'No, Dad, that wouldn't work.' I was mindful of what the solicitor had said about a reference. I saw anger flash behind my father's eyes, betraying his calm exterior.

'I was thinking of a new start somewhere else, I wouldn't want to be known as Sergeant Higgin's lad.' I saw the anger within him dissipate.

'No, I see. In that case I could get in touch with a chap I know in Wakefield: an inspector now — was a constable under my wing at one time. Bright fellow. He's just the man to sort things out.'

So fate clunked forward a notch on its ratchet. I wrote a short, polite letter to the solicitor requesting a reference for a job out of town and within week I was on a train heading north.

I sat a test with several other potential recruits: some basic sums and then we had to read a short piece about the lion being king of the jungle and had to answer questions about the text. The police surgeon measured my height and weight, got me to read some letters off a chart on the wall, asked a few questions and got me to touch my toes. Several days later I received a letter telling me to report for duty at Wakefield. My parents were proud, especially my father, who felt his will had eventually prevailed: his son's resolve had been more malleable than he had let himself hope.

I stood with the other recruits in my new uniform in front of the Chief Constable, a big ex-army captain with severe sandy whiskers who looked us up and down like an eagle might inspect its prey before devouring it.

'As police constables you have an obligation to set standards of behaviour at all times; even when you are not in uniform you remain a police constable; your behaviour will not alter. You will not drink on duty and, if you must off duty, be it in moderation and in private. Your appearance shall be smart. You must remain efficient and informed: you are the eyes and ears of the law at all times. You have chosen a very worthy career: upholding the morality of our nation, preserving the peace and public tranquillity, and protecting property. By good conduct, efficiency and attention to your duty, it is possible for any man amongst you to rise to a superior position in the force. Some constables even get to inspector level or beyond through their diligence.'

I had had my free-will taken away from me, I had put myself in my father's hands, and now it was the West Riding Constabulary in charge of my life, deciding things for me. I didn't have to think, just follow orders. I willingly ceded control; so be it. To try to work my own way out of the mess I was in seemed insurmountable. I felt I was being re-shaped, moulded, and would come out of it different.

I was issued with a tunic and badge, two pairs of trousers, two pairs of boots, a helmet, a great coat and cape. Then there were the toys: a wooden staff that slipped into my right trouser pocket, handcuffs or "snips" as they were known, and a lantern and thick leather belt to attach them to. The effect of the uniform was itself transformational, I became a different person with it on; not only did I look bigger in the helmet, but I sensed the respect I would command – I couldn't wait to get out and test the reaction of people in the street. First though, I had to do the training: we recruits learnt to drill on the parade ground. We learnt the difference between felonies and misdemeanours.

'The definition of burglary is "breaking and entering into or out of a dwelling house between the hours of nine in the evening and six in the morning with felonious intent," ' said the sergeant. 'If it were in daytime what would it be?'

'Housebreaking, Sarge?'

'Good, at least someone is paying attention.'

We were told when we could apprehend and when we had to apply for a warrant, what we should do in certain common circumstances: fires, reports of suicide, prostitution, vagrancy, the difference between a pedlar and a hawker, and their licences, the rules of common lodging houses and that you should only intervene in an assault between a man and his wife in a house upon hearing a cry of "murder."

The sergeant stressed the keeping of good notes in our pocketbooks, and ran through the essential elements of written reports and gave us examples to write up.

'If you've not taken all this in, you will get chances to ask before you are let loose on the unsuspecting public. You won't be out on your own straight away. Other things you will need to know: allowances. If you leave for your beat before eight in the morning, it's one shilling for breakfast, then two shillings for dinner, and a shilling for supper if you don't return before six. You will also receive thirty shillings a year boot allowance – and with all the walking you'll do you'll need it. Your leave is ten days annually plus one day per month: this has to be applied for to your inspector. You see we may expect a lot from you but in return we look after you. If you do well and stay in the force you could look forward to retiring on half your pay in twenty-odd years time. We look after one another, we stick up for our colleagues. You should all be proud to wear that badge.'

For those first few days I was lodged with the others in the section house. Words and numbers banged about inside my head, it was both exciting and terrifying. Most of all, I feared showing myself to be a fool. I had little time to think about how I had got there. My day was regulated: meals, drill, lessons, lights out. I spoke to the others, all a similar age to me; big, often with more than a hint of the countryside about them: boys who would know how to throw straw bales without effort, or help a ewe give birth. I didn't ask questions of them and avoided theirs, sticking to that day's events and prospects for the next. I was unable to call any of them friends.

Then we were ready to go out on the beat for the first time. We arrived at the station early and clung together in a group as the other constables arrived: some were reading the paper, others smoking or telling jokes, some trimming their lamps ready for the night. I checked I'd got everything: the lamp, heavy on my belt, my cape, with its brass lions and chain fastener, folded on my knee; we had all decided on taking our capes – though we weren't sure what was the done thing at that time of year. It approached ten and the inspector gave the order to fall in, and we were each called by number and assigned to one of the beats. Following a "Left turn! Quick march!" we marched out into the cold, damp, night air.

I was with a serious looking man in his thirties, PC 79, Cruikshank; large, untidy moustache already flecked with grey, nostril hairs indistinguishable from the whole mass – like the moustache cascaded from his nose. It made me shudder.

Cruikshank ascertained that I was "Higgins" from Sheffield but showed no interest beyond that. It was not far to the start of the beat by the cathedral.

'The first hour's the busiest lad, then it should be nice and peaceful. Right what's tha know about intoxicating liquor lad?'

What was I supposed to say, that I prefer a pint of Gilmour's stout to gin? He didn't look like the sort to joke with.

'Er, that it's not good?' I said.

'Nay lad. Is tha a copper or what? What have they taught thi about selling intoxicating liquor?'

'Oh, that you need a license.'

'And? Over there – that public? When can it sell liquor?'

'Ah, not between eleven and six.'

'So tha was paying attention. We've got to keep a check on 'em. What about ages? What age can a person be served?'

'Thirteen.'

'Yes, but spirits?'

'Not thirteen?'

'Sixteen lad. Tha needs to learn this stuff.'

I felt like I was a kid at school: not a feeling I had experienced for some time. Some people still tried to push me around but it was not something they carried off. Given my stature, I looked down on most people, and my broad shoulders meant people didn't often take me on. When the solicitor told me to get out, I hadn't crept out tail between my legs. I had retained my own superiority, physical if not of status. But now, in the police, my physique was nothing exceptional and, that nullified, my lack of knowledge and the ever-present awareness of rank lowered my status. I was the new boy. Constable, third class.

'Tip for thi lad – get *The Police Review*. There's always copies in the station and in the section house but tha's better with thi own copy; there's always examples of things we come up against and how to deal wi' 'em, how the law applies. Educate thisen lad, if tha wants to get on. I'm hoping to be a sergeant before the year ends.'

We checked shop doors, shined our lantern beams down alleys, into passages and windows of banks and pawn shops. Cruikshank exchanged banter with a group of colliers who had been washing pit dust from their throats all evening, moving them on, back to their "poor unfortunate wives." He seemed to know them and they him: his authority was natural, came from something other than just the uniform. Shortly after midnight we stopped for some supper; then, when we resumed our beat, the night was still, just the sound of our own boots walking round the same route at the pace set by Cruikshank: a peculiar swaying gait turning up his toes at every step. He no longer spoke; it was as if he were in some kind of trance to assist him through the night. My back ached, I longed to sit down, but round the same hard streets we went, rhythmically, as if suffering some kind of madness, every time the clock on the cathedral advancing another twenty minutes. The sun was not far from rising when I slumped into bed.

Within days the recruits were dispatched to the different parts of the Riding not covered by the borough forces. I was on a train to a place called Liversedge; where that was I knew not, except that it was just beyond Dewsbury, which I had heard of from somewhere. I looked out from the carriage for clues as to the kind of place I was heading to. Windows. So many windows on the vast stone mills that dominated the valley bottoms, mills that were two, three, four storeys high. Somehow very different to the sprawling steelworks of my home or the brick built workshops all round the town centre. And everywhere, in the streets and on the railway sidings and in yards, the populace seemed dedicated to moving bales: onto and off wagons and carts into stacks like some giant baby's building blocks.

I was welcomed by the inspector and took up a recommendation of a room to let: someone who gave favourable rates to policemen.

As I closed the door to my room behind me, a silence fell. I stepped past my tin box and the canvas bag containing my uniform and sat on a wooden chair by the window overlooking the landscape. I leaned my head against the cool glass. The new start.

Chapter Five

It was almost a year ago to the day that I had arrived in that backwater – the sort of place that no one comes to except to work, and then never left. Now I was a married man. I pulled off my boots and poured a drop or two of Condy's fluid out of the little bottle into the bowl of tepid water, the purple drops spreading out in it like drops of blood. I was sitting in my armchair in my shirtsleeves, trousers rolled up, feet in the bowl, eyes closed, when Annie came in and woke me from my half-sleep.

She wrinkled her nose, 'What's that in the bowl?'

'It's for my feet. Most important part of a bobby's armoury, his feet. Got to look after them. How were your mother and sister?'

'Very well. We went for a walk then we had some dinner at the hotel before they left.'

She sat on the arm of my chair and put her hand on my shoulder. 'I can't believe I'm finally Mrs Annie Higgins. Even yesterday I couldn't believe it was really happening – I still have to pinch myself. I have only thought about that moment and had almost forgotten to think past it – at what happens now.'

She paused. 'I thought I might see if there's any work going round here tomorrow – help us save for our own house. What do you think?'

'I'm not sure the police allow wives of constables to work. I'll ask.'

Annie sat on the edge of the bed. 'What will I do all day, John, once I've tidied the room? I've no house to keep, no meals to prepare, no marketing to do.'

'I don't know. I hadn't really thought about it.'

We sat quietly for a while.

'Will we go to church on Sunday morning, John?'

'No, I'm working – we can go in the evening. I've got Easter Sunday off though.'

'I thought you'd get Sundays off at least.'

'I'm afraid burglars and vagrants don't respect the Lord's day.'

She smiled a thin smile at my joke, straightened the bed, then went to her box and picked out some things to set out: a bible and two other books, some little bottles which she placed on lace mats on the wash stand and an inlaid trinket box.

*

During those early days of our married life, I was on day relief and would have time in the morning or the afternoon to spend with Annie. I showed her round the nicer parts of the district – the areas I did not go to for work – past Healds Hall or through Littletown and across the fields to Gomersal, fields worked for many generations, where we would strain our eyes to pick out larks against the bright sky or watch swallows in the evening fly low over the meadows. It was then that I sensed Annie was at her happiest as I held her hand. But when my turn came to be on nights her mood changed; when I kissed her cheek as I left at half-past nine I knew she was trying to hold back a tear as she sat reading in the lamplight. I would sometimes wake her when I returned in the morning; then after breakfast we might go for a short walk before I went to bed. To avoid waking me she took more and more to helping Mrs Shaw about the house, running errands, or just sitting with her in the kitchen while she baked; both of them appreciating the company.

I had to confirm to her that she was not permitted to work. I tried to explain what the Inspector had told me. 'It's the same as me not being allowed to take on other work, which is in the 1856 Act. It could lead to questions being asked. What I didn't add was that he had said, 'When you give her children she'll have no time to work anyway.'

I decided to try to cheer her up. I walked my beat on Good Friday night, and in the morning, when I returned, Annie was at the door to greet me.

'Annie, I've borrowed this suitcase, you'll need to pack some things in it. I've got a surprise for you; our train leaves at five to ten. I've got some leave and am not back on duty until Monday night. Call it a honeymoon, shall we?'

'But where are we going? What do I pack?'

'The seaside. Come on,' I said as I climbed the stairs two at a time. 'And you'll need to change into your best.'

Upstairs, I started kicking off my boots. If truth be told, I think I was more excited than her – I had been keeping the surprise bottled up, making arrangements, writing letters to find a room, and applying for leave from the inspector. The surprise hadn't the effect on her I had hoped for. She didn't put her arms round me or thank me gushingly; instead she was anxious and, if anything, a little irked.

'You should have told me, then I could have got ready properly.'

I had planned to sleep on the train but as it headed up through Bradford then on up through the Aire valley I was eager to see out of the window. It wasn't until people got off at Bradford that we were able to get next to the window to see out properly.

It was about half past twelve when we arrived in Morecambe. I must have missed Lancaster, sleep having got the better of me, and I awoke when the train came to a stop and the compartment door opened. The station was bustling: women in attire normally only seen on a Sunday, with wide-brimmed hats, gentlemen trying to appear in control amidst the chaos of excited children, groups of people standing in the way, porters and piles of luggage.

We followed the "way out" signs and emerged into – the sky! A sky so big that it seemed to merge with the earth. Annie gripped my hand as we crossed the road onto the promenade. Neither of us spoke. We reached the railing at the promenade's edge. I dropped the suitcase and held onto the rail with both hands as if to steady myself. The overcast but clear sky did indeed merge with the earth – it was hard to tell where the one started, the other finished. The sea lapped up against a thin strip of sand. Annie put her arm around me under my jacket and moved close to me as if afraid.

'It's nothing like I imagined,' I said. 'It's just so big.'

'I thought it would be like the sea in the paintings.'

Wooden jetties stretched out to where boats were moored; sail boats and rowing boats, and, just beyond, a pleasure pier thrust boldly outwards as if defying this anxiety: this feeling almost like fear that we both felt of that great space in front of us.

'When you're up on the moors at home you can see almost to the Humber on a clear day, but this…'

'All this water's making me thirsty,' Annie said. The shock was wearing off.

'Let's go to the hotel then, get sorted, then we can go out and explore.'

Along the promenade were carriages, brakes and smaller wagonettes lined up to take people from the station. Horse drawn trams also ran along the seafront. We asked a driver how far it was to the Clarendon. 'I'm heading down that way, hop on.' I handed him a fourpence and we climbed on the back next to a woman and small girl wearing a white dress who nestled up to her mother when I smiled at her. On the seat in front were presumably the father and his son, a smaller replica minus the beard, in the same attire and identical new caps. It wasn't far along the seafront to the Clarendon, past little gardens where groups of young men sat smoking, and shelters where ladies in dark dresses and bonnets sat taking the air. The hotel was not far from the pier and I had already made up my mind what we should do.

'Let's just drop off our suitcase and then go straight out onto the pier shall we?'

'No, I think I need some dinner first.'

Our room was on the third floor on the corner of the building with sloping ceilings and a window looking out over the pier – I gazed out while Annie unpacked the suitcase; she insisted on getting things out so they wouldn't be so crumpled.

We ate in the hotel, then I finally got us out onto the pier. It was magnificent; perhaps a third of a mile of clean wooden boards, as wide as a street, stretching out towards what looked like an oriental palace perched on the end, with ornate gas lights and flag poles at intervals. We sat in a cafe in part of the palace when we finally reached the end and had tea out of fine china cups and ate cake with cutlery.

There was a Punch and Judy show that was just starting when we left the cafe. The booth itself was a masterpiece; covered in beautiful cloth and three flags flying above the framed stage. We stood towards the back of the small crowd; children sat at the front, their parents and other adults in a circle around them. I think we were both shocked at Punch's antics as he first threw the baby against the wall for crying, then beat his wife, and knocked Scaramouche's head clean off his shoulders. However, we soon got used to the beatings and succumbed to holiday spirit in the crowd and laughed as Punch was made to take his "medicine" by the doctor.

'Ah, about time too,' I said when the constable turned up.

'Leave off your singing Mr Punch, I'm come to make you sing on the other side of your face.'

'I don't need constable. I can settle my own affairs without constable thank you kindly. Don't want constable.'

'But I want you and I've a warrant for you.'

I whispered, 'He wouldn't need a warrant for a felony such as that, manslaughter at the very least, if not murder. A triple murder.' Then Punch started on the constable. 'I wouldn't stand for that, I'd have my staff on him first.'

The bottler was doing his round collecting pennies in a hat, I fished a couple of pennies out of my pocket.

There were boos when Punch was eventually arrested and cheers as he escaped the noose by his trickery.

'Why do people like such a villain? They ought to be cheering the policeman.'

'Oh, John, do shut up,' Annie said, which I thought a little disrespectful.

One or two whimpers followed from the children in the audience when the Devil appeared during another Mr Punch song; the all-black, horned puppet with the red glass eyes really was quite scary. Big cheers from everyone followed at the end when, after a terrible battle, Mr Punch hoisted up the Devil's body and twirled it round on his stick.

We strolled along the promenade and were surprised that the sea had vanished. 'I knew the sea went in and out but I didn't imagine it could disappear completely,' said Annie.

We went down onto the strand, past the children getting donkey rides or being pulled along in a miniature carriage by a goat. Further out some children were fishing for shrimps in glassy pools that reflected the metallic sky; the girls with their skirts tucked up showing skinny pale legs like the boys.

'The water looks so clear, John. It's supposed to be salty isn't it, but how do you think it tastes?'

I scooped some in my hands. 'Definitely salty.'

She copied me, but taking more than a taste she coughed after swallowing. I don't think she wanted to appear unladylike by spitting it out. 'Oh, that's horrible, I think I need a drink to take the taste away.'

We went into a public house and ordered whisky and sodas, which seemed rather grand, and which we both agreed was just the thing after seawater. We sat by the window watching people pass by. For tea we had potted shrimps and shared some mussels which we ate from their shells.

By that time I was starting to feel the effects of having been awake for nearly a whole day and night, but for an hour or so on the train.

'I think I'll go back for a lie down,' I said.

'Then I'll sit by that lovely window for a bit while you sleep.'

It was twilight when I was awakened by the sound of Annie being violently sick into a chamber pot like some drunk I would find down an alley on a Saturday night. It was pretty revolting, I must say. When it stopped I helped her into bed; she was shivering and in a cold sweat.

'It was perhaps the seawater,' she said. 'I feel awful John. I'm so sorry for waking you.'

I went downstairs for a glass of warm water and some bicarbonate and also to get some carbolic to deal with the pot – as bad as being turnkey at the cells it was. Once Annie ceased being sick and settled in bed I sat by the window and looked out at the rows of lights on the pier, reaching out into the darkness, even more unworldly; dark figures seen moving between pools of light along its length and along the promenade. I did a mental salute as a policeman passed by – not long till you're finished for the day, fella, I thought. When night fell I slipped into bed. Annie was sleeping fitfully.

I woke early to the sound of arrogant seagulls on the roof and for a while stared at the ceiling, then I crept across to the cool window. It was quiet outside, too early for anyone to be up and about. I got a shock – out to sea there were mountains on the horizon. The day before when I looked out I'd imagined the sea went on and on, but now in the clear morning air were the mountains – I had only been looking out into a bay after all. I wanted to wake Annie and show her. The movement of the curtains, however, disturbed her and she opened her eyes.

'There's mountains out to sea. Come and look.'

Her hair was partly across her face. 'I'll look later. I don't want to move.'

'Are you not better?'

'Perhaps, but I don't want to move. What time is it?'

I took my watch out of my jacket which was hanging on the back of a chair. 'Not yet six o'clock.'

'I'll try to sleep some more.'

'Shall I sit with you?'

'No, thanks, leave me in peace.'

I dressed and went out onto the sea front for a walk before breakfast. The air was crisp and smelt so different. No earthiness or leafiness, not the smell of damp and dirty wool or animal waste that hung over the Spen Valley, or the smell from fires being brought back to life as the day started. I leant against the railing, closed my eyes and breathed, filling myself with the sounds and smells of the sea. Then I watched as the distant mountains faded as a veil of mist from the sea, or cloud from the land, took them away. I walked along the sand, seeing one or two early risers also out for strolls before breakfast. I climbed onto a wooden jetty and hesitantly made my way along, though it seemed very narrow and insubstantial, out into the sea and to the boats at the end. I wondered if it were possible to go out in a boat and what it would be like to be detached from the land, to be adrift.

I smoked my pipe as I walked back along the esplanade to the hotel. Annie was still asleep when I looked in on her so I sat at a breakfast table alone whilst other residents talked in low voices within their family groups to preserve their decorum.

I took some warm milk and toast up with me. Annie sat up in bed and nibbled at the toast; she still wretched a little.

'Shall I get you a doctor? Or go and get you a draught?'

'No, I don't need a doctor. The worst has gone. Perhaps a little something to settle my stomach may help though, if you can find somewhere. John, I'm sorry for spoiling everything – I don't think I'll be getting up this morning. But don't let me stop you going out, I'll be fine on my own.'

I wandered round until I found a chemist and returned with Will's Hygeia Salts, a bottle of seltzer and a newspaper. I was sent out again to let her rest. I followed a sign I had seen to the Summer Gardens. There I walked round the ornamental gardens, casting a critical eye over the planting arrangements. I watched some people playing bowls and wished I could be invited to join in – not that I thought I'd be any good at it. I took tea at a cafe then studied a poster for sea-water baths. It appeared that costumes and towels were provided so I paid my sixpence for a second class plunge.

I had taught myself to swim, after a fashion, over the last year; although I had splashed about in some of the grinding wheel dams as a child – the murky waters of Ibbotson's wheel being the closest. Physical exercise was one of the things the doctor had recommended to provide a release for my energies; he extolled the benefits of bodily fatigue. There was a limit to what I could do – I had always lacked the coordination for cricket, although it was popular in the dark recesses of the West Riding. I had watched football but was not good at it, and anyway it wasn't something you could do in the heavy woollen district. The winter game they called football was not even played with the feet and was to my eyes little more than Saturday night brawling conducted according to a set of opaque rules; the real game of football being like Christianity to the Pygmies. I would have liked to have got a bicycle but it was at least ten pounds even for a second-hand machine in good working order. So, because walking was what I did all day, and of limited use anyway, I tried out the new baths at Wellington Road in Dewsbury when they opened.

I knew I wasn't very elegant in the pool as I thrashed up and down, but it tired my limbs and body which is what was prescribed.

Only, I had not been swimming recently.

I had been resting at one end of the pool in Dewsbury when a man in his prime, in old style bathing drawers, came out of a dressing box and dived into the water at the far end and swam towards me – effortless, graceful breast-stroke, submerging his head and resurfacing. I set off again in my contrasting style, putting in twice the effort for half the gain. Half way down I sensed the man gaining on me, then I watched him overtake, the water rolling off his smooth hairless back, and running off his dark curly hair as he surfaced. I tried to get on with my own swimming, then had to stop once more to get my breath, holding on to the side. This was when the man caught up with me again, slid out of the water and sat up on the side next to me. He grinned down at me and ran his fingers through his hair to get the water out. Dark curly hairs showed on his chest and arm pits. He was muscular, lithe.

'It's good this place, eh?' the man said. 'I used to go to Batley but this is better.'

'I've not been swimming long,' I replied. 'I'm afraid I can't swim like you.'

The man grinned again. 'You're strong though. I've always loved swimming – I learnt in the canal, but this is nicer.' He then stood up, I saw the full length of his body and its contours as he stretched. Then he dived back in. I edged round the side nearest to my dressing box. I ran through in my mind all the things that came within the Town and Police Clauses Act: dangerous dogs at bay, causing obstruction, indecent exposure (no, not that for God's sake); yes, leaving cellar vaults insecure, bonfires, making slides on snow and ice, shaking doormats before eight in the morning. By dint of this list was I able to climb out without embarrassment and gain the sanctuary of my dressing box. I had not been back to Wellington Road baths since.

I was all right by the time I was in Morecambe though – I felt calm as I changed into the bathing costume. It was not too busy in the pool; it seemed most people didn't stray far from the sea front; there were only a few portly, middle-aged gentlemen of the walrus type and a pale gangly man with big feet and hands that didn't seem to belong to him. As I thrashed up and down the pool I tried to calculate what proportion of mile I should swim: four lengths would be about a hundred yards, eighteen would be about a quarter of a mile – that would be a good start.

I washed the salt water off in a cold freshwater shower, dressed and headed back for my dinner feeling ravenous, my body feeling alive. Annie was sitting up in bed reading the newspaper with a bit more colour in her cheeks when I returned. She still wasn't hungry but said she would try a little soup if some could be brought up. I am ashamed to say I felt little guilt as I tucked into the chops on my plate; another afternoon of my own company ahead of me.

I went for a long walk along the sea front after dinner, stopping to watch builders as they worked on erecting new palace-like buildings along the seafront. Further along I also discovered to my surprise another pier, perhaps only half as long but with a ship pulled up at a landing stage at the end.

Building work was underway here too, a pavilion being erected at the end, like something for an Indian prince, perhaps even bigger than on the West Pier. I carried on beyond the edge of the town, then turned back and sought out somewhere for a drink. As I approached the door of the King's Arms someone stepped in front of me and got there first. The man, wearing a double-breasted jacket and blue felt hat, held the door for me with a courteous smile. I had seen him earlier on the pier, something about his confident manner and countenance had drawn my attention. The man was first to the bar and ordered a stout. I waited as the man handed over a sixpence.

'And whatever my friend here is having too,' he said to the potman.

I was slightly taken aback, had I met the man before?

'A whisky and soda please,' I said, before I had thought to refuse. 'I'm sorry, have we met?'

'Perhaps we have, I'm Grainger, you?'

'Higgins.'

'Where from?'

'From Sheffield, but I live in Liversedge. I don't recall a Mr Grainger.'

'No, not Mr Grainger, Mr Balmforth.'

'I'm sorry but I thought…'

The man laughed at my apparent discomfort. 'No, no, common mistake. Grainger Balmforth's the name. My father wasn't content that I should have one surname so he gave me another.'

'Oh, oh I see. My apologies.'

'So you on holiday then? Shall we…?' he said indicating a seat at a table. I felt obliged having taken a drink from him. The man put his hat on a chair; his thick dark hair was longer than usual, slicked back with macassar oil, only slightly receding at the temples. A good-looking fellow perhaps in his early thirties, dark, trim moustache and a definite glint in his eye – a clever man or possibly a criminal type, or both, I thought. I checked my wallet was secure in my pocket.

In answer to his questions I explained about my holiday and Annie's illness.

'Frightful shame that. I've just come up for the weekend to get away from the wife – driving me mad. I sometimes do that – say I'm away on business then come and relax up here. All well and good sometimes, ladies, but can be jolly hard work, if you catch my drift?'

'I suppose you can't always see eye to eye.'

'Exactly so. Especially if you have more modern views like I do,' he paused and looked at me. 'So you recently married?'

'Just over a week.'

'Non-conformist wedding? I believe there are a lot of non-conformists where you live?'

'I believe so, but no, I'm from the old religion.'

'Ah, I see. Intriguing.'

'Why intriguing?'

'No, no reason.' He laughed. 'I suppose it must be marvellous being able to be absolved of your sins by the priest in return for a few *mea culpas*.'

'It's not as easy as that.'

'No, I don't suppose it ever is.'

He sipped from his pint pot then wiped the froth from his moustache.

He asked me what I had discovered in the town, and I told him where I had been. Balmforth got out his cigarettes and we both smoked. I mentioned my curiosity about boats.

'I should give it a go if you get chance. Been out myself before, being free of the land is wonderful, but I'm afraid I got frightfully seasick.'

This reminded me of Annie. 'Look, I'd better get back to see how she's doing.'

'You do that. Tell you what though, if she's still not well and doesn't want to eat tonight, instead of you having to dine alone again, why don't you come around to my rooms, the drawing room overlooks the seafront, and I'll treat you to supper. You can keep me company too. I'll point it out to you, I'm heading that way.'

'That's very decent of you, thanks.'

'Don't mention it. I'll hope to see you at seven.'

We walked without urgency along the esplanade towards the West End. After we'd shaken hands, I headed back thinking what an uncommon fellow Balmforth was – a decent sort though, a gentleman; obviously could discern an upstanding character: clever, not a criminal.

I sat with Annie for a while. When I had got back she was dressed and saying she felt much better. I told her about my day – my swim, what I had seen.

'Got an invite to supper if you're still not up to it – decent sort of chap: quite well-to-do I shouldn't wonder.'

'I'll see, John.'

'Do you think you're up for a little fresh air? We could just step onto the front?'

Annie walked gingerly holding my arm; like I was assisting an old woman across the road whilst on duty. We sat in a shelter for a while, observing the fashions, then Annie suggested we should head back. Once at the room she sat for a while again, while I read the paper.

'I'm not up to supper, but do you think it would be too much trouble for the kitchen to send up a little porridge made with milk? It is all I really feel like.'

'That's good if you feel like something though. I'll go and ask.'

She smiled. 'You go and eat with your friend, I'll be fine here. I don't want to spoil your holiday any more than I have already. You get so little time off duty, you must make the most of it. Hopefully, by tomorrow, I'll be fine.'

I put on a clean collar and a different tie and set off to Grainger Balmforth's lodgings.

I rang the bell and waited. The door was answered by a neatly-dressed, middle-aged woman who led me upstairs to the first floor. She knocked on a door. 'Mr Balmforth, a Mr Higgins to see you.'

'Thank you, Mrs Hall; supper for two tonight please. Come through! Delighted you could make it.'

I was shown into a large room with a bay window fitted with a window seat and which overlooked the esplanade. To one side was a writing desk and bookshelf, opposite a fireplace with a gilded mirror above the mantelpiece, and in the centre of the room was a table set for two. A door in the other wall presumably led to the bedroom.

'It's modest, but it serves my purpose.' He wore a tweed suit minus the jacket, a turned-down collar and a tie.

'Come and sit down whilst we wait for dinner,' he said gesturing to the window. 'Can I get you a drink?'

We sat on the plush cushions looking out across the bay; brightness in the sky out to sea where the sun was throwing light from behind distant clouds depriving it from departing in glory.

'Is she still not well?'

'Much better, thank you, but still not up to proper food.'

'I'm pleased she's recovering, but her loss is my gain. It is miserable having to dine alone don't you think?'

'So, is this place yours or do you just stay here on holiday?'

'Yes, it's mine – or rather I have exclusive use of it – I sometimes let my friends stay here too. It's a wonderful place to escape to, and the housekeeper is very good, and provides good plain meals and keeps herself to herself. I even bring my wife up in the summer for a week; though she thinks I just rent it for that week.' He tapped the side of his nose.

'So tell me about yourself, Mr Higgins. Look, I can't call you that.'

'John.'

'Tell me about yourself, John.'

I told him about my work as a gardener and of my background in Sheffield – I had learnt from experience to omit any reference to the police when I first made an acquaintance – it always caused problems: people invariably took it the wrong way and it killed any conversation. Instead I said I was a clerk working in the law, which was almost the truth.

I learnt in turn that Balmforth was in the linen trade, running the family business.

A lamplighter made his way along the promenade as the sky's strength faded. There was a knock at the door and the housekeeper entered with a tray and placed two bowls of soup on the table. Balmforth poured wine from a decanter into the glasses and pulled back a chair for me. After the soup came a good-sized steak then a gooseberry pie with a thick golden crust and a piece of ripe cheddar afterwards. We sat with cigars back at the window, Balmforth sitting a bit closer to me.

'I don't like to draw the curtains except in winter – no one can see in up here and this seat has such a view: all the lights, sometimes the moon above the sea.' We gazed out. Lights from the pier shimmered on the surface of the water.

'It's delightful to have your company, John.' He then patted me on the knee.

I looked at him, and met his stare. Balmforth's face had flushed; he smiled – not his usual confident grin but almost a shy smile. Then he put his hand back on my knee and left it there. It was happening again: just when things had started to go right. Here was temptation. I looked back into those brown eyes. The other man moved his hand, caressed my knee. Why did it happen to me? I put my hand onto his – it was surprisingly warm and soft. I pushed it away and stood up.

Balmforth looked confused. 'I'm sorry I thought… I've misunderstood.'

'Yes. No. I must go. It's not your fault.'

Balmforth stood up too. He looked pale. 'I didn't mean to…'

'Look I'm not like that. Not now. I'm married. I'm a policeman.'

Balmforth blanched and steadied himself against an arm chair back. 'Please. I'm sorry. I didn't mean anything. It was nothing. I don't make a habit of… . Please don't make any trouble.'

'I won't. I'd better go. Thank you for the dinner.'

Balmforth slumped into the chair. I let myself out and hurried across the road to where people were walking after dinner – as if I could hide amongst them. I walked a short way, past couples walking arm in arm, and gentlemen tap-tapping ostentatiously with their canes. I went down a slipway and sat at the bottom with my feet on the sand; the still night air shrouding me as I tried to make sense of what had happened. In darkness, away from the lights, the sighing of the sea absorbing sounds of voices and wheels on the promenade. It was obvious now I thought about it: all the signs were there and yet I had still put myself in danger – had I been naïve or had I really known and just not wanted to admit it to myself. Why could it not have just stayed as a friendly chat and a nice dinner. And yet, even then, part of me wanted to turn back, to be drawn in to temptation, to fall into the abyss. We all face temptation that is what the priest had said, it was only a sin to yield; that I should pray for strength, for self-control. Since the incident in the stable my sins had not been shared with others, in that at least I had succeeded despite temptation – but to what extent had opportunity been missing from the crime. What was it those clever types said in court: there was no crime without a guilty act – actus reus they called it – as well as a guilty mind. Edward was taken away from me in body but he was in my mind, in my dreams. In those dreams I let myself go. Dreams with physical consequences; I enjoyed it and was without shame unless I awoke remembering. Was it the Devil that sent those dreams?

Where I had failed, however, was in the sin I did not share. I was weak-minded and it enfeebled me even more. That little booklet I had sent away for – put on the fire before Annie came – how to regain manhood and prevent exhausted vitality and premature decline – just a waste of five penny stamps. It had promised a cure but all it did was increase my guilt, made me worry even more, not stop my yearnings. Then there were those soft wax crayons that were supposed to soothe and restore – the insertion of which was not as painless as was claimed and which just made things worse. Just what damage had I done to myself through my weakness? To have a worry so great that it outweighed the shame and led me to the doctor! The doctor was reassuring – it was common he had said. Exercise, hard physical exercise – hence the swimming. Then the bromide which just made me drowsy and ill. I had bought pictures of Lillie Langtry to stimulate my romantic feelings and the doctor suggested that I try falling in love with a boyish woman.

I must re-double my efforts – after all it had been working. I must avoid dangerous situations, being lured into intimacy. Be thankful for what I'd got; be good to Annie. After all, she had come to my rescue. One letter of apology, explaining that I had had a difficult time with my employer and was asked to leave, and she had agreed to meet me again. A few weekend visits later, and a meeting with her mother, and it was all agreed.

I had to do the right thing.

I shivered as the damp air penetrated my clothing.

Annie was asleep when I returned. She stirred when I got into bed, there was just enough light entering the room to see that she opened her eyes briefly, smiled at me, then closed them again. I put my arm over her as I lay, but she did not respond.

In the morning Annie came down to breakfast and even managed a boiled egg. Not feeling up to a walk she suggested we go for a drive. For a shilling we hired a landau and were taken for a drive along the front where I had gone the day before: I looked up as we passed Balmforth's lodgings – did I see someone at the window? We had a light lunch, wet our feet in the sea and had one last trip along the pier before heading for the ten to six train back.

'You've been very quiet all day, John. You've no need to worry about me, I'm fine now – it was nothing serious. I'm sorry for spoiling it for you.'

'You didn't, I had a nice time anyway. Not that I mean… I should have enjoyed it more if you'd been well, but I tried to make the most of it.'

She leant against my shoulder on the train. 'I never got to see your mountains.'

'No. And I didn't get to go on a boat. I could hardly have suggested it today.'

'Well, we'll just have to come back another time.'

*

We arrived back at a quarter to nine, and, an hour or so later, I was walking down Gasworks Street towards Providence Mills, shining my bullseye into corners, water trickling off my helmet, down the back of my neck; the leather of my boots already soaked. The rest of the world was tucked up in bed or fondly cradling their last pint before the landlord rang the bell for closing time and they pulled their caps down and hurried home to cold receptions.

Chapter Six

Annie

I've long kept a diary – since I was a girl in fact. It's foolish really, I know. I ought to throw them away after I've written them because they are of no use. There is a little pile of old ones, written in school exercise books, at my mother's house in a box in the cubby hole. They'll never be looked at again. But that's not the point – it is writing them that matters – being able to sift through my thoughts and set them down, like I'm talking to someone. It helps put it all in the right order and sometimes helps me decide what's important.

John's just gone off to work so I've been writing about my awful weekend. It's not just because I was ill, though that was bad enough, but the whole way it came about set me off on the wrong foot. He can be so thoughtless at times. I know he wanted to surprise me, but if I'd had time to prepare I could have been in less of a fluster and packed the right things. As it was, spending most of the weekend in bed in my night-dress meant my hurried choice of clothes made no difference.

He can be such a chump, but I've always known that, right from the start. Him thinking I didn't know he was up there on the shed roof all those times! But it's that almost childlike nature of his that attracted me to him, that slight awkwardness: like he doesn't really know himself yet. And yet, he is a fine figure of a man and my friends thought him quite a catch. It's just, well… it's like he almost has this image of himself as a gentleman and doesn't quite appreciate his shortcomings, in the way most people do in order to try to cover them up.

I think the world of him though. I suppose being vexed occasionally by one's husband is just the way of the world. Don't we all have a job to do in taming them?

The way he took that Punch and Judy show so seriously – and to think at first he thought it beneath us to even stop and watch. Taking to heart the insults to the policeman! And that bottler collecting pennies was smiling at John like he knew he was a policeman – like he had sniffed out an old foe – wouldn't surprise me by the look of him. Shifty he was. John though wouldn't have noticed something like that; they talk about a "copper's nous," well, John certainly hasn't got one yet.

His earnestness, it just makes him come across as pompous sometimes. I know he is nothing of the sort, but so often he sees things as one or the other, and rarely in between. Give me a straightforward man like John any day, rather than one with any "side" to him. I'd rather have someone you can read like a book, to someone with hidden depths.

I worry about him sometimes. He is easily taken in by people – only John would get himself an invite to dinner from a stranger like that. Perhaps it's just that I'm too suspicious of other people and him too trusting – perhaps it's me that's the odd one. But I didn't have the strength in me to question him about it. He works terribly hard, and puts in long hours without complaint, in all weathers, so he deserved a break too – and I didn't want him moping around in the room with me feeling so dreadful – it was better that he got out and made the most of it. I'm not sure he had such a nice time himself though. I don't think his evening and dinner were quite up to his expectations; he has been subdued most of today. I can't help feeling guilty for spoiling his surprise weekend – he must have spent quite a lot of money on it after all, though I'd rather he saved it so that we can get out of this one little room. I'm just relieved to get on so well with Mrs Shaw – had it not been for her I would have felt like I was in a prison. Her companionship saved me from going mad. There are only so many times you can straighten a bed and do the dusting in one small room. That's typical of John too – not to think things through, to think ahead. You'd almost imagine he'd given no thought to what I would do all day or whether I'd want to live here – he was happy in his own mind with the arrangement, therefore I would be too. That's my John.

It's all been such a whirl, I haven't worked it all out for myself yet – to think it was not so very long ago that I thought he had walked out of my life forever. I had even convinced myself I was better off without him – that he really was a rotter and that he didn't care one jot for me. Then he came back into my life after a year and swept me off my feet with his enthusiasm. He's still not really explained how he lost his job, it was clearly a serious falling-out with his employer. He doesn't like to talk about it, so it is wrong of me to ask and bring back memories of what were clearly unpleasant circumstances. People like that can be vile sometimes and very cruel in the way they deal with servants. I should know. It does nothing for your self-respect, being bullied and treated like dirt. But he finally replied to my letter – that he had kept it showed me that he really did care, though. I was really very down-hearted when I did not hear from him when I first wrote. I thought we were getting on so well. Better than I had with any young man who'd courted me – not that I can boast many – and not that I thought any of them who'd tried worth encouraging. But John – how he hadn't had girls lining up for him, if only for his looks, I'll never know.

That pain only reduced slowly – I really must have fallen in love with him for me to be so affected – so, if truth be told, when he finally replied it was easy to forgive him, especially since he was so apologetic and remorseful. It was me who ended up apologising to him, though exactly why I wasn't sure.

And he had clearly rebuilt his life and wanted me to be part of it – and there is something about a man in uniform!

Anyway I am very hopeful for our life here. There are things I want to do, and part of that is to not let John just drift, as I am sure he would without me at his side.

Chapter Seven

Bill

Josiah blocked the shot on goal and threw the ball to me. It splashed right in front and I grabbed it with my left hand and swam down the pool. One of the Bramley men appeared from nowhere and grappled me round the shoulder but I wasn't going to let go that easily. I twisted, my skin burning, and broke free then launched the ball to Walt who was screaming at me from the other side. Free from the man, I splashed my way forward to help. The pass from Walt was intercepted but the ginger-haired youth was slow to react; so, seizing my chance, I threw myself forward, arms aloft to stop his pass and landed on the youth grasping round his bony torso with my right arm, my left gripping his hard upper arm as he tried to quell it and wrestle the ball free. I took a mouthful of water but the ball was mine – I scooped it up and threw it as hard as I could. A Bramley defender rose out of the water and stretched but only succeeded in distracting his goalkeeper – the ball hit the post and went in, putting us in the lead.

I watched Josiah climb out of the pool, his smooth back arch then straighten. The captain, tall, self-assured, pulled off his cap and ran his fingers through his dark curly hair and passed his hands over his face and moustache to dry them. Josiah held a strong arm out to help me out of the pool. I had had a good match.

He gripped my shoulder, his arm warm across my back. 'Excellent shot that Billy. Well battled. We deserved to win that.'

'Thanks Josiah, tha stopped a few to keep us in it, solid as ever.'

We changed and headed down Wellington Road to the Old Anchor with Walter: the other four deciding to head off home to the spend the rest of their Saturday with their families. Neither me, Walt nor Josiah had anything in particular to rush home to. Josiah lived alone and both me and Walt still lived in the family home. In no sense of the word was there a warm homecoming to be had. My mother would be sitting in her black dress, ready to chide me when I got home; for what I didn't yet know nor care – there was bound to be something new; and my brother, Thomas, though invariably more soused than me, would be held up as a shining example of industriousness, thrift and devotion to his poor, widowed mother. Thomas, older by three years was always the favourite, and Fanny, well, Fanny, being a girl, was incapable of doing anything wrong in her mother's eyes.

Josiah returned from the bar with two pints, a soda for himself and a box of dominoes.

'Tha ought to get a piece of steak to put on that eye, Walt,' he said.

'I'll ask mother for a nice piece of fillet steak when I get back shall I? P'raps I'll get the butler to bring it wi' a drop of champagne.'

'Fair point. I suppose a chunk of stewing mutton will do nearly as well.'

'I reckon I'll just put up wi' it, eh?'

I laughed at them. 'Not long now to the Whit gala, five weeks is it? Do we know what we're doing yet?' I said.

'The club chairman wants us to put on an exhibition match, so we'll try and get enough players for two teams – we might need to ask around. It will have to be nice and genteel though, since there'll be ladies there. No rough stuff. In fact probably no grappling at all.'

I shook my head and made Walter laugh.

'Sometimes I think it's all you play for,' said Josiah.

I felt my face warm and my ears redden. I smiled and supped my pint – not much point denying it, I knew and they knew; in fact I would almost go as far as saying it was what made life worth living. I choked my way through the week in the stinking dusty filth of other people's discarded clothes with the only break from feeding the rag-puller being to salvage the occasional button or crawling under the garneting machine with a broom to shift six inches of dust whilst trying to avoid my scalp being ripped from my head; my life ordered by machine and overlooker; ten hours a day of relentless, monotonous, deafening, whirring of leather belts on pulleys, interspersed by abuse barked by the engineer for not moving fast enough. Then on a Saturday afternoon, I rushed home, changed, grabbed a crust of bread and was away to the pool. There I shed my clothes, like emerging from a chrysalis, coughed up the dust, stretched and plunged into the water cooling my body, freeing myself from my ties, escaping the dust and relieving the dullness in my ears, bathing my mind as well as my limbs. And then there was the excitement of the contest, the challenge for the ball, the sense of your own strength, the power, the muscles of my fellow players. I went all week with the only contact with others being a guarded slap on the back in the pub after work, or the pain of the engineer's boot on my backside. But there in the pool I was free to hold, to feel, to be held, free to live that precious time in the game. And Walter and Josiah knew because they felt it, or something like it, too. Walter, sweet little Walter, who people suspected wasn't quite right, who worked behind a counter and rode his bicycle around making deliveries, and who carried his basket to the door like a girl. I smiled to myself at the thought – how could there be a difference in how you carried a basket? – yet there was. But in the water I knew I transformed into an aggressive, assertive, small but powerful, masculine figure who would turn many a girl's eye.

'What's tha smiling at?' Josiah said.

'Nowt. I'm knocking. No fours.'

Josiah narrowed his eyes at me, and 'hmm-d' before looking back at the little black domino barricade on the table in from of him.

Josiah on the other hand was different. No doubting that he was a real man. Strong, self-assured, knowledgeable. Something almost foreign about him, what with his dark curly hair, just a little too long, and a head above all the other men in the wool towns, something perhaps of the look of an Italian organ-grinder or ice-cream seller about him. And, unlike most men round about, he was good looking – beautiful in fact, and he seemed to know it, and maintained that beauty somehow – he had good, clear skin, was always well-shaven, his moustache neat and trim. He dressed well, like he was a class above everyone – even though he was just a gigger in a mill. Then there was his intelligence – he read newspapers and poetry. He would sometimes go to the free library after practice and join us in the pub with a book under his arm. As far as I knew he had left school at thirteen like me but perhaps more of it had sunk in. I didn't know where Josiah came from – he would only say "not from round here" but it couldn't have been far, given the way he spoke. It was, though, like he had just been dropped in from somewhere else.

The girls adored him and he was often seen out on a Sunday with a different girl on his arm, but I knew he was more at ease with me and Walt and our friends. He was warm and friendly and knew all about us, but he was somehow out of reach. I adored him. I loved him, couldn't believe he could hang around with someone like me. There he sat puffing on his pipe, somehow being brilliant even at dominoes; smiling at us, protecting us, enfolding us. He was my brother, my father. I could touch, I could hold him, be consoled by him – but that was it. Josiah had a boundary that wouldn't be crossed – not for me – not for anyone I knew. He was pure, chaste. Perhaps it came from his religion – he was a lay preacher – had taken the pledge – or perhaps it came from wherever he had descended from, but that was how it was. Josiah was always in my hopes and dreams; I would do anything for him, but just to be able to be near him, to breathe his smoke, to hear his voice, I felt lucky.

'Tell you what,' said Josiah, scooping the dominoes back into the box, 'if it's nice tomorrow, shall I come down after chapel and we'll go up to the park? We could take some beers and a pack of cards. Perhaps see if any of the others want to come?'

'Sounds good. Meet by the fountain like before?' I said.

'I'll see if I can smuggle out some stuff – speaking of which I'd better be getting back. Don't want to push my luck – don't want him putting a stop to my Saturday break from the shop. I'm lucky he lets me.'

'Aye but it's not like he don't sweat you to make up for it.'

'Still, I'd rather work till eleven than miss out. See yer.'

I headed up Pinfold Hill on my short walk home, already looking forward to the next day.

'Where in God's kingdom have you been. I'm waiting for my tea.'

'Nowhere, mother. I'll get the kettle on straightaway.'

'Don't give me that. Frittering away our money. Wasting it on getting wet again when there's a perfectly good bath hung up in the scullery that costs nothing.'

I had nineteen shillings left from my wages and dropped seventeen of them into the tin on the sideboard. It only contained a few coppers. Thomas wasn't back yet. The jar would be lucky to see its contents double when he returned.

'Our Fanny not in, Mother?'

'No, she's away to do the marketing, so she is.'

I shook some coke onto the fire and filled the kettle in the scullery and put it over the fire. My mother sat and watched me from her chair. She was not yet sixty but could have been much older the way she behaved. She had once been beautiful and vivacious, and when all the Irish families had got together loved to dance to the fiddle. The fiddle stopped when my father died; my mother stopped too. No longer living, just existing, her once blue eyes, now grey, empty, following me round the room. Resenting my youth, that I was still here when her husband was not, blaming me – my very being. She had lost her "Albert" and, like Victoria, now wore black and sat on her throne immovable. Like a parasite, controlling them all, defining them. And yet how could I not love her; you had but one mother. She had borne me, raised me, loved me and she had done her best; only now she was spent. And I had dealt her the blow that led to all this.

I got a panchion out and tipped in some oatmeal and a sprinkling of salt. I scraped some dripping out of a pot then started mixing.

'What you up to?' my mother's voice croaked at me.

'Oatcakes mother.'

'I'd rather have drop scones.'

'No eggs, Mother.'

I had to go through for some hot water for the dough – I ran some from the stove into a cup.

'Not from there – it's better from the kettle.'

'That's not boiled yet.'

'It would have been if you'd been back earlier.'

I went back through. I mixed, moulded and rolled the cakes onto a pastry board then waited for the kettle to boil so that I could exchange it for the girdle.'

'Is that all we're having?'

'I daresay Fanny will bring something back – we can do some colcannon or something.'

'No meat?'

'Let's see what she brings, shall we?'

While I was stood baking the oatcakes, the front door opened and Fanny entered, all smiles, radiant, still living her life outside the house – where she had no doubt been strolling with the son of the Sligo Connellys from the down the road. I watched her smile fade as she removed her hat and mantle and hung them up.

'Hope you managed to get some meat, Fanny dear.'

'Yes, Mother, I'll get on with it as soon as William's out of the way.'

'You are good to me.'

She took her basket through and returned with her apron on and her long chestnut brown hair now tied up, a pan containing sheep or lamb's brains in her slender arms. While I finished turning my oatcakes, Fanny mashed some tea for mother and poured the rest of the water into the pan to boil. I tipped the oatcakes onto a plate.

'Leave the girdle, I'll use it for the braincakes. Could you chop some of that parsley and make some breadcrumbs?'

I was glad to get out of the living room.

I was crumbling the stale bread when Fanny came through. She started unpacking the rest of her basket, then she got an egg and cracked it in the panchion.

'Everything all right?' she said. 'You seem quiet.'

'Yeah, it's just 'er,' I said in a low voice nodding towards the front room.

'It's perhaps that next week's the anniversary of Dad's passing away.'

'I suppose so – but you know how it is. Just me and 'er.'

'I'll go and sit with her while she drinks her tea if you mix all that and add salt and pepper and a bit of vinegar.'

'Just me and 'er,' I repeated to myself. 'Me and 'er.'

The anniversary of our father's death – that also meant the anniversary of my what? – awakening – too. I had never understood how my father had been so quiet that afternoon. Normally he made such a noise around the house, asserting his dominion, doors banging, boots being flung. Or was it that I was so – absorbed? – enraptured? – that I hadn't heard the approaching footsteps, and so was surprised by the opening door. The door to the room where I shared a bed with my brother, and which right then I was sharing with one of the other apprentices, a sweet, blond-haired but incredibly dim boy called James.

My father had shut the door again and gone downstairs. I led James down and we had crept out past the turned back of my father in his chair, motionless, facing the empty fire. I returned later for my tea, and my father, face black with rage, swept past me and out of the door without a glance. That black, furious face was the last image I had of my father. My mother didn't speak when she put my tea in front of me, and she didn't look at me when she told me to go to bed as soon as I had finished. There was a separate mattress on the floor now for me. I didn't sleep. It grew dark and I was still awake in the room on my own. Then I heard a low voice downstairs – my father had returned. I didn't know what to expect, but knew it was likely to involve my father's belt. Then I heard a wailing noise, some sort of animal having its neck wrung – I crept onto the landing. My father wasn't there. The voice was that of a policeman, helmet in hand; the animal noise came from my mother wailing and sobbing "Oh, Michael!"

I went downstairs and was told by the policeman that my father was dead and that I had to be a brave boy for my mother. My brother and sister were nowhere to be seen.

A neighbour came round and I was removed to their house where I stayed for quite some time. I remembered looking out of an upstairs window seeing the black horse with black plumes, and thinking it strange how the street was lined with sacking. I did not go to the funeral or the wake, though I later learnt that my brother and sister had, along with most of the street. It was also not until later – and this from one of the others at the factory – that I learnt that that my father's body had been fished out of the Calder from a gravel bank down near Albert Mill. Someone had seen him go over the parapet – drunk they assumed.

I went back home a few weeks later and found my mother gone. Instead there was this thing in black, continually sat, often sobbing, muttering about "her own dear Albert" – back then I didn't understand why: because she had always called him Mick. Poor little Fanny had to sit with her and have her hair stroked. My brother and the fat "aunt" – not really an aunt at all – who came in to cook and clean, kept me away from her. For weeks I ate alone in the scullery while they sat at the table and talked in low voices, if at all.

My brother tried to apologise to me: 'I don't know why she's behaving this way. She seems to blame thi for what happened, but that's ridiculous. Tha don't know what she's on about, does tha? Nah, I don't see how tha could. To be honest I think it affected her mind. She keeps saying tha killed her Albert. But I think it's best to go along with her for now and hope she gets over it. Don't know what else to do.'

Fanny came through with the hot pan and stabbed the brains with a fork.

'I'll keep this stock for stew tomorrow.' She chopped the brains, mixed them in, and then together we shaped the cakes ready for frying. Tea would happen as soon as Thomas rolled in from his end of the week celebrations.

'I'll not be in for dinner tomorrow – after mass I'm going up to Crow Nest park. But I'll have some stew for my tea when I get back if that's all right. When she's like this it's better if I'm not around.'

'Don't be like that.'

'But it's true, isn't it?'

Fanny had to concede that it was.

The next day I arrived at the lake by the fountain. Walter Ripley was already there, looking round nervously, his face lighting up when he saw me approaching.

'Does tha ever get that feeling when tha's meeting someone that they'll never turn up and it was just a joke to get at thi?' Walter asked. 'That's what I've been worrying about for the last ten minutes. And I'm sure people have been staring at me. I've not got ink on my face or summat, have I?'

I laughed. 'No, tha's fine, Walt, just relax!' I lowered my voice, 'Tha can be such a girl.'

'I asked Jesse to come down too – he was sat outside looking bored this morning when I went past. Look, I've got some food.' He had a grocer's basket and pulled back the cloth revealing some bread and jars of potted meat.

'I've only managed a few oatcakes and a couple of bottles of beer.'

'The others'll have brought stuff. Does tha know who's coming?'

'No. Or, rather – I think so – because isn't that Josiah now.'

Josiah Hinchcliffe (Big Josiah) was strolling casually towards us, a cloth bundle over his shoulder, flanked by Josiah Longley (Little Josiah) and Walter Johnson (Big Walt).

'It's the old Walter-Josiah-Josiah-Walter confusion again.'

' "Pass this bottle of beer to Walter will you, Josiah," and there's a right bloody tangle!'

'Makes for easy whist teams though.'

There were handshakes, and we waited for Jesse.

'It'll be the daylight blinding him, and he's got lost with not having a tunnel to follow.'

'Or the arse of the man in front.'

'And they say it's just 'cause it's hot down there!'

'Keep your voices down for God's sake,' hissed Big Josiah. 'Ere 'e is. Get a shift on Jesse.'

Jesse broke into an ungainly trot and greeted us all.

We set off to find a spot by a group of trees across the grass on the edge of the park away from the bandstand and flower beds and the Sunday strollers. We were alone and able to spread out and relax, pooling the food and beer. We ate and played cards and drank and smoked. I pulled my cap down over my eyes and leant my head on Big Josiah's thigh. Josiah gave my hair a little stroke.

I woke a while later and heard some pages rustle.

I didn't get up or open my eyes. 'What's tha reading?'

'The Bible.'

'Really?' I sat up. 'I didn't think that was the sort of thing for a trip like this.'

'Why ever not? it's perfect.'

'But it's…'

'What just for church?'

'No, but…'

'Look. It's full of great stories and you can never finish reading it – you can always discover something more, or a new meaning. Tha still looks surprised. Tha believes in God don't tha?'

'Yeah, but…'

'There can be no buts.'

'I don't think God approves of me, does he?'

'Approves? God loves every one of his children.'

'But what about sin.'

'What about it?'

'Isn't what I am sinful? I fear God and what he will do to me. Turn me into a pillar of salt or something.'

'What on earth for? Didn't God make thi the way tha is? He must have a purpose in that. Why would he create thi with feelings that he considers sinful?'

'Did he create me that way?'

'Tha don't think tha could choose to be any other way does tha?'

'No, but…'

'But nothing – Christianity is the religion of love – it is not the religion of "this sort of love" or "that sort of love" – all flames burn pure – remember that. You have to see it through the eyes of Jesus – he interprets the Bible for us. Let me read thi a bit from John's gospel after the last supper: Jesus "riseth from supper, and layeth aside his garments; and he took a towel, and girded himself. Then he poureth water into the basin, and began to wash the disciples' feet, and to wipe them with the towel wherewith he was girded." And does tha remember later on Jesus says that someone will betray him? It says: "There was at the table, reclining in Jesus' bosom one of his disciples…" – it is presumed to be John himself – "one of his disciples whom Jesus loved. Simon Peter therefore beckoneth to him, and saith unto him, Tell us who it is of whom he speaketh. He leaning back, as he was, on Jesus' breast saith unto him, Lord, who is it?" Wasn't tha leaning on me a minute ago? See Jesus's love for his disciples was like my love for thi.'

The game of whist continued a short distance away as we spoke, piles of coppers getting higher or threatening to disappear altogether.

I was more interested in Josiah. 'So does Jesus say nothing bad about men like me?'

'No. He says nothing bad. He may even refer to you directly: he talks of marriage between men and women. It says then: "The disciples say unto him, If the case of the man is so with his wife, it is not expedient to marry. But he said unto them, All men cannot receive this saying, but they to whom it is given. For there are eunuchs, which were so born from their mother's womb: and there are eunuchs, which were made eunuchs of men: and there be eunuchs, which made themselves eunuchs for the kingdom of heaven's sake. He that is able to receive it, let him receive it." Don't you say you were born like you are; could that not be a reference to you: a eunuch "born from their mother's womb?" Jesus teaches love – everything else is just the opinion of men – often men with axes to grind, with hatred in their hearts – who read the Bible only to justify themselves.'

'But what about the pillar of salt? The destruction brought on that place?'

'Even that is distorted by priests and vicars. We don't really know what the sins of Sodom were: in the earlier chapters of Genesis it just says that they were wicked and sinners. Lot had two angels as guests in his house and some thugs tried to break his door down to rape them. Jesus says something about this.' Again he riffled through pages towards the other end of the book. Jesus was speaking to his disciples: "And he said unto them, In what place soever ye enter into an house, there abide till ye depart from that place. And whosoever shall not receive you, nor hear you, when ye depart thence, shake off the dust under your feet for a testimony against them. Verily I say unto you, It shall be more tolerable for Sodom and Gomorrha in the day of judgment, than for that city. And they went out, and preached that men should repent." So you see, the sin is not welcoming God. What the thugs in Sodom tried to do was evil, but it doesn't mean that it was the love that men may have for men that was the sin. What about the rape of the maids of Judah – do priests and vicars condemn all bodily acts by men on women because of that?'

I thought how nice it would be to lay my head on Josiah like John did with Jesus, to put my cheek against those little tight curls of hair. 'Don't you worry about sin then? Have you no doubts, Josiah?'

'Everyone should have doubts – they should continually question themselves. Something that Paul said to the Romans I haven't worked out… hey fellas listen to me,' he spoke to the card players, 'act natural, don't look round, I think we're being watched – come and sit round me.'

Everyone did as Josiah asked. As they did so I saw a copper heading our way. I felt sick and tried to get up to run, but Josiah put a hand on my shoulder and pushed me down.

Josiah took out some coins from his pocket and in a raised voice said to Walter Ripley: 'Here Walt, here's my share, thanks for bringing the food.' Walter looked puzzled but went along with it, his back being turned to the approaching policeman.

'Good afternoon, sir,' said Josiah. Those who hadn't seen, now turned to see the large figure towering over them: bushy black beard making him look untidy despite the uniform. 'It's a beautiful afternoon, isn't it?'

'Would you gentlemen care to turn out your pockets.'

By now I was shaking and my mouth was dry – I didn't act, I couldn't now that the only path open to me, to run, had been blocked by Josiah.

'What on earth's the matter, sir?' said Josiah.

'Could you just do as I asked, please.'

Handkerchiefs, coins, a couple of battered watches, pipes, tobacco, latch keys, a bag of toffee and two packets of cards were produced for perusal. Still I couldn't move.

'I thought as much. Gambling in public,' said the policeman.

Josiah laughed as if he had heard the best joke in years. The policeman turned to him. 'What is so funny?'

'I'm sorry, sir – they were playing cards but not for money. The only money you saw changing hands was to pay for the food. Walter here works in a grocer's and he brought more than most, so we were settling up. That's why he's more coins than the rest of us. It's funny because we're a Bible study group.' He held up his Bible: I was reading some texts to them.

'I must apologise to you gentlemen for my mistake. I'm glad you see the funny side of it,' the policeman said taking off his helmet to scratch the back of his head. 'You can't be too careful – there's a lot of gambling goes on.'

'Yes, and it is a good thing there's fellows like you around to protect us from it.'

'Thank you, sir, and sorry again for disturbing you. Good day.'

Josiah opened a page at random and started reading: 'But I would not have you to be ignorant, brethren, concerning them which are asleep, that ye sorrow not, even as others which have no hope…' The policeman's boots flattened daisies as he made his way down the slope. One or two of them grinned at Josiah but I just stared at the ground.

'It's all right, Bill, he's gone. I told you there was nothing better than the Bible for a day like today, didn't I?' He put his arm round my shoulder. 'Mustn't run from coppers unless you know you can outrun 'em – it only makes 'em think you've done wrong – it's like a wolf: you don't run from it or it instinctively chases.'

I looked up at him. 'Thanks; it's just coppers. Summat about them. They're no good. Always bad news.' I couldn't explain it any better – I always crossed over the road from them or turned and went the other way if I saw one coming towards me. It was just a thing I had to do. The sort with helmets were bad enough but then there were some with round flat hats with leather peaks. Worst of all were the ones on horses – devils on horseback who trampled striking miners in ninety three. That constable who brought the news of my father's death that night – always kept calling round, popping up and giving me a fright. I'd be playing in the street and the copper would ask how I was and call me "son": "come along, son – you know you're not supposed to play cricket on the highway causing a nuisance. I'll overlook it this once. How's your mother?" As if it were any of his business. Then during the Fenian scare, the same copper, then with stripes on his coat, had tried to get all friendly with me, asking about my brother or my Uncle Patrick, where they'd been the night before and so on. Sometimes I'd open the curtains in the morning and see a policeman passing by the house, looking up.

For me the afternoon was ruined. 'I'd better be getting back and see to mother's tea.'

'Righto, Bill, see thi on Saturday.' I headed down the slope trying to avoid the route marked out by crushed daisies.

Chapter Eight

John

Later on in that same week that I returned from Morecambe, whilst parading for duty, we had a visit from Superintendent Midgley.

'At ease men. Now I have been speaking with the Chief Constable and we are concerned at the level of behaviour on our streets. There have been a number of complaints from eminent persons and we must do something about it. We have the powers to prosecute foul-mouthed offenders – those who use abominable expletives – fines up to ten shillings may be levied. If you know the offender then you should summons them, if they are not known then you have the powers to arrest.

'Speaking of arrests, we have noticed an unaccountable variance in rates of arrest. In fact some of you have gone for several months without a single apprehension when your colleagues manage a number of arrests every month. The only explanation can be that some of you are too soft, too lazy or not attending to your beats properly.'

I kept my gaze on Midgley's highly polished boots. I just didn't seem to come across crime, though I wished I did. It never seemed to happen when I was around.

My last arrest had been for an assault – I was passing a courtyard entrance when I witnessed a man assaulting a girl – I was almost pleased. I took down the details: the man's name and address, the name of the girl – the man's niece as it turned out – and what I had heard: "I'll teach you a lesson you'll never forget" and that I had seen a blow which knocked the girl into the wall causing a cut to her head. I escorted the man – now crestfallen and apologetic, and saying his temper had got the better of him and that he had never done anything wrong before – to the police office. The sergeant asked me the girl's age. I didn't have that information in my book. "Thirteen," said her uncle. The Sergeant asked me whether the man had cooperated. He had. "You are free to go sir," the sergeant told him.

'So. Higgins?'

'Sergeant?'

'Aggravated assault.'

'Yes, Sergeant.'

'Did you ask the age of the victim?'

I looked down, wishing I was somewhere else. 'No, Sergeant.'

'Did the assailant provide you with information when asked?'

'Yes, Sergeant.'

'You cannot arrest without a warrant for an assault on a minor except when you are not provided with information.'

'Sorry, Sergeant.'

'Get out, Higgins.'

It was then I resolved to study more, and, remembering the advice of the copper who took me out that first night in Wakefield, I paid my six shillings subscription to *The Police Review*, and, since then, its arrival through the post had become quite an event for me.

Midgely continued: 'to address this discrepancy we are going to pair you off more often so that you can learn from each other. Sergeant Hebron will give further details.'

I set off on my beat with PC Love.

'So, Higgins, out to see how it's done then eh? Or does tha think I'm here to learn from thi? No, didn't think so.'

I didn't reply. Love was not really the sort I get on with.

'Well if tha's any questions just ask and I'll try to give thi the benefit of my experience. Tha knows tha trouble? – just too damn prissy.'

'I beg your pardon?'

'Exactly my point.'

We walked on for a bit towards the start of the beat.

'This is just a game, tha knows: keep thems at the top happy with arrests and they in turn can keep the chief constable happy – who in his turn can show the ratepayers how hard we're working on their behalf. The Chief has to report monthly – you've got to give him summat to write up. It's all about covering arses. If you don't cover yours, it gets kicked, the Sergeant, has to cover his, the inspector his, the Superintendent his, the Chief his. The only way you can keep your own arse from being kicked is to kick someone else's – that's where the vagrant, the pedlar, the cart driver comes in, see? And all they've got to do now is use obscene language and we're on to a winner: the Super doesn't want his arse kicked again. Right here we go…'

In front of us were two men leaning on each other as they made their way along the street heading away from the Swan Hotel.

'Good evening, gentlemen,' said Love. The two men parted and swayed slightly in doing so, like stacks of toy building blocks.

'Good evening, constables,' one of them said, raising his cap and grinning a little more than politeness warranted.

'There has been a burglary nearby, can I check your pockets for a picklock that may have been used?'

'We're not fucking thieves!' Love grabbed him by the arm. The other man lowered himself carefully on to a wall and sat dumbstruck, watching.

'Gerroff us!'

'I need to search your pockets, sir.'

'Fuck off and leave us alone.'

The man struggled to free his arm and, failing to do so, pushed at Love with his free hand.

'I'm arresting you for being drunk and disorderly. PC 188, please note this down in you pocket book.'

'Go the hell, tha bastard!'

'And for use of obscene language. I'll take him back to the office, you speak to the other man. I'll catch up with you later.' And off he went with his first arrest and a smile on his face, leaving me with the man slumped on the wall evidently trying to focus straight.

'Get yourself home, sir.'

The man pushed himself onto his feet and ambled away as fast as he could with a gait like he had one leg longer than the other.

I could not believe what I had just seen. Was that really what was expected of me? It was wrong. Of course I'd heard tales of such things, but that was so blatant. I continued the beat brooding over it. Half and hour or so later Love caught up with me.

'Got a quick cup of tea while I was waiting for him to be booked into his bedroom for the night – good result all round – didn't tha get the other fella for anything? Tha got it all in thi notebook though, for corroboration?'

'Yes. I put that PC 182, Love, was struck whilst questioning the gentleman and that he was arrested after for being drunk and disorderly and for using obscene language directed at PC 182, Love. Said gentleman was clearly intoxicated with liquor.'

'That's good – to the point.'

We continued round.

'Look, I'm thirsty – I think we should just check in at the Black Bull, make sure the landlord is no longer selling.'

There was still a light on downstairs. Love banged on the door. It opened an inch and someone peered out into the dark through the crack.

'George. I wondered when you'd be dropping by, come in.'

'Evening, Barnabas, everything nice and quiet? This is PC Higgins; have you met?'

'Come in and take the weight off. It's been quiet tonight. I reckon everyone's saving their pennies for tomorrow night to celebrate Batley bringing home the Cup.'

'Didn't Villa win that two week ago?' I said.

They looked at me as if I'd spoken French.

'It was a joke. Villa beat Everton three – two?'

Love spoke, his voice like he had just trodden in dog mess, 'We're talking about *The* Cup. Not just any old trophy.'

The landlord pulled two pints and put one on the bar next to me, where I sat, ignored. He and Love got down to the important business of the Northern Rugby Union Challenge Cup and Batley's chances against St Helens, especially after their win over Warrington.

'Will we see you on the train over to Leeds, George?'

'I've not been allowed leave. I couldn't believe it – that bastard of an inspector. We're on afternoons after tonight, but I'll see you here after I finish.'

I wondered how long they would be – I'd rather have been out on the beat, doing what I was supposed to. These people really did believe they were the centre of the known universe. Their parochial little game. I'd had to wait for Stan to post a page from *The Sheffield and Rotherham Independent* to be able to read a decent report of the English Cup. They'd probably read all about it in India before I had.

'Come on then, can't sit there all night, sup up, Higgins; off your fat arse. We've got the law to uphold. Thanks, Barnabas. Cheer them on for me tomorrow.'

Back outside, Love spoke. 'See it's important to keep in with the landlords. Vital part of the job. They know, and get to see, all the criminals; they overhear things. Keep 'em sweet and they'll pass on information. In return you overlook certain – minor indiscretions, shall we say. Works to everyone's benefit – especially to ours in upholding the law – and the odd pint's welcome too.'

We looked into courtyards and back gardens, shone our lanterns into empty shops and checked that the doors of the pawn shops were secure. We then went round the beat again, going over our footsteps at the same even pace, each long hour being counted down by a distant bell. After four o'clock, as we were heading past the end of Crown Street, Love spoke: 'Just wait here for me for ten minutes, I've got to go and wake someone,' and he disappeared up the street before I could object. I waited more than ten minutes. Should I carry on the beat or go and see where Love had got to. I got my snuff tin out; it seemed like an age. My breath hung in the night air. Eventually Love returned with a smile on his face.

'Where the hell's tha been? If I'd been seen by someone hanging around and got reported!'

'No one about, is there? Well then. Anyhow I've been on important police business. Like I said I needed to get someone up.' He smiled a faraway smile. 'Ever so polite and welcoming. Lovely lady. Fast asleep when I shone my lantern in, fair squealed she did, till she recognised me. Showed her one or two tricks with my staff.' He pulled the wooden staff out of his pocket and twirled it.

I walked on disgusted. A married man.

'Look 'ere Higgins, don't get all above thisen. I thought tha had a sense of humour. We've put in a successful shift – including an arrest. You've a lot to learn.'

'I don't approve, that's all.'

'Well, I don't ask thi approval. Just keep thi neb out of what doesn't concern thi.'

I carried on walking, ignoring him.

'Tha really is a queer sort.'

'Change the subject.'

'As long as tha don't go getting any ideas about blathering or causing trouble. Who does tha think has the aces in their hand – the constable with a shining record of arrests and convictions, or thi?'

'Well, I now see why they call thi snatcher and shagger anyhow.'

A pain suddenly shot up my arm and I was forced to my knees as Love put me in an arm lock.

'Just don't get the wrong side of me, Higgins, tha hear?'

'All right, let me go!' My arm was released.

The rest of the night passed in silence. Not until we returned to the office was another word spoken.

'Good work tonight, gentlemen,' the sergeant said. 'Let's get the occurrence book written up then you can go and get off home yourselves.'

*

It was getting on for eight in the evening when I got back from our detachment's annual outing. I felt sick and was unsteady on my feet as I climbed the stairs.

This year the committee had arranged a trip to Harrogate and each of us had paid in four shillings for the hire of the brakes and for a slap-up dinner at the White Hart Hotel. On the way, George Love spoke at length of the recent police versus tradesmen cricket match in which he had scored sixty and had taken three wickets. I tried to ignore him and take in the countryside as Love then rattled on about his clever detection and told tales of his famous arrests, embellished with explicit details, much to the amusement of the others. He told of how he had arrested a man for assaulting him. 'In court he claimed he had not assaulted me at all. No. The man said, "I was merely saluting this wonderful officer!" ' The others then tried to out do each other with their own tales, each time more exaggerated, to put them in a good light.

We stopped at an inn on the outskirts of Leeds for refreshment. More beer accompanied dinner, or lemonade or ginger beer for those who had signed the pledge, then more was downed in toasting the Chief Constable and the Queen and her Diamond Jubilee, the Outings Committee, the waiters, and anyone else they could think of. Then Inspector Knight gave a fine speech extolling the virtues of the Constabulary and thanking all of his men for their hard work and serving the citizens of the Heavy Woollen District. This was followed by cheers and a round of "for he's a jolly good fellow."

After a walk on The Stray and taking the sulphurous waters we got back in the brakes and headed for Knaresborough for tea, stopping at the first inn on the way as a matter of necessity because the drivers wanted to take away the aftertaste of the Harrogate water. In the shadow of the impressive viaduct, sandwiches, tea and cakes were piled on top of the earlier soup, boiled mutton, goose, beans, peas and cabbage, potatoes, suet pudding and ale, before we all climbed back on the brakes to be shaken and jolted all the way back to Heckmondwike. I was ill over the side on the approach to Batley to the strains of "The Girls of Yorkshire" led by the voice of PC Love, best tenor in the West Riding Constabulary choir:

'To cheer me when my manhood has passed its happy prime, and comfort me when troubles come in dark dull winter time.'

Everyone joining in the chorus: 'the girls of dear old Yorkshire who know no care nor fear. The happy girls of Yorkshire. The loved ones and the dear.'

My illness and the subsequent big cheer, interrupted the singing to the annoyance of Love and the Inspector who was dabbing a tear from his eye. I tried to blame it on Harrogate's disgusting water, which caused great mirth.

I steadied myself at the top of the stairs and lined myself up for the few strides to my room – no to *our* room. I pushed it open. 'Hello, Annie dear. I'm sorry I'm a bit later than…'

I realised I was on my own, so pulled off my boots and lay down on the bed and tried to lie still in the hope that the unnerving sense of movement would stop.

A few moments later Annie entered and I tried to sit up.

'I'm sorry, Annie, dear. Hello. I'm a bit later than what I had wanted to be.'

'You're drunk.'

'No, it's more a case of seasickness from being on the road – no, roadsickness.' I giggled at this joke.

'John, I'm disappointed.'

'So am I. Very much so in fact.' I giggled again.

'I'll put you to bed.'

'No, thank you. You can manage. I mean, I can.'

I got my jacket off and fumbled with my shirt studs before giving up on the pesky, fiddly things and letting Annie do it.

Fortunately, I had the next morning to sleep it off before going on duty. She had made me drink an egg beaten with salt and a little brandy, then later I managed some porridge and dry toast and Annie went to the shops and came back with ground coffee which she prepared milky and sweet. I started to feel better and got up after midday.

'I've been offered a little job,' said Annie after I had soaped my face and had my razor poised.

I stopped, looked at her, then carried on. One thing at a time.

'It's at Zillah Law's refreshment rooms. Mrs Shaw recommended me to her.' I glanced at her through the mirror.

'Don't look like that at me, John. I've nothing to do all day and I might as well be earning some money so that we can move out, get our own place and start a family.'

She was many steps ahead of my thinking. It shocked me. I couldn't even contemplate a family, but I supposed it could happen. I dried my face.

'But what will the Inspector say when he finds out?'

'I don't know, but then I don't see it's any of his business. He can't stop me can he? It's not like I'll be the only one.'

'What do you mean?'

'Several of the other wives work.'

'Do they? How do you know?' I started to get dressed.

'Well, do you expect me to sit here all day waiting for you to get home? Yesterday I had an invite to Mrs Watson's house. While you were all away getting drunk she had a little tea party for the wives. Very pleasant it was too.'

'Why didn't I know about that?'

'Because you weren't here.'

'I still don't think you should accept work.'

'It's too late. I already have. In fact I start this afternoon.'

'Don't you think you should have asked me first?'

'It wouldn't have made any difference, John. I can't stand it here all day.'

'But I'm putting money aside for furniture to get us started, aren't I?'

'But how much? Perhaps if you got on up the grades a bit faster.'

'What? Where did you get that nonsense from? Have they been gossiping behind my back? Even my own wife questioning me now, is it?'

'I'm sorry, John, it just slipped out. I didn't think.'

'No, you didn't.' I put on my tunic, picked up my helmet and left.

I brooded over this all the way through the afternoon on reserve duty. Hanging about in the station wasn't really what I wanted; keeping an eye on a couple of vagrants in the cells – poor sods who had been tramping for work – out Lincolnshire way they had started – and were unfortunate to find that their luck ran out at the same time as their money whilst on The Green when one of Love's acolytes was on duty. They only had a bottle of beer between them which they tried to claim amounted to "visible means of subsistence." At least while they waited for the magistrates to sit in the morning they would have a blanket to cover them and a crust of bread and tea. Their names were chalked up on a board next to that of a pedlar arrested for going from house to house grinding scissors without a certificate.

At teatime Art came in with his pocket book to get it endorsed after his afternoon's duty. Art was one of the "regulars" – there was a steady stream of them who came in to the police station – people who were in trouble and needed advice, or people who were just sad or lonely. Some came in for minor first aid or even money. Sometimes there would be a whip round for them.

Art had the mind of a small child but the body of a man – he was nearly six feet tall and walked with a stoop. Art loved the police. We were his friends and he felt that he was one of us. He would wander around pretending to be an assistant constable, scribbling hieroglyphs in his official pocket book. Art's mother was getting on, but for our kindness to her son she brought cakes into the station on a regular basis.

'Good afternoon, Constable Higgins, sir,' Art said.

'Good afternoon, Arthur. Have you finished your duty for the day?'

'Yes, Constable Higgins, sir,'

'Notice anything suspicious?' I flicked through the squiggles in his pocket book.

'Not today, Constable Higgins, sir.'

'Jolly good. Keep up the excellent work, Art. I'll tell the Chief Constable you've done well. Give my regards to your mother.' Art gave a huge grin and a salute and went home to his mother, happy with his day's service to the community.

I had some quiet moments when no one was around, so I got out *The Police Review*. I studied what to do if I was called to a collapsed scaffold. I rehearsed it in my head: PC 188 Higgins reports that at around 2.15 p.m. the scaffold at the Town Hall gave way suddenly causing 2 men to fall to the pavement. PC 188, Higgins, arrived at the scene to find one man unconscious and the other injured. PC Higgins conveyed them in a four-wheeled cab to Dewsbury Infirmary where the house surgeon declared that the first man had a broken neck and that life was extinct, the other man had a severe scalp wound and a broken right arm and was detained in a ward. The body was taken to the mortuary. The wife of the deceased and the Coroner's officer were informed. Property of the said man amounted to 7½d in bronze, a box of snuff and a broken pocket watch. 2½s in expenses were incurred by PC 188 Higgins.

I practiced some maths questions: reduce 863,412 halfpence to half-crowns, and wrote out some common spelling problems. I read the letters and the questions and answers. "Question – what do you do if you find someone insensible in the street? Answer – keep people back, loosen their collar and send for a doctor. Send word to the station for an ambulance or a stretcher. Keep their head raised and inclined to one side and notice carefully their breathing and odour of breath. Obtain if possible name and address. Note the positions of the body and the surroundings…" "Question: you see a man bathing in a pond so near to the highway that he was exposing his person. Would you charge him?" I shut my eyes. The scene was vivid. I saw trees overhanging the pond and bushes from where I was observing the man. It was Edward, no – it was the man I had seen at the swimming baths, the one with the dark curly hair, only this time the bathing drawers were discarded. Of course I wouldn't charge him. I would observe the situation carefully, note the particulars and with an eye to detail. I shuddered and opened my eyes. "Answer – You would charge him only if you could show or prove there was intent to insult a female. If not caution him."

I went home resolved to apologise to Annie; I badly needed her help. I had to make it up to her. I took a loop round the back of Liversedge Hall on my way back – there was a lane where dog roses grew. Stars were coming out and the air was cool and scented – I couldn't make it out, but there was honeysuckle somewhere. My lantern wasn't lit. I breathed in, letting the scent fill me: if only Annie were here with me now. I located the dog roses and picked half a dozen, putting them inside my helmet that I carried under my arm.

When I got back there was a candle on a chair by the door. Annie was already in bed. She stirred when I entered.

'I've brought you these.'

'What are they?'

'Roses.'

'Can you put them in some water?'

I arranged them in the vase and stood them on the wash stand. I put my arm over Annie when I climbed into bed.

'I'm sorry about earlier.'

'Don't worry. I've forgotten all about it.'

'Thank you.' I kissed her cheek.

'I've had a busy day, but it was good.'

Without actually saying "no" she had turned down my unspoken request. Would it be so very bad to force myself on her? I lay awake trying to think of other things, of nothing at all. Then, when I started to drift off, an image of water and a swimmer came to me and I jolted wide awake again. I lay awake, tormented, for quite some time.

In the morning Annie had leapt out of bed and pulled on a skirt and blouse before I had fully come round – I had reached out to find only an empty space beside me.

'The roses are lovely, John. I thought I half-remembered you bringing them in last night; I must have been sleepy.'

'I think you were.' I lay staring at the ceiling as she moved about the room.

She leant over me to kiss my forehead and I made an attempt to catch her wrist but she was too quick for me – she skipped away laughing; like a mountain stream. 'Come on lazy bones. Mrs Shaw has the bacon on; I can smell it.'

Over breakfast I decided I needed to resume my prescribed vigorous exercise. I had enjoyed being in the water again at Morecambe. I would go to the baths at Batley – plenty of time before I was due on at two; just as long as I avoided Wellington Road I would be all right. Thrashing up and down the baths for an hour and a brisk walk was just the thing.

I covered the two miles or so in long strides, the thought of the cool water spurring me on down the dusty hawthorn-edged lane into Batley. I was warm when I got there and once in the dressing box I got out of my clothes quickly and into my costume. The water was cold as I splashed myself to get accustomed to it. Then I set off in a great disturbance of water. The pool was quiet, only a group of white-haired and balding men, everyone else being at work. I counted the lengths – my aim was fifty. I got halfway to my total and then the pressure of the water on my bladder was too much and I got out to find the urinal. When I got back in the pool someone else was swimming amongst the group of old men – and overtaking them. I got my head down and ploughed on through my lengths not stopping. Twenty-eight, I counted; as I touched the edge I felt a tap on my shoulder and stopped, lifting my head out of the water.

There, grinning at me, was the man with the dark, curly hair, an immaculate set of teeth flashing: 'How do you do. I thought I recognised you. Haven't we met before at Wellington Road?'

'I don't know.'

'Yes, I'm sure it was you. I recognised your swimming action first. Quite unique!'

'Yes, sorry about that. I don't really know what I'm doing – but it gets me there.'

The man laughed and held out a hand. 'The names Hinchcliffe – Josiah.'

'Higgins – John.'

'Don't let me stop you.'

I was glad to be released. I would just carry on to fifty then get out and go. What was all the fuss about?'

The other man swam up and down nearby, sometimes doing breast-stroke, sometimes overhand backstroke, efficient, elegant swimming.

I got out and went to change. I headed to the lavatory again – I tended to swallow a lot of water as I went. As I emerged onto the street, the man was perched on the wall waiting for me. I must have looked startled.

'I'm sorry. I wanted to catch you before I left. I've got a proposition for you. Let me buy you a drink.'

'Thank you for the offer, Mr Hinchcliffe…'

'Josiah.'

'Thank you, but I'd better get back. I'm working this afternoon.'

'So am I, but I shan't let you go that easily: I insist.' He smiled and my defences crumpled.

'All right then, but I haven't got long.'

'Excellent. Which way are you heading?'

'Towards Heckmondwike.'

'Then I'll walk with you as far as Healey. The George is on your route and it's a nice country pub, nicer than the ones round here.'

'So, what's your proposition?'

'I've got a water polo team and, the thing is, we're short of players. We've an exhibition match coming up at a swimming club gala and we need to get a few more players to make up two teams.'

'You can't mean me?'

'Of course.'

'But you've seen me swim – what's the opposite of a fish out of water?'

'A fish in the water?'

'No. I mean I'm like a fish out of water when I'm in the water – but that doesn't work does it?'

I cracked out laughing and Josiah had to stop walking as he creased up. When he regained control he said: 'I know what you mean, but it's not important. You're strong and as long as you can move the ball down the baths you'll get along fine. Look, I'm bigger than the other players I know and you're taller and bigger than me – you must be what twelve, thirteen stone or so and none of it wasted.'

'No… I don't know.'

'Tell you what, why don't you just come along on Saturday afternoon and give it a go. Two o'clock at Wellington Street – we've just got a muck about. If you don't like it you needn't bother again.'

'I might then.'

'That's good.'

'Why were you here today if Wellington Street is where you play.'

'I prefer it there but I only live round the corner from here – just felt like a few lengths before work. Glad I did.'

'Me too. I mean, wanted to swim before work.'

As we left Batley and headed past fields towards Healey village, Josiah explained how water polo was played, how you could tackle but not hold someone under. Strength and fitness were the most important thing.

Josiah would make a good evangelical preacher, I thought; I was already sold on the idea, though I didn't let on. It would be good to put my swimming to use and perhaps it would be like Josiah said – I might be quite good at it, even if my swimming was ungainly – my size would give me an advantage. Having friends outside the police would be nice too – if I could call anyone in the police "friends" – one or two were decent enough but I didn't have much in common with them except the job. I hadn't really slotted in to a social circle since I'd moved here.

'Anyhow you have to come on Saturday,' Josiah said, 'It's been determined by fate.'

'What do you mean?'

'Well I was told by the gaffer to take the morning off and work late tonight instead – they didn't have the cloth ready for my machine, see. So I said yes and took the chance of a swim. I normally go to Wellington Street but I didn't have time so it had to be Batley – and, if I'd not, I wouldn't have met you. See, it's fate.'

'I don't know about that.'

'Come on, I'll buy you a drink. What are you having?'

The bar was empty, just an old farmer with his dog lying at his feet, one hand on a stick, the other on his pewter mug, gazing beyond the here and now.

'So what's you line of work?' Josiah asked.

I took out my tobacco pouch, offered it to Josiah, and filled my pipe bowl. 'I'm a clerk – in the law. Boring really.'

'And are you married?'

'Yes.'

Josiah was looking straight into my eyes, holding my gaze, his brown eyes shining, drawing me in.

'And are you happy?'

'What? Yes, of course – it's not been long – you know how things are – you're always two different people, it's never straightforward is it.'

'No.'

'What about you?'

'No. I've never… never met the right person. I love being with people but it's probably that I'm… too selfish – it's complicated. I can't see as I'll ever be able to share my life with someone.'

'Surely not.'

Josiah smiled. It struck me that there might have been a touch of sadness in that smile. I felt I had known him a long time, was strangely at ease with him, like I was with Stan and Harry – friends I had known for so long that it was often enough just being with them – no need for superfluous conversation.

'You will come on Saturday, won't you?'

'Yes, I will.'

'Good. That's good.'

There was a warm handshake when we parted. I headed off at a quick pace. I felt alive. Swallows dived and turned over the cricket field, and a blackbird swooped across the lane and into a hedge, it's beak stuffed with worms. I had not met such warmth in a person – not since I had left Sheffield anyway. I found most people round about to be cold and guarded – treating everyone with suspicion, and I knew I had come to do the same. Everyone I met was a potential criminal: someone who beat their children, or stole from their employer. But that was not there with Josiah; he was open and could be trusted. But how did I know – what was it? Why should he not be just a clever, confidence trickster? There was a lot more about him – I wanted to get to know him. Damn! I didn't finish until two on Saturday – I'd have to take a day's leave. I couldn't miss it – not now; it was already forming into the thing that would drag me through the rest of the week.

Chapter Nine

Bill

I sat on the pavement opposite the Old Westgate entrance to the second class baths. I hadn't been home since finishing work, not wanting to get dragged into an argument, have guilt piled on me for wanting to do something for myself – for pleasure. This was my time; all morning I had been cutting bales of cloth to feed that devil of a machine – roaring and rattling, ripping and tearing, spitting out dust and fluff, concentrating to keep clear of its jaws so that it didn't do the same to my skin, my flesh, my bones. That would put a stop to my catching a ball.

I'd see my mother later – she could vent off then, but now I was sitting waiting for the others to arrive, as if by arriving early that would hasten our allotted start time in the pool. Just as I had anticipated that first pint to slake my thirst and wash away the dust and filth I had breathed in, so I quivered with the thought of that first dive into the water to wash away the marks of enslavement, to restore my humanity.

Soon Walter arrived and came and sat next to me.

'Ay up W alt. How's tha doing?'

'Not bad ta. Knackered though – been tearing around on that bone-shaker trying to get all my deliveries done in time – I'm glad we've not got owt serious this afternoon. What's Josiah got planned?'

I didn't reply – my attention was fixed on a man over the road – about my age, not in mill worker's clothes, no ill-fitting jacket covered in dust, no neck-cloth, no greasy cap or wooden-soled boots. Instead a jacket that hung properly on his broad shoulders, a neck tie and a turned down collar, a felt hat and polished boots. He was tall, rather stiff-looking with a well-groomed, sandy moustache. He was pacing slowly backwards and forwards in front of the entrance to the baths. Then I saw Josiah turn the corner of Wheelwright Street; I raised my hand, but instead of crossing over Josiah went up to the man and shook his hand. The man greeted him like a long lost friend. Me and Walter got to our feet; 'Come on let's see what's what.'

Josiah introduced them: 'Bill, Walter, this is John – he's come to give it a go – to make up teams for the gala.'

I shook his hand – I felt like a child shaking hands with a grown-up. I was uncomfortable looking up at him.

'Pleased to meet you, Bill,' he said. I wasn't sure about this man. Who was he – in what way did he know Josiah? What was he to him?

'You'll have to go easy on him. He's never played before.'

That made me feel better, relieved – the stranger's status had just fallen below mine – I would show him how it was played. That pool was my territory.

We went in and I went into my usual dressing box. I tied the string on my drawers, flung open the door and flew through the air straight into the pool. First one in. I swam up and down and dived under the surface until my chest scraped along the bottom of the pool, enjoying the claustrophobia that would smash when I went back up. Dressing box doors banged as others arrived at the pool side or emerged to dive in. The stranger came out in a full length red and white striped costume and sat on the pool side with his feet in the water. I smiled to myself as I watched him turn and lower himself slowly into the water, splashing his head and shoulders as he did so; he then stood there at the pool side not knowing what to do. Can he even swim? Where did Josiah get *him* from?

Josiah threw a ball to me and set about erecting the goals at either end before diving in himself – a dramatic dive, emerging above the surface quite a few yards into the pool.

I couldn't resist throwing the ball to the stranger out of sheer devilment – landing it just in front of him, spraying him in water. Josiah went over to him and started talking to him – explaining something to him. I dived under and sought out Walter's ankles to grab – then the two of us ended up wrestling in the water trying in earnest to drown each other. I tried to get Walter's neck in a lock and hook my legs around him. Then we got a ball and much the same sort of thing ensued but with the ball as an object not the drowning. After a few minutes Josiah shouted me over.

'I've shown him the basics of a tackle, let's see how he goes on. Bill, you have the ball and try to get past him.

I grinned at him, 'You ready?' The man smiled a half smile and nodded. I swam at the stranger with the ball in front of me, then I took the ball in my right hand. The man's right arm went up. I leapt forward and reached under the man's armpit, let myself sink, twisted, turning onto my back and pulling the man forward, I then kicked out and escaped, ball firmly under my arm. When I surfaced, I turned and smiled at the man who was grinning back. 'That was clever,' he said.

'Have another go,' Josiah said. 'You know what to expect now, John.' I went back at him the other way. This time though as I touched the other man, I felt an arm round me. I tried to sink and twist but the man tightened his grip and pulled me in. I was going nowhere and ceased my struggle. I was released from the strong grip and laughed.

'Not bad for a beginner. Now you have the ball and come at me.'

In a bizarre thrashing stroke the man swam at me ball in hand – he wasn't looking where he was going. I stroked good and hard and pushed high out of the water onto him – an arm round his neck, pulling him to my chest, throwing him off balance with a leg hooked round and releasing the ball which I grabbed, then I twisted and was away.

'Thanks for that, Bill – I can see I'm going to have to learn fast,' John said, as he came up coughing.

'Don't mention it. Happy to give anyone a ducking.'

'That's enough of the basics. So, shall we get caps on and have a knock about? I'll be in a team of six with John, against a team of five.'

John's swimming was a right laugh – absolutely hopeless – but somehow he managed to get down the pool. Most of the time I got the better of him and enjoyed showing him up; but once or twice the sheer strength and size of the brute meant I couldn't. Once he leapt onto me like a salmon out of the water and grabbed me round the shoulders and squeezed – not a tackle I had ever encountered before, more like a bear hug and I'd had no option but to let go of the ball.

I was annoyed when afterwards Josiah invited John to go with us for a drink: we would have to remain on our best behaviour and I'd have to share Josiah.

I walked behind with Walter, trailing Josiah and John like two small children walking behind their better turned-out parents: Josiah in his matching jacket and trousers, looking handsome in his straw hat, and John, his felt hat perched on his carefully combed straw-coloured hair. If only I had been bigger too, perhaps I could feel Josiah's equal.

Josiah patted John on the shoulders and asked him how he liked it.

'It was better than I'd imagined. It's brutal, but fun.'

'How's your cheek?'

'Nothing to it.'

'It looks quite a nasty scratch though.'

'Does it?'

'Was it a finger nail?'

'Don't know, could have been a toe nail – I thought I got kicked once.'

We sat round a table in a gloomy corner of the Old Anchor; three pints of porter and a pint of soda.

'Thanks for inviting me along,' said John. 'And thank you, Bill, for going easy on me – it must be frustrating having a beginner holding you back and not being able to play the way you normally do.'

'That's all right.' I had made no concessions at all for John, but wasn't going to say.

'So you think I'll be up to scratch in time for that match of yours?' John said to Josiah.

'Oh yes, no doubt, is there fellas?'

'If he keeps learning at that rate,' said Walter.

'I don't think I'll ever get the hang of scientific swimming though.'

'I've never seen owt like it, that's for sure,' I said.

'Call it a unique and rare talent,' said Josiah, which set us all off laughing.

'We might try you in goal though so that you don't soak all the spectators. Glad you enjoyed it anyway.'

'I did.'

'So you'll come next week too.'

'Yes.'

I was studying John. He was good looking – blue eyes and a wave in his hair, strong jaw line – his face almost sculpted, like one of those Roman statues you see in pictures. He would have a thick sandy beard if he let it grow – like a heathen. And yet there was something vulnerable in that face: eyes that moved rapidly and cheeks that were prone to flush. I was more at ease with him but still needed to know more about him – what he meant to Josiah, where he was from.

'Some bloke at work said that that Oscar Wilde's been let out. He said he should've been strung up for what he did,' I said.

'Look I'd better be going,' John said. 'See you Josiah. Walter. Bill.' He pushed his stool back and headed for the door.

Josiah gave me a black look and went after John. I shrugged at Walter.

Josiah returned a few minutes later. 'What the hell did tha say that for?'

'What?'

'Tha knows, that Oscar Wilde thing.'

'I just wanted to see how he'd react. Test him out.'

'Tha's a bloody fool. I think I reassured him that tha wasn't being deliberately offensive – but I had to explain tha could be stupid sometimes. Tha could've scared him away altogether. I'm trying to get two bloody teams together and I'd appreciate thi help!'

'Well, is he on our side or not?'

'How the hell am I supposed to know, eh? I just know he's a nice bloke. What the hell did tha think tha'd learn?'

'I thought if he stood up for Oscar Wilde we might know.'

'No one sticks up for him whether they sympathise or not. Either he was offended because he thought tha was suggesting summat of him, or he was offended because he's a ladies man, or he didn't think a conversation about hanging Oscar Wilde was proper. See tha's none-the-wiser. And we want him to come back don't we?'

'Sorry, Josiah, I didn't think.' I couldn't bear being attacked by Josiah. Anyone else and it wouldn't have mattered, but I craved Josiah's respect and had destroyed it. I felt my eyes start to prick. 'I'm sorry.'

'Look, forget it. I think he's all right.' Josiah put his arm round me. 'I'll get thi another drink.'

Walter looked at me and rolled his eyes after Josiah got up.

'All right don't rub it in Walt. I know I'm a fool.'

'So do we.'

'What did tha reckon to John, then?'

'I liked him. I hope he is a non-conformist. I'd like to see him again.'

'Just your type, eh?'

Walter smiled and finished his pint.

Josiah returned.

'So do you think he sympathises, Josiah?' Walter said.

'Not sure, Walt – not that it is any of our business. He's married, but that's all I know. He's a decent chap though, and I think he could make a good player so that's all that matters.'

Chapter Ten

John

I had left the pub in turmoil. I had had such a good afternoon and believed I had been accepted into the group better than I could have imagined.

I had been about to head off for the train as I left the baths, but they'd invited me to the pub. Then Bill had come out with that – like he had been suggesting something – he'd even been looking at me when he said it. Oscar bloody Wilde! All I knew was that everyone said he was done for sodomy and got off lightly. Josiah had caught up with me and told me to ignore Bill – has had a hard time of things – had a habit of saying the wrong thing at the wrong time – would get himself into a lot of trouble one of these days – he didn't think that Bill meant anything by it – he was just a stupid little *get* with no manners, but his heart was in the right place. I said that wasn't why I'd left – I'd just better be getting back, that's all. But, still I had a lingering suspicion that Bill suspected something about my character. Something that, no matter how hard I had tried to push it under, just kept bubbling back up to the surface. I wasn't sure I could go back the next week, despite Josiah's assurances. Had something really been that obvious? – what could it be? My hair, moustache, everything was just like any other man who tried to present a respectable image – I didn't wear strange clothes or odd colours – there couldn't be anything, but then there was something that Edward and Grainger had gone for, something that the likes of George Love picked on. Some signal I must unconsciously send out, a sign saying: 'here's a man whose manhood it open to question.' And it was.

I had been terrified getting into the pool – I had had no idea what to expect. Then, when Josiah had explained the rules, the tackles – what was going to happen, I'd wanted to run away. But there could be no running. Josiah had demonstrated the tackles on me, grabbed me round the neck, held me in his arms, then told me to do the same on him! I tried not to think about it, and found I didn't have to try too hard – any thoughts of passion were ended by a combination of the cold water and the kicking-in of my instinct, in a battle for survival to avoid drowning or being physically humiliated – then later by the pursuit of the ball. This was pure physicality. No room for thoughts. I had thought that after Josiah, Bill would be a pushover – small skinny Bill, not much higher up the physical scale than a boy with rickets. Then he'd been pitted against me: more like trying to catch an eel, the way he'd slipped past me and got away – and his strength in taking

the ball off me! Bill would have been no match for me out of the water – I
would have batted him away like a kitten, but in the water he seemed to turn
every bit of his strength into wrestling the ball away. I'd had great respect for
Bill; I'd liked him – getting the better of him that time was fun: that firm grip
I'd got around him and he'd just gone limp in my arms like a child. But then,
it was also fun, though frustrating, being tackled by him; being submitted to
the strength of the other. From never touching another person other than
Annie, except by handshake or a slap on the back since I was about six, that
one incident excepted, here I was able, allowed, encouraged, to be in such
close contact with other men. It was liberating. It felt all right, it felt good and
it had happened without arising any passion in me. This was perhaps the
release I needed to allow me to feel normal. There in the pool, different rules
applied. I could separate off that side of myself – dedicate it to water polo,
where it was safe. I would get some old-style bathing drawers like everyone
else wore too. I could see myself spending time with these new friends –
going for a drink every week after water polo. And then Bill had come out
with that.

I didn't see Annie when I got back – she was out at work so I had tea
brought up to my room and I ate alone.

In fact I didn't see her much that week at all. I was up early while she lay in
bed; then she was out when I returned and didn't get back until bed time.
Coming back to an empty room in the afternoon, I reflected that this wasn't
how I had imagined it – I had had in mind a wife waiting for me when I got
home to sit me down with a cup of tea and something on a plate. Perhaps
finding our own place would be the answer.

I sat and read *The Police Review* by the window and watched the puddles
form in the muddy street, or would fold it in my pocket and go out when the
weather was fine to find a quiet spot against a tree to read, or to close my eyes
for a while. I read of campaigns to provide summer clothing for the police: in
Huddersfield they had been given a more lightweight summer uniform rather
than having to sweat it out in the heavy woollen tunics that the rest of the
county had to endure – I lost pounds in weight on warm days.

There was a portrait of a PC James Morfitt from Bradford, and it told of
his exploits: rescuing a woman from a burning building, catching thieves. He
had caught someone breaking into a pawn shop and someone else breaking
into a plumber's workshop. It made you sick – just a matter of luck that's all.
My study was paying off though. Earlier in the week I had reported the
owner of a dray and issued a summons against him for driving it without the
name and address marked on the side. I had spotted it turning off the street
through an archway and went to inquire. The owner had said he'd just got it
re-painted the day before and that he couldn't do the lettering until the paint
was dry. I had touched the paintwork. 'I think you'll find it is now dry, sir –

and shouldn't be used without the requisite details marked.' Then the next day I had made an arrest – a cyclist who was overtaking a cart without warning of his approach by sounding his bell. He had not thought it necessary he had said, and inquired whether I should not be catching criminals. 'Not only is it necessary to sound your bell, it is the law and that does make you a criminal, sir,' I added. The youth, dressed in a grey cycling suit and chequered stockings, would not give his name, so I arrested him. Only when he was addressed by the sergeant did the youth give his name – he was the son of the owner of Castle House and his father dined with the Superintendent. I feared at that point that I had made another serious error but Sergeant Hebron had said: 'In which case you ought to know better, sir.' I was jubilant though I kept a straight face. At last I had a decent tale to tell the others. Love had summonsed a poor builder's assistant for pushing his bicycle along the pavement the other week. Mine was a far better application of the law, and, that it should be someone well-heeled, added to my enjoyment.

*

In the early hours of Saturday morning, I walked down Church Lane and past the graveyard. The world had survived another night under my watch and was slowly reviving again. Something was stirring and any minute now the dawn chorus would break out. I waited in anticipation. Always one of the highlights of night duty, especially if I could work it so that I was away from the mills and gas works which the birds avoided. A tawny owl hooted. I stopped and waited. Somewhere a song-thrush was brave enough to sing the first song for the day. It liked its little melody and repeated it a few times, found another even better one, so repeated that. Next, a robin started to tune his instrument and that encouraged a blackbird. Then, as if a conductor had tapped his baton, the songs started up one by one and the sound grew as all the birds in the valley started to compete. Here I am. Over here. This is me. Me. Me.

It had been an eventful week – my summons and my now famous arrest. Then the chaos of the explosion at the colliery – I had felt as helpless as most people. I had tried to keep order along with the other police on duty, keep the roadway clear. But news had spread rapidly and wives and mothers had gathered and miners from other shifts came in to see if they could help. At first it was feared that firedamp was the cause, but it turned out to be a blasting operation that had gone wrong. The two men, were rescued quite quickly and brought up – two brothers it turned out. The poor mother. They lived in New Scarborough just round the corner from me and were wheeled there by ambulance, the younger of the two being taken on to the Infirmary later on.

I deserved the light relief that water polo would provide. There was no reason not to go. I had promised Josiah and I wanted him as a friend, wanted to get to know him. I was reading things into situations that didn't exist.

I reported back to the police office, then went home. Annie awoke as I moved about the room, removed and folded my uniform. She waited in bed just long enough for me to get in and kiss her before getting up herself.

Chapter Eleven

Bill

I whistled across the street. 'John!' The big, new bloke raised his hand and crossed over to where I stood. He held out his hand and I enjoyed my own being engulfed in the other's; warm and strong.

'Tha come back for more, then? Didn't put thi off last week?' I grinned.

'No. No, I enjoyed it.'

There followed an awkward silence. John was the first to break it. 'You got any more players?'

'Don't know, that's down to Josiah. He will have though. He has a way like that – hard to say no to.'

'Yeah, I can see that.'

'I'm glad tha came back an' all.' The big bloke was all right.

Walter arrived, then the others from the team, lastly Josiah accompanied by two strangers who were introduced to everyone – experienced players from Huddersfield.

I was first in the pool again. I was swimming on my back when I saw John come out – not wearing a full bathing suit this time but navy blue drawers. He looked good in them. They showed the fine hair on his chest and in a line down to his navel. I was going to get him. I swam over to the side, took a breath and dived. I could see his ankles and grabbed them and pushed my shoulder into his legs to topple him over. I gave him no chance. While the big bloke was floundering I leapt on him, putting my arm around him under his armpit and across his chest, then rolled him over taking him under with me. I let him go. John came up spluttering. For a moment I thought I'd gone too far and that I had upset him again. A look of anger flashed across his face, but I smiled, and he started laughing – a glint in his eye, too.

'I'll get you for that, Bill, you runt. Just wait.'

I then deliberately turned away. I knew – I hoped I knew – what was coming. Then it did; I was gripped in those strong arms, in a bear hug. I was lifted off the bottom of the pool, then just had time to draw a breath before I was submerged under the weight of the other man.

'All right, that's enough,' shouted Josiah as we re-surfaced. He divided us into two teams, putting John in goal. 'You'll do better in goal – less swimming to do and your size will be an advantage.'

I was playing on Josiah's side with John in the opposite goal. At one point I found myself swimming past a defender with the ball in front. I scooped it up and saw John reaching up to block the shot; I then threw it hard down and watched it bounce off the surface into the goal.

At half-time I sat on the side of the pool with some of the others.

John had remained in the water. 'It would be much easier if I could put my feet down.'

'Then we'd never get it past thi.'

'That's the point. Even just staying afloat is hard work.'

'That's 'cause tha's not doing it right.' I perched on the side to demonstrate. 'That way there's less bobbing up an down see. If you keep your head still, you can focus on the ball better.'

'Tha coming for a drink, again?' I said to John as we met on the pool side after getting changed.

'Thanks, I will.'

Josiah also brought along one of the Huddersfield men, called Wilson. I recognised him from a previous match: clean-shaven, giving him a boyish look and very attractive blue eyes and mop of brown hair. Obviously someone Josiah trusted.

I sat next to John in the pub as Josiah was taken, speaking to the Huddersfield man.

'So, what's tha do for a living then?' I asked.

'I'm a clerk.'

'Oh.' I admit I was surprised and a little disappointed. I had him down for something more physical than a pen-pusher. Something requiring work from that body, like a farrier or a woodcutter – not that there were many woods around – I could just picture him with an axe over his shoulder.

'What about you,' John asked.

'Nowt much – just work in a mill like most folks.' I tried not to paint too bleak a picture of work at the mill or my home as I talked about my life; it required lots of detail to be left out or lightly sketched. I didn't want John thinking me a rough sort or pitying me – I wanted to be regarded as an equal. Like we were in the pool. 'I gather tha's married.'

'Yes, for seven weeks.'

'She a local lass?'

'No, she was a friend from Sheffield – I moved here last year and she agreed to follow me.'

'Not straight away then?'

'No, I… things didn't quite fall right at first.'

I noticed John flush slightly, very charmingly. I looked him directly in the eyes, soft blue, and smiled. He looked embarrassed, flushed again and looked into his pint. I felt there was more to this man than met the eye; I was sure of it. I decided the best thing to do was not be too forward, to play out more line.

'And does tha like it here?'

'Yes, it's nice.'

'No it's not, it's awful! Don't lie. I'd rather be somewhere like Manchester or Sheffield. London even. Where there's more to life.'

John smiled, 'I didn't want to offend your home town.'

'The only people who come here are the desperate – turnip-crunchers looking for work that pays, people fleeing famine like my folks did. It's a place people leave if they have a choice.'

'Well, it was work that brought me here too I suppose.'

Josiah interrupted: 'Bill, has tha got any of that liniment left that tha made up?'

'Yes, nearly half a bottle or so. Why?'

'Jim here has done summat to his shoulder, could tha have a look at it for him?'

By way of response to John's raised eyebrow, Josiah said: 'Bill's our unofficial trainer, didn't he tell you? He's got a gift in those hands. When I ricked my back he had me back in the pool the next week. I keep telling him he should get a job as a Turkish bath attendant.'

'That's all very well, but where can I see him?'

'What about little Josiah's – if he's not in, I know where he hides a key – he won't mind.'

'I'll bob home and get my stuff then. Back in five minutes.' I scuttled off, flushed with the idea of feeling the young Huddersfield man's muscles slip under my hands.

Chapter Twelve

John

I'd not wanted to wait around for Bill to return to the pub with his liniment. For some reason I was irritated by the situation – vexed. I told Josiah that work meant I couldn't make it the following Saturday but that I'd be there for the match on the Monday.

'How about we meet up at Batley instead then – get a bit more practice in. It's gone six when I finish, so if I see you there at half past? I'll take some shots at you. Not Wednesday though – it's ladies on Wednesday.'

Josiah was waiting outside when I arrived, tossing a ball from hand to hand.

'Won't they mind us using the ball?'

'Not if it's quiet. I'll sort it out – they know me.'

We swam for a bit until the deep end became free when two men climbed out. Josiah pounded me for twenty minutes from different angles – shots through the air, bouncing off the surface, some struck, some thrown; and he showed me what to look for in the opposing players movements and eyes that would give away what he was intending to do. We stopped when some more people got in.

'Thanks for that,' I said as we came out into the evening.

'Don't mention it – you improved two-fold there. No one would know you've only been playing a couple of weeks. Look, how about coming back to mine for a quick coffee before you go.'

Josiah led the way through a maze of alleys and courtyards in the old part of town. Here what had obviously been farm buildings still existed, surrounded by mill workers' cottages, shops and brick privies, forming a haphazard array of little yards on which the Corporation were in the process of striving to impose a sense of order by building streets through the middle and knocking down the worst cottages, before old age and gravity got there first. Josiah's room was on the first floor of a short terrace of four. He got some water from a filter and put it in a tin coffee pot over a spirit stove to boil.

'Sit down, I'll not be a minute.'

I looked round the room which was plain and simply furnished. There was an iron bed against the back wall, a fireplace with a brass fender and a small wardrobe down one side; and, down the other, a wash stand and a bookcase holding a dozen or so books and a few magazines. Under the small window that overlooked the yard, was a table with two wooden chairs.

Josiah punctured a can of condensed milk and put it on the table next to me, then poured the coffee.

'So you looking forward to the match then?'

'Very much. Will there be many there?'

'When we've done it before there has been quite a crowd. If it rains and the park empties it will soon fill up I imagine. There's some swimming things first, then we're on towards the end.'

'I'll see if Annie wants to come.'

'Annie?'

'My wife.'

'I'd like to meet her some time.'

I looked directly into Josiah's brown eyes. 'I'm sure she would like that.'

Josiah put his hand on top of mine where it rested next to my cup. I flinched and pulled my hand away.

'It's all right,' said Josiah still holding me with this gaze.

'What do you mean?'

'To like people; to like anyone you want.'

I looked away.

'I know you are troubled,' Josiah said. 'I can help.'

I got up and stood looking out of the window onto the broken yard where some sparrows were beating their wings in the dust.

'I don't need help, I'm happily married. I don't know what you mean.'

'There is nothing wrong with loving more than one person. There is nothing wrong with a man… loving another man.' The room went quiet – only the ticking of a clock somewhere. I continued to stare out of the window. I wanted to be somewhere else.

'But it is sinful.'

'No. Not sinful.'

I turned round.

'God made us the way we are. You, me, Bill, Walter.'

I sat down, trying to take in what Josiah had just said.

'You mean…' It seemed so obvious now.

'You didn't think Walter was a ladies' man did you?' said Josiah laughing.

'I don't know, I suppose now you've said.'

Josiah shook his head smiling. Then he became serious again. 'No one should feel shame for the way they are.'

I couldn't find words to say anything. Perhaps I should have just left, walked away; but I was under Josiah's spell. Josiah had answers. 'You said you could help?'

'I've helped quite a few people. Too often people seeking help fall into the hands of doctors eager to make money, or a name for themselves, wrapping up their prejudice as cures, or snake oil merchants, or men who call themselves God's, who just sow hatred in the name of religion.'

I was conscious of having experienced all of these.

'But I am fine – I am determined to make my marriage work.'

'Good. If that works and it makes you happy, but it can also make people unhappy when they deny themselves and make another human being unhappy at the same time.' Josiah again put his hand on mine, it was rough and dry. This time I let him.

'We're moving into a new century – the twentieth century – soon we will sweep aside old ideas – people will decide for themselves and not be ruled over by masters and told what to think, what to believe.

'But it is a sin. I must struggle against it.'

'I can prove to you it isn't. You're a Christian aren't you?'

'Yes.'

'It is the teaching of Jesus Christ that you follow above all else?'

'Of course.'

'Nowhere does Jesus say it is a sin for a man to love a man.'

'But doesn't it say in the Bible that a man who lies with a man will be put to death and bring a curse on the whole nation – it is this sin that brings so much trouble on the world.'

'That is a load of tripe. It is Leviticus.'

'But Father O'Sullivan says…'

'Oh hang what Father O'Sullivan says. Did your Father O'Sullivan also say that it is a sin to eat fruit off a tree in its first three years? Or to reap the corners of fields, or to wear clothes where wool and linen is mingled? To eat black pudding? Or sausages? Did he say that anyone who curses their father or mother should be put to death? Did he say that he would be sacrificing rams or sprinkling blood around the altar or burning sacrifices? Or dipping his finger in bullock's blood and sprinkling it seven times? Did he condone slavery of heathens? And the God of Leviticus says you must obey all of these commandments or – let me read this to you…' He went over and pulled a Bible off the bookshelf. He read of terror, consumption and burning ague, sending wild beasts among them, eating bread but not being satisfied, eating the flesh of their own children. Don't you see it is all nonsense and your Father O'Sullivan was just reading bits that suited his bigotry? There is so much in the Old Testament that can only be described as nonsense. The word of Jesus overrides it all. He interprets it for us.'

'I'd better be getting back.' I went to the door. Josiah followed to open it for me. He put his hand on my shoulder and looked into my eyes.

'Look, why don't we meet up at the George in Healey tomorrow. At the same time; and we can talk further. I'll bring my Bible and prove it to you.'

I offered my hand. Josiah returned the firm shake.

I was pleased I had night duty. I had a lot of thinking to do and there was nothing better than quiet streets and lanes, moonlight and your own company for resolving thoughts. My spirits were light to start with – I felt relieved that I could now talk openly to Josiah, someone who understood; not to have to hide my feelings, keep up a pretence. And yet I was scared. I had to uphold my reputation and professional standing. Any loss of privacy was unthinkable. The moon faded from view as clouds built up; then, halfway through the night, the rain fell, a passing shower I thought, but it just seemed to get worse as the night wore on until it leaked into my boots and breached the wool of my tunic and seeped onto my skin. My feet were sore from where my wet toes rubbed. I had to make this marriage work. No other life could I contemplate, but I should go and see Josiah if only to impress the need for discretion on him. The thought occurred to me that Josiah could be seeking to blackmail me – I had read about those things. But I had said very little, done nothing – it was all deniable. I could still turn away. No. Josiah was genuine.

We stopped for a drink at the George. Then the rain having finally stopped, Josiah suggested we walk over the fields towards Carlinghow and then round to White Lee. We crossed several hay meadows. The path through was narrow – I walked behind. Little was said then, other than Josiah making sure I knew to bring my full length bathing suit for the match. Nothing had been said of why we were really there – as if our previous conversation had never taken place. It couldn't go on.

To Josiah's back I said: 'How can I be sure that anything I say remains secret?'

Josiah turned and stopped. He looked me in the eyes and took both my hands. They were dry and rough.

'None of us stands to gain anything by anyone finding out about us. Some day we will be able to be honest but not now – there are too many enemies out there. People who would lock us up, beat us up, or report us to the police just for loving someone. What? Why are you smiling?'

'Because. Because I'm a copper.'

Josiah blanched and pulled away. He looked anxiously around him. Suddenly Josiah looked small and vulnerable; a boy needing my protection and reassurance. I felt for the first time our roles switch: the valet had become the master.

I took his hand and impetuously kissed his cheek. 'See I'm genuine. I'm a copper *because* I loved another man. Bloody ironic, eh?'

I led Josiah by the hand to a broken stone wall where it was dry enough to sit, and then explained how I had left Sheffield – running away to join the police like others ran away to the circus, or to sea.

'You were part of the problem, don't you see? I tried to ignore feelings – to cure myself as the doctor said. But that first time I saw you in the pool at

Wellington Street – you set me back months. Little did I know that you…' I put my arm round him and kissed him again. 'Now I don't know what to bloody well do. What to think. You bastard. I suppose I should arrest myself.'

'There's nothing wrong with you. Start with that. You are safe with me. With Bill. With Walt. We all know the score. I'd best not tell them you're a copper though – especially Bill. He hates the police for some reason – so that's one thing between you and me.'

'There's another thing.'

'Yeah?'

'How did you know?'

'That you were not – straightforward – so to speak? I didn't to start with. Then just the way you looked at me. I wondered. The way you… call it intuition if you like.'

'Is it that obvious?'

'No, not at all – very, very subtle.'

'Do the others know?'

'No, and I won't say anything – if you want to that's up to you – but Bill and Walt can be trusted. I'll at least let them know that you can be too.'

I smiled. 'Thanks, Josiah.' Josiah was rightfully back in the master's chair, but I felt I at least now sat at the table. 'You said you'd prove to me it wasn't a sin.'

Josiah took out his pocket gospel. This is God's truth – the Old Testament is full of contradictions. You mentioned Leviticus yesterday but in Samuel it says that the love of David and Jonathan was "a wonderful love passing the love of woman."

He explained away the destruction of Sodom and then read to me from the Gospels: about John at the Last Supper, about the choice of the house for the Passover supper: that the disciples had to follow a man bearing a pitcher of water.

'That is hardly a manly man is it? Water carrying was women's work. The trouble is that those who claim privileged knowledge of the Bible use it to their own ends. For centuries they tried to stop people reading it for themselves, they wanted to keep the ability of interpretation, to use it to retain control over wealth and power. It still goes on. Your church: why does it use Latin if not to keep ordinary people subjugated, to deprive them of inner knowledge – to make them dependent on the priesthood. Look how easily those in power skate over what Jesus said of the rich – he could not have made it any clearer. They will not enter heaven and yet those same rich people who ignore those clear words spoken by Christ himself seek to condemn people for loving others and to twist words to fit their bigotry.'

I stood up and stretched. 'I'm glad I met you Josiah.' I offered my hand and pulled him up onto his feet.

I kept his hand in mine and looked at him. I felt giddy, ecstatic, happier than I had for a long time. I sensed my cheeks had reddened. 'Can I kiss you again, properly this time?'

Josiah smiled. 'I don't mind. But I don't look for physical expression of love.'

I dropped his hand.

'I don't judge others. It is just not what I want. I can love you and Bill and Walter without that.'

I tried to smile. Josiah had firmly re-established his superiority. So far above me that he was out of reach. My own feet were in the mud, Josiah floated in the air. It felt like I had reached up for a cake on the table and had had my hand slapped.'

'It's not important, John. Come on I'll race you to that next stile.'

He was fast and well ahead before I, with the instinct of a lurcher after a hare, set off in pursuit. I gained on him but Josiah put on another burst of speed, yards from the stile, and fell against it panting and laughing as I caught him. Josiah put his arm round me. 'You all right?'

'Yeah,' I said, struggling for breath. 'You're a strange one, Hinchcliffe.'

'So are you, Higgins. Anyway is strange that bad?'

We climbed the stile and headed down past the quarry; the Black Horse at White Lee whinnying to us.

On the following Sunday morning, me and Annie strolled up Frost Hill on our way to St Patrick's. The day was already warm and, wearing our best clothes, normal walking pace was out of the question.

'You know I've been going to the swimming baths?'

'Yes.'

'Well, I've also taken up water polo.'

Annie looked quizzically at me.

'It's like football but in the water. It's great exercise: quite a spectacle I should say. I'm playing in a match tomorrow. Do you think you would like to come? There will be plenty of other ladies there as it is part of a swimming gala that the club is putting on.'

'I'm sorry, John, I can't. It will be a busy day at the shop tomorrow and Zillah has given one of the other girls the day off to be with her family.'

'But my friend Josiah, the team captain, would like to meet you. You'd like him, everyone does – he's very charming, well-mannered.'

'I'm sorry, John, but I promised, and anyway we can't exactly invite friends round can we? Perhaps once we have our own place... That's why I'm working after all. We need to get our own home.'

I had hoped to have her there – I felt sure she would be impressed and look at me in a different light – I didn't feel I commanded the respect I would like and that perhaps such a display of manliness would change her view of me. I wasn't a sergeant or even a first class constable and didn't have my own house, but if she'd seen me in the pool – if I could stop shots and be seen at the side of the others of lesser stature... The truth was I also wanted to show to Josiah that I was settled and happy, that I was all right without him – and, if I admitted it, get one back at him.

'I'll meet your Joseph another time,' she said smiling.

'He's called Josiah.'

I saw Father O'Sullivan and the mass in a completely different light. Josiah had opened my eyes. I had started reading parts of the Bible for myself in a new way: no longer reading just the words but looking for meaning. For the first time I resented the Latin, and the ritual, the silk and the silver. Just as Josiah said, it was all there to control, conceal – not to impart the truth.

I removed my jacket and slung it over my shoulder as we headed back to Liversedge. Annie took my arm. I had no inclination to speak, lost in my thoughts. I could handle this; there was no contradiction. I could be happy with Annie and still have friends I could be at ease with in other ways, with whom I didn't have to pretend. I could be like Josiah – in a better position even – because at least I didn't live alone and adrift; I had a home where love was physical.

'John, I need to talk to you about something.'

'Yes, Annie love, what is it?'

'You know I said we needed to get our own home?'

'Yes, of course.'

'Well, there's a reason for that. A pressing reason.'

I stopped and looked at her. She smiled up at me.

'John, my prayers have been answered.'

'What prayers?'

'We have been blessed by the Lord – the precious gift of new life, John – I'm with child.'

I looked at her; she looked no different.

'But how do you know?'

'I just do. You're pleased aren't you? You want to be a father?'

'Yes, of course. Of course.'

She took my arm and set off walking again. 'I've been dying to tell you but I wanted to be sure of it myself first. I gave thanks in church today – in my prayers. I felt God watching over me and our baby.'

We walked on. I was going to be a father. A father? I let out a little smile. It had somehow seemed too strange to believe it would happen to me – when I had tried to contemplate the idea of a smaller version of myself or Annie following us around it had seemed fanciful. But now it was going to happen. We would have to get a house now: we perhaps had enough money to get by already – not enough for much furniture but we could manage the three pounds for a bedstead and mattress, and thirty odd shillings for a table. But then there was crockery, cutlery, linoleum, wringing machines, chairs, wardrobes, and goodness knows what else… Annie was bringing in fourteen shillings a week extra though, but then…

'But shouldn't you stop work now and rest?'

'Don't be silly, John; I can't until the start of next year. And besides, mother was still scrubbing steps all round town until a few weeks before I was born. And we need the money more than ever now.'

Within a few steps my life had taken on a much more serious meaning. I was now clear of the way ahead.

'I am very pleased, Annie. It is marvellous news.'

'Isn't it. I wasn't sure it was what you wanted. It happened quite soon didn't it? But it is after all the reason for marriage.'

'Yes. Yes. I suppose so.'

'If it's a boy I would like to call him John.'

*

There was applause as the club secretary announced the winner of the forty yards handicap race. Inside one of the dressing boxes I was slowly getting ready – I didn't want to be sat in my costume waiting – I wanted to be straight in the pool when I was ready, so I sat with my shoes off and my jacket and tie hung up. I had never performed in front of an audience before – not since school sports day anyway. I didn't want to let Josiah down, but most of all I didn't want to make a fool of myself. In a way though it was a relief that my over-riding emotion was fear.

I had impatiently sat through the display of scientific and ornamental swimming that had preceded the prize giving – having to watch some pompous, bearded wonder perform high dives, "execute his perfect breaststroke," ludicrous feet-first swimming, underwater somersaults or something he called "ornamental floating" which consisted of doing nothing, every time expecting, and lapping up, rapturous applause for the last breathtaking feat. I had enjoyed the barrel race where in teams of two they had to either ride on the barrel or propel it for two lengths of the pool: watching them struggle to stay afloat on the barrel was hilarious. The biggest laugh of the day though came when the club chairman had moved aside to let one of the female dignitaries take up her seat on the raised platform and had stumbled and fell backwards into the pool. His morning coat tails were like the fins of some monstrous skate as he flapped to reach the side. He had been a renowned swimmer in his day and had worked hard to earn a reputation as an esteemed and respected chairman. All his dignity drained away with the water running off the fine worsted and now limp, starched collar as it departed from his shirt. He stood briefly, frozen on the side of the pool, in that soggy state, as if slowly dismissing his options one by one before audibly harrumphing at the audience's mirth at his misfortune and hurrying out not to return, leaving the officiating to be done by the secretary.

The door next to mine opened and someone splashed into the pool – I removed the rest of my clothes quickly and pulled the knitted costume up over my shoulders, conscious of the visible bulge lower down and the fact that ladies were out there; heavy rain outside making sure that anyone who had resolved to leave after the prizes changed their minds and now, looking favourably on water polo, decided it was just the thing to finish off the afternoon. I heard other splashes, so loosened the catch on the door and with two steps I jumped into the water. I pulled on the blue cap that was thrown to me. Bill, also in a blue cap, swam over to wish me luck as I took my position in goal. 'Get the ball out to me if tha gets chance, yeah?'

'Have a good game, Bill.'

The ten minutes to half time passed quickly. The score stood at one-all. I had made a couple of good stops but the one that got in I had no chance of blocking – whether it was just a good shot or whether I was wrongly positioned I didn't know. At least I had held my own. The cheering when I saved a shot was gratifying. Then I'd tried to respond to the shouts and get the ball out to Bill.

Tiredness crept in in the second half and it was harder to avoid touching the bottom in the shallow end. I let in another two but Josiah was having a tough time at the other end also and the final tally was three-all. I climbed out much relieved and acknowledged a "well played keeper" from the referee.

Afterwards I just couldn't stop smiling – people kept patting me on the back or shaking my hand – it was just a shame that Annie couldn't have seen. This was more than politeness or good sporting behaviour – this was recognition of my achievement and it felt good. And, in a year or two, Annie could bring our son, little Johnnie, to come and cheer for his dada.

'I think we might have found ourselves a new keeper, eh, fellas?' said Josiah. 'Maybe I can go back to playing where I did before Tom left.'

I bought Bill a pint and we stood by the bar in the quiet corner.

'So, what's tha going to do with thi time now then, eh?' said Bill.

'What's tha mean?'

'Now we've finished polo for the summer?'

'We have?'

'Yeah. We take a bit of a break; then start again mid-August.'

'Oh, I didn't know.'

'We'll have to meet up and go for a swim – I can perhaps teach thi how to improve that awful stroke of tha's.'

'Thanks, I'd like that.'

'I live on the High Street in Daw Green – near the park, number twenty seven – leave a message if I'm not in, it should get to me.'

I saw Bill differently now – felt a little sorry for him, appreciated some of the difficulties he must have faced. We were both second generation Irish; born to survivors of the famine, escaping to find work and life in Yorkshire.

Both of us shared a secret, lived with shame. I studied him more closely. There was a spark in his eyes, blue Irish eyes with long lashes. His face was boyish, with only what would be a thin beard if ever he grew one – he hadn't shaved that day and his moustache needed a bit of a trim as did his hair sticking out in light brown clumps from his cap, worn too far back on his head. His skin was clear, unlined except for a deep line in his forehead, unusual in someone so young. Many passably good looking boys took on ugly features as they passed into manhood – their features hardened, jowls broadened or drooped and eyes went cold, but Bill had retained a youthful charm. There was something about him – something unconventional, impish even… Something in his manner… almost like Mr Punch.

'What's tha smiling at?'

'Nowt. Tha just reminded me of someone.'

'Who?'

'Oh, just someone I met at the seaside.'

As I headed home, I still couldn't stop smiling. People would think me simple. Let them. Things were really looking up. I was going to be a father, of all things! That would make people see me differently – treat me with respect, like a grown up. A father. A patriarch. We would get a house and my eldest, little Johnnie, would run up the path to greet me when I got home and then my daughter would approach shyly and I'd scoop her up in my arms too – one on each arm, and Annie would be waiting by the door and there would be the warm smell of baking drifting through. I would not be like my own father, cruel and self-centred. I would guide them with a loving arm; protect them.

I was getting on in the job; going about it quietly, not making a fuss, keeping my head down, my nose clean, making sensible arrests. Behaving like a sergeant in waiting. Playing a smarter game than the others. I would get on; I felt more self-assured as every week passed, no longer just pretending to be a policeman. And I was no longer the new boy at the station since Wilf had arrived. And I had a sporting pastime, and some good pals – men I could be at ease with, have a laugh with, be physical with, not worrying about dropping my guard – as long as they didn't find out I was a Bobby.

Chapter Thirteen

Annie

I don't know why, but I really wasn't sure how John would react when I told him about the baby. Silly of me really, he was clearly delighted. It's funny how these things always come as a surprise – as if it is something that only happens to other people. But it was surprising nonetheless, for me as well as him. It's not like we've had lots of opportunities, especially since I've taken on my work at the dining rooms – I'm just too tired and can't really be doing with John bothering me. I've been quite shocked by him at times; he's even tried to get friendly towards me in the morning when my mind's already on the day ahead, and it doesn't seem quite right to me in the daylight.

Anyway, it is God's will and I wanted to thank him first – properly in church before I told John – it felt the right order to do things in. I had all on not to laugh at him when he asked me how I knew. I suppose there's nothing to show as yet on the outside and he can't feel what I feel inside, but I think he really has little idea about such things, despite his, shall we say, interest in the act itself.

It's not come at an ideal time, but you don't get to choose. I would have liked to have built up a bigger nest egg first – a good few months' of saving money. I'll have to tell Mrs Law and stop as soon as my bump starts to show, I expect. I would have liked to have been set up in my own home by then – we might still be able to, if we are prepared to get by on the basics. Nothing will make me happier than running my own home, having an oven for baking, and a pottage on the go in winter.

I mentioned it to Mrs Love, she's the wife of one of John's colleagues, and not long married herself, and she said she got a lot of help from everyone at the police station – help with moving and donations of unwanted furniture and bits.

I've found the other wives to be a great support. I first got invited when the men went off on their beano – when we all went around to Mrs Watson's for tea – a case of when the cats are away, perhaps. Although, if there were any cattiness, I suspect it wasn't amongst those who were away: there was more than a bit of gossip – about life in the police and the misfortunes of a policeman's wife. It was there I found out quite a few of them do work on the side, despite what police rules might have to say about it. I went straight round on my way home and accepted a job at Zillah Law's.

I was so cross with him when he got home from Harrogate. I couldn't believe how drunk he was, and he stank. That was the first time I've got short with him. Our first exchange of words. We both regretted it afterwards.

I must say I am enjoying being in work again, meeting people and getting away from that awful room of John's. I'm trying to get in all the hours I can, while I'm still able. Some of the customers are quite offensive and treat you like a skivvy, but most of them are very polite and appreciative, especially the regulars. There's one gentleman, who I believe lives on his own, who takes all his meals with us: breakfast, dinner and tea.

I'm glad to see that John is pursuing an interest outside the police – I worry about his single-minded obsessiveness at times – putting all his efforts in one basket. I get sick of hearing about the police, so for him to have this water-football thing as well can only be good for him. And to have friends outside the police – I think policemen get a jaundiced view of the world, always seeing the worst side of everyone. He seems to have made at least one good friend through his swimming thing, Joseph, or somebody.

I wasn't so sure about moving to a place like this at first. I'd never heard of Liversedge – the fact that it didn't sound very nice either didn't help. I found it quite claustrophobic to start with; I was quite lonely, but things are much better now. I can see us building a happy life here.

Chapter Fourteen

Bill

I lay on the mattress on the floor staring at the wall – my brother's snoring having woken me. Too light to get back off. I wasn't sure of the time but it didn't matter – no work today, even though it was Tuesday. A blessing even if the cause were sinister. A shame John wouldn't come over though. I'd have to make do with Walt.

I still didn't know quite where I stood with John. After the match I'd met him a couple of times to go for a swim and I had tried to refine his swimming style – all about getting him to breathe regularly. It was nice to have him to myself – it confirmed that he must like me for myself – not just being polite for the sake of the team. We chatted over a beer about not much in particular. John had grown on me. True, I had disliked something about him at first but he had pluck – there weren't many people who would take to polo quite as quickly as he had done. He was perhaps just shy to start with. Now though he seemed self-assured and warm towards me, listening to what I said, sympathising when I complained about my mother's latest whims. It made me happy. I hoped I could continue to get to know him. He was a challenge for sure. But until I was confident I'd keep playing it long.

For weeks now, people had been obsessing about the Jubilee. Shopkeepers vying with each other to put up ever more tawdry bunting and banners, unnecessary electric lights and gas jets arranged in arches or, even, round the back of the baths, in the shape of a crown. And pictures of the Queen were everywhere. Those frog-eyes really gave me the creeps, yet no one shared my sense of repulsion, and the only time I had, at work, dared to voice an opinion – all I had said was that I thought it was a fuss over nothing and the money could be better spent – I was practically accused of treason. So after that I just kept my mouth shut. I wasn't the most popular of people at the mill as it was. I was the only one who could see it – that they were all being duped; they were all being blindly led over the edge. How did England end up being in thrall to the Germans anyway? They had been sending over carrier pigeons in the thousands to fly back to Germany – all in preparation for an invasion, and a frog-eyed German squatting parasitically on the throne, waiting. Yes, I was better keeping such views to myself, for now. I didn't want to be discovered.

My mother had been stirred into activity – for the first time in ages she had gone out into the street to look at the bunting strung between windows and lampposts, and she had declared she was going to watch the procession; it was what her own dear Albert would have wanted her to do.

I went downstairs to make a fire and sat on the cool flags feeding sticks underneath the little pile of coal and blowing on it as I got it to take. I filled the kettle and sat watching the coal hiss – little black dragons breathing fire from their nostrils, devils dancing in the smoke. I heard boards creaking overhead so scraped some fat out of the pot ready – at least Fanny had bought eggs and bacon as it was a special day.

'Thomas and Fanny will accompany me to the cemetery this morning whilst you stay here and tidy the house – it's not fit for a Jubilee, so it isn't. Then you can have the dinner ready for when we get back,' mother announced when I placed an egg on her plate. The other two looked at each other – clearly this plan was new to them too.

'There is the meat I boiled last night's soup with, Bill,' said Fanny. 'I thought we could mince it with a bit of suet and have it with potatoes.'

'After breakfast you can go and get some flowers for the grave. No. Fanny, dear – you shall go and get the flowers.'

'But mother, all the shops will be shut today.'

'Nonsense. One of them will open up for flowers for your father.'

Fanny didn't argue.

'Then this afternoon, Fanny dear, we will go to the park.'

'Yes, mother.'

I knew that Fanny would have to change her plans – whoever it was that she had arranged to spend the morning with would have to wait until evening for her charms. I wondered where she would get flowers from, but she would, somehow, knowing Fanny.

Walter called round after I had cleared away the dinner things.

'Quick, get me out of here before I kill somebody.' I whispered. 'I need a pint or two of hops and malt tonic to revive me.'

Walter led a mercy mission to the Crow Nest Inn. It was already busy with people on their way to the park, so we only stopped for one before heading to the Rising Sun which was a bit quieter.

'Don't tha think it's all a bit much, Walt? All this fuss.'

'I quite like it.'

'But we did all this Jubilee thing ten year ago.'

'I were only eleven. I don't remember it much – and I were too young to get served then. Anyway, I'm looking forward to seeing all the fine fellows in their holiday clothes parading through the park.'

'Yeah, with girls on their arms.'

'Sometimes I think tha's no imagination,' Walter said in a low voice. 'Tha needs another. Same again?'

'Nah. Let's try the Anchor. See if anyone else is there.'

The Old Anchor started to empty as four o'clock approached.

'Come on. Are we going to watch this procession then or what?'

'I can't be arsed. Can't we just stay here?'

'No, come on. I'm not going on my own.' Walter grabbed my arm and escorted me out of the pub. As we stepped outside, the Borough Band was coming down the hill from the Western Church schools, leading their diminutive Christian soldiers onwards on a roundabout march through town to the meet up point on Willans Road where all the tributary processions would merge to march on the park. The edge of the road was thickly lined with people as the band went past and I just caught glimpses over people's shoulders of small banners and flags waving, straw hats and white and cream muslin and lace that foolish mothers had spent the best part of a week's wages on. Some were singing along to the band and others waving at people they knew or anyone who would wave back, so proud were they of how splendid they looked and so taken were they with celebrating German dominion.

'Come on Walt – we can't see nowt here.'

'I'll just wait and see if I can see our Liz.'

'Come on. If we go up to the park tha can see 'em when they come back round again. We might meet some of the others there too.'

'Tha's getting right on my bloody wick.'

'Sorry, Walt. I'll be good now.'

We headed slowly over to the park – no one was going anywhere fast – the whole of the town was out and quite a few who'd come in by train from round and about: some following the children, others trying to go the same way as me and Walter.

There was no chance of finding anyone else when we got to the park so we made our way to where it was less crowded and found a spot to sit where Walter could see the procession when it arrived from the top end of the park.

'It's too hot here, Walt, I'm going for a lie down by the trees.'

I closed my eyes to the sounds of one of the brass bands drifting up the slopes. I was woken some time later by the toe of Walter's boot in my ribs.

'Tha missed it.'

'Did I? That's a shame – what exactly?'

'The children arriving and singing the National Anthem, hymns and Rule Britannia.'

'Never mind, eh. I'm sure they were lovely.'

'I'm surprised all the cheering didn't wake thi up.'

'That's the sleep of the righteous that is.'

'Good God! The sleep of the intemperate more like.'

'Come on, there's some stuff going on.'

There were three platforms created for entertainment, but the children had been let loose and were now milling about, getting under our feet, and all of Dewsbury tried to get near enough to hear what the Negro comedians were saying, or to listen to the Excelsior Minstrels, or watch Professor Ainsworth's sleight-of-hand tricks. Me and Walter settled for barging our way close enough to gawp at the Moravian Athletic Club performing gymnastics.

'That's a bit more like it,' said Walter. 'A fine display of athleticism – can't beat it. Can't beat a few well-honed muscles, I always say.' I kicked him hard on the shin.

'Ow! What was that for?'

We watched the athletes swing clubs in time, balance on each others shoulders and perform somersaults and handstands.

'There's a lot of coppers around.'

'They were parading earlier – tha were asleep. A fine body of men – must be bloody hot in them uniforms though.'

There were some in caps, but most in helmets. Some of them wore medals and fancy braid – not like they normally were.

As soon as the gymnasts finished their routine I suggested going to get another drink.

'Tha needs to go steady, mind,' said Walter.

'We'll stop at mine and get a biting on first then.'

I was relieved to find the house empty so invited Walter in and we helped ourselves to some bread pudding; then we headed towards town.

'Black or white?' said Walter, meaning the White Lion or the Black Bull.

'Black then white, and then perhaps the King's for afters.'

I had cheered up, now I was away from the kids and coppers. I even laughed at the way the carved white lion had been done up and adorned with a crown for the occasion. Suitably refreshed we sought out some chips then went down to watch the pictures in the market place. In front of the Town Hall a large screen had been built, onto which were projected views of Buckingham Palace and other things that I assumed were in London. Then there was a picture of the Prince of Wales and then the Queen herself, from earlier in her reign, and in her full, frog-faced, menacing scowl. I turned away. The Town Hall was festooned with small, red, white and blue electric lamps, and, illuminated by an arc lamp, was a huge portrait of her in the centre. Police were everywhere too. I was being watched from all angles.

'What have you been up to!' There was a hand on my shoulder which made me jump. I ducked like someone had swung a punch at me. Jesse Hirst laughed. 'Who did tha think it were? Someone's got a guilty conscience.'

I tried to regain my composure. Walter laughed. 'I'm afraid he's a bit the worse for wear. He'll be reminded of this Jubilee in the morning even if he don't remember much of it.'

'Toasting Her Maj, eh? Isn't this great – beats working any day and I'm getting paid for it – good ol' Miner's Fed – made sure of that.'

'Look, I'd best be getting back. Tha's right, I've had enough, I'll leave you to it.' I shook hands with them and with a glance over my shoulder hurried away up Market Street. My heart was pounding in my chest.

Why did coppers have to be always snooping about? Why couldn't they leave me alone? Always watching.

Heading up Daisy Hill I saw a tall dark figure approaching so I headed down a side street. I broke into a trot and came back out onto Church Street where people were spilling out onto the pavement outside the Market House Inn and the Royal Oak; I had to step out onto the road to pass. Flags flew over the shops, another portrait of the Queen stared down at me; it was noisy, and bright from gas jets and arc lamps. I cut up a side street and started running again, then took a left. I turned alongside Providence Mills, also flying flags, and found myself at the river.

I stopped to catch my breath. The river flowed putrid and dark the other side of the wall. Opposite I could just make out a shingle bank that ran up to the bridge. I realised where I was. Opposite was Albert Mills. That meant those stones, were where they had found my father. I threw up over the wall. Albert. Always bloody Albert.

Chapter Fifteen

John

June gave way to July and with it I had hopes of some drier weather. On those cold, wet nights in February and March when I held my lamp in both hands to warm them, it provided solace to think about the balmy summer nights that were not far off. But now, even though the nights were shortened, I felt robbed when I returned home as cold and as wet as I had been back then. Autumn was only eight weeks or so away and time was running out. Spring would leap straight through to Autumn with no respite in between. There had been one or two nice days but no prolonged warm spell; hopes of summer were quickly dashed as it turned cold or thunderstorms ripped the summer sky apart.

The Jubilee had been a welcome interlude. Even though I had been on duty it did not feel like it; and I was paid double. Everyone was pleasant and well behaved; the thieves and thugs apparently having taken the day off too. The sun even came out to broaden smiles and show off pretty white dresses. Heckmondwike Old Band marched through the streets and there was a little parade of children and a couple of carriages. This was followed up by sports on the field in the afternoon. Nothing special, but nice. Annie worked all day but we went together to see the bonfire in the evening. I worried about her feeling sick all the time and again tried to talk her out of working, but she was driven by a passion for someone other than herself and nothing short of the best of her efforts to provide would do. I felt the intensity of her passion and saw it on her face as she knelt by the bed and said her nightly prayers. My own desires were now secondary. My role had changed. I would cradle her and the child inside her but was not hopeful that she would touch me and attend to my wants.

There was pleasant late afternoon sunshine when I headed out to get my tea: I was looking forward to a nice bit of meat, a pudding and a glass of stout.

The door to Zillah Law's dining rooms was wedged open to allow the light breeze inside. Plain wooden tables were arranged either side of the narrow gangway that led to a door to the back of the shop. There were a few customers in, some eating silently, others reading newspapers whilst they sipped their tea or ate their toast. I slid onto one of the bench seats towards the back of the shop and picked up one of the hand-written menus that was propped up against the cruet set – it was Annie's neat writing. She came out from the back wearing a white apron, carrying a pot of tea and a plate. As she turned I was surprised. The rosiness in her cheeks was gone and she looked tired; she only smiled a half smile when she noticed me.

'Annie, you look dreadful, sit down.'

'I can't, I've customers to serve.'

'Oh, blow them. Sit.'

She did as I said.

'Look, I'm going to take you home to rest. You're not well enough to be on your feet.'

'No, John, don't make a silly fuss.'

'You'll do as I say. Wait there.'

I went through to the back, PC Higgins in all but uniform, and I was met with no argument from the proprietress. I took Annie home and got her into bed.

'Thank you, John,' she said as she settled onto the pillow. 'Could you get Mrs Shaw to come up to see me please.'

'Why?'

'Please John, just ask her for me.'

I trailed behind Mrs Shaw up the stairs and was about to follow her into the room when she stopped me.

'Mr Higgins, it might be best if you waited here.'

I stood on the landing unable to make out the low voices in the room. Then a few minutes later Mrs Shaw emerged.

'I'll look after her, Mr Higgins. There's nothing you are needed for, and just having you lounging around will only upset her. Why don't you get your uniform and everything else you need for the morning and put them in the attic room. You can sleep up there tonight; that way you won't disturb her. You should go out and get some tea. I'll let you know as soon as she's feeling better, it's probably just a touch of flu or something.'

I entered the room and Annie forced a smile for me.

'Annie love, is everything all right? Shouldn't we send for a doctor?'

'I'm all right, John. Just you go. Mrs Shaw will look after me.'

I did as I was told and gathered my things, kissing her cheek as I left. Mrs Shaw was waiting at the top of the stairs, an enamel jug of water and a towel in her hand.

She smiled at me a confident smile.

'Don't you go worrying now, she'll be just fine.'

I slept badly up under the roof – it was too warm with only a small skylight to prop open and the little miner on the mattress was asleep and snoring before I had even arranged the blankets and a pillow to sleep on.

As the daylight illuminated the cobwebs, I woke and looked at my watch as I heard the miner stirring. I dressed and went downstairs. I listened at the door to mine and Annie's room, but could hear nothing.

I returned in the afternoon; every hour of duty having been slow and drawn out. I had tormented myself thinking what it would be like if Annie was gravely ill and left me, and hated myself for my selfishness when I was trying to think of her. I prayed as I walked round, prayed that Annie would be well. I was being silly. Didn't women often get sick early on when they were carrying children? And Mrs Shaw didn't seem too worried. But then I would spiral into black thoughts again. I made a pact with God. Let Annie be well and I would be devout. This made me feel better and I expected to see Annie back to her normal self again as I climbed the stairs to our room. I pushed open the door, it was a bit dark inside, the curtains being half drawn. Mrs Shaw was at the bedside. Annie was sitting up, propped by pillows. She burst into tears as she saw me.

I approached. 'Is everything all right? Annie?'

'I'll leave you two alone for a bit,' said Mrs Shaw. 'I'll bob back up later and see if I can get you anything.'

I sat and took Annie's hand.

'What is it, Annie?'

'John, I'm so sorry. I've lost our baby.' She burst into tears again.

I felt sick. 'Are you sure?'

'Yes. It's all over.'

'And you. Are you…'

'I'll be back to my usual self in a day or two the doctor said; but, John, I'm so sorry.'

'It's not your fault.'

'Then who's is it?'

'Nobody's. These things happen.'

'But I wanted to give you a child.'

I sat on the edge of the bed and put my arm around her and there we stayed for quite some time.

I tried to remember what I had said to God – Annie may well get better now, but this wasn't playing fair – that wasn't what I'd agreed. If she was well but the baby had died, that was just playing games with me. What sort of God would do this to Annie? What had she done to deserve this? And if God was punishing me, then why take it out on Annie and a baby to get at me? I went round and round this in my mind as Annie lay broken against me.

Some time later there was a knock at the door and Mrs Shaw brought in a tea tray.

'I thought you might welcome this.'

'Thank you, Mrs Shaw,' said Annie. 'You've been very kind.'

'Perhaps you should have some tea and then go out for a bit to leave her to rest,' Mrs Shaw said. 'You'll be all right sleeping back in here again tonight.'

I headed out in a fury, not intending to go anywhere in particular. After walking for half an hour, each turn off my route made on the spur of the moment I found myself heading along the side of a dry-stone wall at Popeley Fields. Behind me to the west stretched the Pennines, to the south, in the distance, the hills of Derbyshire, to the north the outskirts of Bradford. A few white clouds travelled across the sky but down where I strode through the long grass the air was still. Grasshoppers chirruped then stilled as I pushed onward through the narrow path, wildly thrashing down nettles in my way with a stick. I found myself alone on a wide flat hill top, open to the summer evening sky; a black and white flash in the field, a solitary lapwing landing some distance off calling "hoo-wit."

I looked up at the blue grey above my head, turned around and back, and shouted: 'You bastard! How could you do this!'

The still evening air swallowed up my words as if they were no more than the wing-beat of the lapwing.

'If it's me you've got a problem with you bastard, go on strike me down! Go on!' I opened up my arms. 'Go on! You bastard! Go on!' But again there was nothing, not a sound. No hand reaching down to throttle me, no thunderbolt from the blue sky.

'Ha!' I slumped down against a stone gate post and sobbed.

When I got home and staggered to bed, Annie was fast asleep, which was just as well since I was blind drunk.

Chapter Sixteen

A week later I was back on nights. I popped down to the kitchen to get a snack before I left and was about to enter the kitchen when I was waved away by Mrs Shaw who sat with her arm around Annie, consoling her as she sobbed. Having nothing better to do, I set off to work early and once there sat and read *The Reporter* that I had bought on the way in.

I was paired off with PC Ashbourne for the first half of the evening.

'We are expecting a busy night tonight,' the Sergeant said when we fell in. 'The warm weather is bringing folks out and the pubs are busy. For the first hour we will do the shortened beats covering just those streets with public houses or beer houses. Visibility is the key. Let them know you're there. Then we'll split up and return to normal beats for the rest of the shift come eleven o'clock. Drunken behaviour is to be dealt with firmly. We must have order on our streets.'

Me and Ashbourne walked round the top of Huddersfield Road, Frost Hill, Wakefield Road and part way up Station Lane, taking in all the pubs and beerhouses in Millbridge. We walked side by side, ploughing the pavement of anyone thinking of loitering or walking slowly, pricking guilty consciences, and forcing people to step aside or hasten away as they saw us coming. We nodded to people we recognised and said "Good evening, Sir" to the few respectable looking gentleman who were out. We called in at the Black Bull where the landlord whispered an invitation to us to drop by later. The Swan was busy with people quenching their thirsts after a hot day and the bar was several deep as customers looked to get a couple more in before the bell.

We heard raised voices as we pushed open the door to the saloon bar of the Globe.

'Even if tha were Lord Salisbury or the Prince o' bloody Wales I wouldn't serve thee.'

'My money's as good as the next fella's!'

'Get away home, tha's 'ad enough.' The landlord saw the two figures in dark blue entering. 'Just in time gentlemen. This fella 'ere is refusing to leave and is quite clearly intoxicated.'

'Come along, sir, just leave quietly and we'll hear no more about it,' said Ashbourne.

'I'm an Englishman, I've a right to my drink after a hard day's work bringing up coal just so's you lot can burn it and make yourselves rich.'

'Would you like to summons this gentleman for refusing to quit, sir?' I asked the landlord.

'Can't you just arrest the b–, I mean, the gentleman?'

'No, sir, we'll get his name and address for you. Come outside, sir.'

'A'reight. I'm going. Come on Cecil. We're not wanted.'

I looked around for another man, but instead a movement on the floor drew my eye as a large, light brown dog got to its feet: a scruffy looking beast with a mastiff somewhere in its make-up.

Outside the pub the man swayed a little as he drew in the fresh air.

'Right then, sir,' said Ashbourne, getting out his pocket book, 'name please?'

'Cecil, after Cecil Rhodes. There's a man!'

'Very funny, sir. Not the dog. You,' I said.

The miner looked up at me as if struggling to adjust his focus. ' 'ere, don't I know thee? I do. Never forget a face. Tha tried to stitch me up for burglary when I done nowt wrong; thee an' that other bastard, Love, it were. Is it 'im?' He looked up at Asbourne. 'No, not 'im, t'other un. Anyhow tha's not getting me again. This time my mate'll stop thee.'

He bent down and fumbled with the dog's muzzle. 'Nice set o' teeth, eh?'

'It's an offence under the Town and Police Clauses Act to have a ferocious dog unmuzzled.'

'Sod off!'

The dog snarled and started barking, standing between us and his master.

'Bad men, Cec!' The dog jumped up at Ashbourne who retreated, drawing his staff. I moved to grab the miner's arm to get it behind his back. The dog, seeing this, turned to defend his master and sprang after me. I feared the dog most and let go of the man's arm, to try to pull my staff out of my pocket as the dog snapped at me. Then the man jumped on my back and I lost my footing. The dog was in my face now and I tried to get to my feet, then I felt an excruciating pain in my hip and I looked up just in time to see the miner's boot strike me again, hard on the thigh. I shrank back from the beast of a dog, barking and slavering, its foul breath in my nostrils. The miner saw Ashbourne move towards him and kicked at him. The dog left me on the floor and went to join the attack on Ashbourne. I got to my feet and with my staff struck the miner on the back of the legs and felled him. The drink that had seconds before emboldened him now combined with his exertion to drain him of any remaining fight. I gave him another blow to the kidneys for good measure and then handcuffed him. Several men had come out of the pub to watch and one of them helped Ashbourne get the muzzle on the dog and they tied it to a lamppost.

At the station the man was identified as George Alderman. He was charged with being drunk and disorderly, with assault, and with having a dangerous dog at large. He was shoved into a cell where he collapsed on the floor, even his cursing had been knocked out of him.

Stiffness was now setting in to my leg, and the soreness made me limp. The police surgeon was called and examined me. Two red and purple patches showed where the toe of Alderman's boot had landed. The surgeon didn't think anything was broken, but advised me to return home and not to report back until Monday morning. The sergeant told me to write up a report for the occurrence book then to go home.

It was gone midnight when I limped home and up the stairs to bed. Annie murmured something in her sleep. I climbed into bed and tried to lie comfortably, my leg throbbing from the dull pain.

I woke the next morning as Annie got out of bed.

'I didn't hear you get in. Go back to sleep, I'll be quiet,' she said.

'No, it's fine. Anyway shouldn't you be the one that's staying in bed, resting?'

'Oh, don't fuss, John, I'm much better in myself. I need to just get on with things. Not lie about brooding.'

'I'll get up in a minute as well.'

'But you can have only just got to bed.'

'No, I got sent home early.'

'Why, John? Is everything all right?'

'Yes, don't worry, we just had a difficult arrest. He cut up a bit rough and I got a kick to the leg so they sent me home.'

'Oh, John, you must be careful. Let me see.'

'No, no, it's nothing really.' I felt under the covers at the bruises – they were raised and felt very sore.

'John, do let me see.'

'No, it's fine, there's no need to go on about it.'

She paused. 'Does that mean you can come to mass after all?'

'Oh, yes... I suppose.'

How could I share with her my feelings towards God? That would hurt her even more.

'I would like you to come. If we pray together we will find comfort and peace.' I must have given something away in my expression, for she continued: 'God knows what it is like to have a child die – on the cross. He shares our pain. We have got to believe there was a reason for this. Perhaps it is more than we'll ever understand. But just think, John, we shall have our own little angel looking down on us now.'

I turned my face to the wall, a tingling across the top of my nose. If God really cared... existed even, then he wouldn't let this happen. There could be no higher reason.

'I went to see Father O'Sullivan; he has helped me. It's not unusual to lose a baby – I am still blessed. It will make me stronger, a better mother when the time comes – and it will, John. It will.'

I could see through this brave front she was putting on for me. She was trying to protect me, shield me from the pain of her thoughts. She was finding her comfort, her strength, elsewhere – in Mrs Shaw, spending a lot of time with her as she convalesced, and in her church and its non-existent deity.

'No, perhaps I'd better get a bit more rest this morning, after all.' I watched her dress, then brush her hair at the glass, tying it up behind.

'I'll be down for breakfast in a bit,' I said as she left the room. Only then did I sit up to examine my leg. The bruises had come out, an angry pink and purple, covering just about all of my thigh. The other bruise extended across my hip to somewhere on my backside, as far as I could tell. That afternoon I was supposed to be meeting up with Josiah, Bill and the others to go for a drink and to see a Welsh choir that were touring the country. I had not seen Josiah since the Whit Monday match and had last seen Bill before the Jubilee. So much had happened since, I was in need of some joviality.

I pulled my trousers on, bending my leg as little as possible and tested my ability to walk. I did not move very freely but I was determined not to miss out on the afternoon.

It was more of a hobble than a walk from Ravensthorpe station to the Anchor where we had arranged to meet. There was already a pint on the table for me when I got there. Walter and Josiah had the dominoes out but Bill was just sat balancing his pint on his knee.

'He's been watching the door for thi coming in,' said Walter.

I shook their hands and sat down cautiously.

'Tha all right,' said Bill.

'Yeah fine, just a bit of a strained muscle I think.'

'Oh yeah? What's tha been up to, to get that?' asked Walter looking up from his dominoes again.

'Nothing, don't know what I did. So, what do we know about this thing this afternoon?'

'It's a Welsh male voice choir,' said Josiah. 'They're supposed to be very good. They're from a slate mine in North Wales. They were locked out by the gaffers for trying to organise a union. So there's a whole load of them on strike now. By touring and singing they are raising money for the strike fund: for their families.'

'Best save a tanner or two between us to throw in the hat then,' said Walter.

'Poor sods,' said Bill. 'No working man wants to go round cap in hand. But if we're paying to be entertained that's different.'

I kept quiet. I wasn't always sure about strikers. They abused the police just for trying to do their job. It wasn't our fault if we had to keep law and order and let the workers in past a picket; and, after all, workmen had a duty towards their employer too and towards their country.

'It's not like they've done anything wrong,' said Josiah. 'The quarry's owned by Lord Penrhyn: a nasty parasitic bastard living in his castle, entertaining royalty…'

'Ptthh!' interjected Bill.

'…raking in vast profits at others' expense – they started off making money out of slaves in Jamaica. He probably resents the abolition of slavery and is trying to enforce another kind of slavery on his workers in Wales. The bosses don't want to even allow working men to put their case for a better share of the wealth they help create, for money enough to feed their kids, for decent conditions, for hours of work that allow them to do things other than work and sleep. And then people like him try to keep people down by pointing to Christianity: telling people to be grateful, that their happiness lies not through being able to clothe and feed their family, not through having the necessaries of life and the benefits of civilisation but through the love of God. They ignore what Jesus said about the rich.'

'But if striking is against the law…' I said.

'But who makes the laws, John? Who sits in Parliament and makes those laws? The bosses themselves: people like Penrhyn; those who have the power and want to hang on to it.'

'But surely the Liberals and Radicals are on our side.'

'Liberals, pooh! Always think they know what's best for others. Couldn't deliver on employer's liability – even a Tory party, scared though it is, looks like conceding a bill on workers' compensation – that's more than the Liberals could ever achieve. And they're just as Imperialist as the Tories. No, socialism's the only thing for it. Workers need to own the means of production, to get more than a few shillings for their labour. How can someone like Penrhyn even claim to own the slate under those Welsh mountains? Those mountains belong to all of us, like the rivers, the sea, the air we breathe.'

'But that'll never happen,' said Walt.

'Perhaps not yet, but soon. Once all men get the vote, and women too. The current system will be overthrown. Once we get a truly universal franchise and get our own men into Parliament.'

The voices of the choir added a rich emotional substance to Josiah's words. They stood at the bandstand in front of their banner which read "Penrhyn dispute – Bethesda Quarrymen's Choir – all you contribute is for the suffering women and children." They looked nothing exceptional, a disparate, rather untidy bunch, but when they sang to the accompaniment of Dewsbury Old Band the hairs stood up on my neck. Thousands of people crowded round the bandstand in the park, everyone awed into silence as they sang hymns such as Lead Kindly Light. I strained to pick out the words of The Comrades Song of Hope – "a joyful day for caring to follow the night of despair." "He that is mighty will not fail you, he shall be your strength." "Men that toil in the battle of life, listen to the strains that will sweeten the strife." Their voices went straight to my heart. These Welsh miners were not broken men, they were proud and had right on their side. "Play the man and win the fight, the cause is right and right is might." I felt close to tears when fortunately they finished and I was allowed to smile and applaud. Speeches followed. They spoke of the dreadful conditions they worked in and that life expectancy was around forty. And for no more than three and seven a day for a labourer. And they were up against an employer determined to crush them into the dirt. I willingly threw my sixpence in the hat when it came round. I had gone from being sceptical about unions to being convinced of their necessity.

We dispersed slowly afterwards with the crowd.

'That was something wasn't it?' I said to Bill as we headed towards the park entrance.

'Aye, it was that. I wish I could sing like that.' He looked at me. 'Tha's in some pain with that leg isn't tha?'

'No, it's nothing.'

'It is, I can see. We're heading past mine. I'll get some pain-killer for thi. We'll catch the others up at the pub.'

Bill found the door locked. 'Oh, I forgot mother's gone round to her cousin's for tea. Since her Jubilee outing she seems to have discovered that she's got legs again.' He got the key from under a stone and went in.

'Come in a minute. I'll go and get it.'

The living room was very simply furnished with just a deal table and half a dozen wooden chairs and a sparse dresser against one wall. But it was clean and tidy.

Bill disappeared upstairs, then shouted down: 'Come up, there's no one in.'

I went up the stairs which were covered with a strip of patterned linoleum down the centre. On the landing I saw a door open.

'I've got it,' said Bill, emerging with a small glass bottle. This is good stuff: expensive, but it works: it's got myrrh in it — the stuff they gave to the baby Jesus — and opium. You could put some on now then it will get to work quicker. Let me take a look. I'll rub some in — it's more effective if it's rubbed in in the right way. Come on, nowt to be shy of. Sit on the bed.'

I did as I was told. I undid my belt and let my trousers drop onto the uncovered boards.

'That does look nasty,' Bill said looking at the bruise on my thigh. 'That's no muscle strain — what happened?'

'I got kicked — in a sort of fight.'

'Bloody hell. I hope the other bloke got what he deserved.'

'You could say that.'

Bill dripped some of the liquid onto his hands. There was a heady smell of myrrh and camphor. He started to apply it gently to my thigh.

'Did he get thi anywhere else?'

'On the hip as well.'

'Shall I rub some in there too?'

The thrill and embarrassment were unbearable. I shuddered. Bill had noticed the effect he was having on me, and touched me.

'I can sort that out for thi, too,' he said.

Bill grinned up at me as we approached the pub, and slowly shook his head. I cuffed him round the ear.

'What? What did I do?' he complained.

'Tha knows damn well.'

'Well, tha weren't exactly timid.'

'Bloody cheek!' I laughed at Bill who was rubbing his ear, so I cuffed the other one as well. 'There, at least they'll match now. Come on what you having?'

We sat down, and were passed a little pile of dominoes each.

'You're just in time,' said Josiah. It was as if nothing had happened.

On the train on the way home I re-entered the real world, Dr Jekyll once more. I was conscious of people's faces turned towards me in the compartment. Could they sense what I had done – was there anything to show for it? I was weak – there was no escaping it – I had succumbed to disgusting thoughts, to baseness. I knew this time I had stepped over a line, but if the same temptation was before me again I knew I would be unable to resist. Bill was such a rogue. How could you not like him; he clearly felt no shame. Unlike Annie, he had known exactly what I had secretly wanted, exactly how to give it: like it was the very thing he wanted too. I could never be that bold with Annie, nor even contemplate that she might be so with me. I felt a bit guilty as well – perhaps for cheating on her – but it was not as if I had been with another woman – and she had not wanted me recently.

'What's that smell, John?' Annie said as I snuffed out the candle and got into bed.

'What smell?' Panic bubbled up.

'A heady sort of smell.'

'Oh, that'll be the pain-killer.'

'What pain-killer?'

'I just rubbed a little on my leg, but it's nothing.' I had taken Bill's little bottle out with me to the privy and applied some more, re-running in my mind the earlier episode.

'Where did you get that on a Sunday?'

'From a friend, the trainer at swimming.'

We lay quietly for a while, then Annie sought out my hand. 'Why not come back to church, John. I missed having you there with me today. It was not God's will – I felt a warmth come over me as I prayed to Our Lady for help today. You must find time for God and me and not neglect us for your friends. I know you're hurting and angry but you will find peace if you let God in.'

I didn't know what to say; I couldn't find the words that would speak the truth and not hurt her. The bad stuff was never God's fault, he only took credit for the good things in the world. So I lay still and silent.

Then she whispered: 'We could always try again soon, as well. When I'm fully better.'

I squeezed her hand by way of response and waited for sleep to overcome me.

Chapter Seventeen

I reported at the station in the morning, and was told to go with PC Ashbourne to the West Riding Court at Dewsbury. The pain in my leg had changed from being sharp to a dull, not unpleasant, ache. I had rubbed on some more painkiller into the now lurid, multi-coloured bruises. I was confident of being able to return to duty that evening.

The courthouse was close by the station in Dewsbury which was a relief: I didn't want to walk through the streets of Dewsbury in my uniform. I didn't want the two aspects of my life to encroach on each other.

I sat on the bench outside the court next to Ashbourne as far away from the public and criminal classes who frequented court as we could manage; we were helped in this by no one particularly desiring to sit next to the two large figures of authority.

'I hope they put that bastard away. My leg's still killing me,' said Ashbourne. 'Not even the decency to fight with his fists!'

'Yeah. Thank God that beast didn't sink his teeth in though. I thought I was finished at one point; I've heard of many a dog bite go bad and finish people off, not just from rabies either. A dog's mouth is full of microbes.'

'What you going to say when you give your evidence?'

'Just tell it how it happened.'

'Don't forget to mention the foul language as well.'

I was called into court first, the usher leading me to the witness stand and handing me the bible. All eyes were on me: all of the Justices of the Peace, an array of side whiskers and beards, sombre and aloof, the chairman peering over the top of his spectacles, the gilded coat of arms like a halo above his head, the rabble of spectators on the public benches and a reporter, pen poised. Only the miner, Alderson, was looking at the floor as he stood in the dock.

I tried to steady my shaking leg; this was not the first time I had given evidence but it got no better. It was worse than anything in life for making me feel small and insignificant. I felt on trial myself. And after all, had I not done wrong in the eyes of the law? I could get penal servitude for what I had done.

The clerk looked up from his writing, his voice crackling with contempt for everyone around him when he spoke, except when addressing the chairman for whom he reserved a special obsequiousness. I held the leather bound book aloft and tried not to let it waver as I spoke. I then waited for my cue to give evidence. I folded my arms, then unfolded them, dropped my hands to my side and then finally settled for folding them behind my back, out of sight.

I answered the questions put to me and felt more at ease; though I was conscious of the hawk-like gaze of the Chairman. Alderson looked up occasionally, expressionless, sober, drained of all his ferocity of the Saturday night. He was not represented and declined to cross-examine.

Much relieved that I had survived, I sat at the back and watched Ashbourne give evidence, apparently self-assured and in control of his scene in the performance. The chairman conferred in whispers with those on the bench, first to one side then to the other.

'We take into account your previous record which does you no favours. This is an extremely serious offence. Your behaviour was disgraceful…'

He is going to prison, I thought.

'… and if you appear before us again then your liberty will be at risk. You would do well to abstain from drink as it clearly leads you astray, do you hear?'

Alderson looked up and nodded clearly attempting to suppress his innate scowl.

'You will pay a penalty of ten shillings and costs of one shilling for damages done to a police lamp. You are free to go and let that be the last we see of you.'

'Can't believe he got off that lightly,' said Ashbourne as we left the building. 'No worse than if he was a normal Saturday night drunk. What did you say to 'em?'

'Nothing, just what happened.'

'Them magistrates don't stick up for us – we're assaulted and it's seen as no worse than any brawl outside a pub. Like we are expected to take a beating. Well, at least we stick together – we'll keep an eye on him and make him pay. Make sure he's back in court again, eh? No one gets away with kicking us.'

I went straight home afterwards, glad to be away from Dewsbury in my uniform. I went to bed when I got in, ready for reporting for duty late that evening. I would be put on reserve duty so that I didn't have to walk my beat.

Another week or so passed before I could get away to see the others again, but on my first free Saturday afternoon I went into Dewsbury to track them down. It wasn't hard. I tried the Anchor first. The corner was empty so I asked at the bar. They had just left, leaving a message that if anyone was looking for them they were going to the Crow Nest.

I found them in the lounge bar: Josiah, Walter, Bill and Jesse. I shook them all by the hand and stood a round for them. When I sat down Bill patted my leg. 'How's that pulled muscle been?'

'It's fine now; good as new. Oh, and I've got the rest of your painkiller.' I pulled out the bottle which I'd wrapped up in brown paper and handed it to Bill. 'There's not much left – it's good stuff is that.'

'Tha's welcome to borrow it any time. I'll have a ready supply for the start of the season.'

'I'm looking forward to starting again.' I sipped my pint and leaned back, listened to the conversation and observed. Yes, the physicality of starting polo again would be welcome. It was as if nothing had happened between me and Bill. Not that there could be any mention of it, but there was not even a wink to it. He had patted my leg, asked after me, but that was it. What could I do? I couldn't ask him directly; it had just been spontaneous; perhaps it was just a one-off.

After a few drinks and a game of cards we spilt up, Bill saying he'd better get back to sort out tea.

'Next week then?' said Walter as they got outside.

'How about Friday after work? We could go into town for a change, see some of the others?' said Bill.

'Right let's meet at the usual place,' said Josiah. 'You up for that, John?' I nodded. 'Tell you what why don't you come over to mine first and we'll head down together.'

I watched Bill head off down the street, head bowed. It was indeed as if nothing had ever happened.

I walked back towards Ravensthorpe station with Walter.

'How's everything with thi, John? Tha's a bit quiet.'

'No, I was just thinking.'

'About what?'

'Oh, this and that.'

'Tha seems to be getting on well with Bill these days.'

'Yeah. Bill's all right. Kind.'

'Yeah… he is, but… tha wants to be careful with him though.'

'What's tha on about?'

'Don't rely on him overly much; tha knows. Don't attach too much to thi friendship wi' him. I made that mistake.'

'How?'

'Bill's all right, but he never gives much back, not… I dunno… commitment. I don't think he knows what love is. I've just come to accept him for what he is.'

Walter shook my hand as we parted, leaving me trying to weigh up what had been said about Bill, pondering exactly what it was I wanted anyway.

*

The tram engine fussed its way down Bradford Road from Batley, shaking and juddering; screeching as it stopped, wheezing steam as it started away again. The odd patch of green grass, remnants of pasture land, now looked incongruous between mill buildings that now came one after another: vast monuments to their founders' pride and wealth. The engine and its trailer crept along their iron track, delivering fresh workers to the mills and removing the depleted.

I yawned. I shouldn't have come out really as I had a long night ahead of me and I had only slept fitfully that afternoon: it was too warm with the window shut and, with it open, the curtains billowed in the breeze, letting in the light, and the sounds of the street drifted in. I had given up at about half past five and wandered over to Josiah's, the thought occurring to me that I might be missing out on something. I would only stop for a couple, then make my excuses.

'You're making me yawn too, stop it.'

'I'm sorry – it's always hard changing shifts. I'm not tired really, not yet, but I was just thinking what I'll be like at four in the morning.'

We got off the tram at the bottom of Bradford Road and crossed over. I spotted Walter, talking to another man, as we picked our way past carts returning from the last deliveries of the day and people heading home.

'John, has tha met Josiah?' said Walter. 'Another one I'm afraid – as if one wasn't enough. We call him Josie or little Josiah, even though he's not that little – '

'I'm not little.'

I was struck by the beauty of him. He was young, smartly dressed, perhaps not yet twenty, had a perfect, honest smile and bright blue eyes, that sucked you in. His cap was worn too far back on his head, like Bill's, showing a mop of brown hair. He was completely clean shaven which lent him an even more youthful look.

I shook his hand – compliant in my own firm shake, 'Pleased to meet you.'

'Likewise,' said the youth, meeting my gaze with a smile.

'So, tha coming for a drink, Josie?' said Walter.

'I don't know,' he said.

'Oh, go on,' I said, surprising myself by my forthrightness.

'Well, I suppose it's a bit quiet; you've twisted my arm.'

'Come on then, there's no sign of Bill.'

We sat around a table in the Railway Hotel, me next to little Josiah.

'So, how's tha know this lot then?' Little Josiah asked.

'I met them through swimming. Josiah dragged me into playing water polo. How about you?'

'Just one of the gang.'

I found out that he was a mill hand and lived alone; I didn't have to reveal anything about myself really, other than that I came from Sheffield. The shove ha'penny board was brought across and, while we were playing, an old, sickly-looking man with rosy cheeks entered the pub and came up to Little Josiah.

'I wondered where tha was. Not working?'

'Nah. I came for a drink. Might see thi later though, Henry.'

'Right ho.'

'Tha knows Josiah and Walter.' The man shook our hands. 'And this is John.' His hand was warm, soft and flabby. He smiled at me, showing gaps in his teeth.

'Tha stopping for a quick one, Henry?'

'No, I'd best get back.'

'We going to sort out another supper party some time?'

'Yeah, we should. I'll ask Tom about it. See thi later.'

I looked at little Josiah as the man left.

'He's all right is Henry, once you get to know him. Wouldn't hurt a fly. Would do anything to help a friend.'

'What do you reckon to another party? You up for that?' Little Josiah asked the other two.

'Count me in,' said Walter.

'Tell you what, I'll sort summat out with Henry and Tom. Why don't we meet up again early next week? Monday?'

'That's the holiday.'

'Oh aye, make it Tuesday then. Tha'll come too, John?'

'Yes, I'd like to. Thanks.'

I got up to leave for the nine o'clock train, to give myself enough time to get back and get changed.

Little Josiah got up to go as well. 'I'll come with thi. Good evening gentlemen,' he said.

We left Josiah and Walter in the pub. Little Josiah stopped when we got near the railway arch where we first met earlier.

'Nice to meet thi, John. I look forward to seeing thi next week.'

'Me too. Thanks, Josiah.'

'Tha can call me Josie, if tha likes, all my best mates do.'

I strode quickly to the station. As I waited for the train to pull in, it occurred to me to wonder where Bill had got to. Strange. I'd not really missed his company. Josie was charming though. A long time since I had seen such warmth in a person. What about that Henry bloke though? And what was this supper party? I'd never been to a "supper party" before. I thought of the dinner parties at the solicitor's in Broomhill, with ladies in gowns and the men in morning coats. What was I letting myself in for? I looked forward to getting to know Josie better though.

I put such conjecture out of my mind and got on with keeping villainy at bay in the dark streets and alleys of Liversedge over the next few nights, separating out these two parts of my life – of my personality; it worked and it was exciting.

On the bank holiday, I woke towards midday. Annie greeted me with: 'Get your boots on lazy bones we're going for a picnic.'

We walked along the lanes up towards Robert Town and Hartshead. It was warm and still, a slight haze in the air blocking out any distant views we might otherwise have had.

Annie said, 'You seem a lot happier in yourself, John.'

'I am. And you – being back at work again, you seem more like the old Annie?'

'Yes, keeping busy is good for me and I get to meet so many people – I really have nothing to be ungrateful for.'

'And no one at the station has commented on you working. I suppose they can only tell me to stop you if they know about it.'

We moved aside for some cyclists coming down the hill.

'I'm glad you're coming to terms with what happened. It will make us stronger, John.'

'Yes.'

'Will you be seeing your friends again soon?'

'Yes, tomorrow.'

'They are obviously good for you. It seems to cheer you up.'

'Yes. Yes, it does.'

We spread out a blanket in the shade of a hawthorn down by Tanhouse Beck and set the basket down.

'We're saving up nicely now, aren't we? We should soon have enough to set up our own home. Everything will be all right then. You can invite your friends and their wives round for tea.'

We had a bread cake and a chicken leg each, and bottles of lemonade and a pie made with gooseberry jam. Clouds of small, annoying flies led us to hurry our meal and move on. We stopped for a drink in Robert Town before heading back.

'We really should do this more often, John. I've had a lovely afternoon,' she said.

'Me too.' But already I was thinking of the following evening.

When I arrived at the viaduct I saw Josie standing talking to a man. The man moved away when I approached.

Josie stuck out his hand: 'John, good to see thi again,' and held my hand in the shake. 'Who else is coming?'

'No idea,' I said. 'Walt and Josiah said they would didn't they?'

'I've not heard any more from Henry about holding a dinner party. Well, I say dinner party, that makes it sound grander than it is. It's more a group of friends getting together and sharing a meal, some beers, and having a bit of fun. We'll go round to the house and see, if everyone wants. See if he's in.'

Josiah arrived, followed by Walter.

'Bill couldn't come. His mother's not well or something,' said Walter.

'Let's go up to the Junction and get a pint,' said Josie. 'Then we can call in at Tom's about sorting out a party.'

The front door to the cottage on Lidgate Lane was set down from street level, with a small yard which it shared with the adjoining cottage. I could see it was back-to-back with cottages in the next street down.

'Wait here,' said Josie, 'I'll see if they're in.'

I sat on a wall with Walter and Josiah. The door was answered by a rather jowly man, perhaps in his fifties, thick-set, with fair, or perhaps fading, brown hair. His sleeves were rolled up revealing thick forearms like those of a sailor. He was soon laughing at what Josie was saying, a face that was accustomed to laughter: lines readily forming round the eyes. Josie went inside.

'Who's the old fella?'

'That's Tom Brown. It's his house,' said Josiah. 'It's him that opens up his house to distinguished guests.'

'So, who's that Henry bloke we met the other night?'

'He's Tom's lodger.'

'So, what are these parties like?'

'They're good,' said Walter. 'Good food, plenty of beer and no one to tell you to behave.'

Josie re-emerged with another man who came up to shake our hands.

'This is Walter – big Walter, or Wallie, to distinguish him from the runt.'

'Not nice that, Josie.'

'Sorry, Walt.'

Big Walter greeted them: 'I'd have come up for a drink if I'd known.'

'We might have asked thi if we knew tha were here.'

'Look, we're on for Saturday night,' said Josie. 'Tom's given me a book to keep tabs on subs. Who's in? A shilling up front.'

Josiah gave him a shilling, Walter a few pennies with a promise of more, and Josie noted it down.

'I've not got enough,' I said, going through my pockets. I only had enough for my train fare having bought generously at the pub.

'So, are you going for another drink?' said Big Walter.

'Come on then, scrounger.'

I said I'd better be getting back.

'I'll head down that way with thi,' Josie said.

We rounded the corner onto Mill Road.

Josie said, 'So tha'll come on Saturday, then?'

'I'd like to, it depends whether I can get away from work.'

'Well, why don't tha meet me one evening and bring the money if tha's coming. Tha'll find me in the usual place, and if I'm not there just wait a bit. I hope tha can come.'

He looked up at me and smiled; then touched my arm, gently, subtly. A gesture that a passer-by would not have noticed, but which to me was like a tingle from an electric generator, a signal of... desire? – of intent?

It was frustrating: we were walking through the streets of the town, like everyone else. I wanted to steer the conversation, to say things, but couldn't; wanted to move to something – spontaneous, but every window had eyes, every door ears, every person in the street was dangerous.

As he left, Josie said, 'Come and see me.'

That evening I asked the inspector about taking the Saturday off. The Inspector said no, but if I asked again the following evening he would have a better idea depending if one of his officers reported back from illness. There was no point going to Dewsbury until I knew, so I'd have to wait until Thursday. The night was still and warm – a good night for burglary. I had been ordered to keep a particular eye out on certain premises, premises of certain respectable gentlemen with whom, I thought special arrangements had probably been made; gentlemen who were recalling favours or expecting entitlements for discreet subscriptions. I had to follow orders and took extra care to look all around Ings House and down the footpaths at the back.

I wondered about this supper party idea. What would it be like? When I first had to face the idea that my feelings for people weren't quite like everyone else's I had tried to ignore them – perhaps those thoughts would go away. It would remain buried within me forever and that was how it would be. Then Edward came along. Something had been unleashed that I couldn't control. Fear had overcome me, fear for my health and for the consequences of sin and I had had to seek help, both spiritual and medical. I had fought against it but it took Josiah to soothe my torment, and now I felt a freedom when I was with my friends. I was not questioned, they accepted me for who I was, for what I was – whatever that might be. Self-expression was open to me, opportunities were opening up and it was exciting. I was amazed to find that there were lots of people who were different: a whole underworld, a secret society which I was now on the edge of. It did not operate according to the rules of society – how could it? But I was not yet part of it. I didn't really understand the meaning of everything; the language, the gestures, the looks, the things that everyone who was part of it seemed to just know: the meeting places, who everyone was. I felt a certain jealousy; and yet I was being admitted. I was invited to the party. And then there was Josie. I stopped, closed my eyes, and took a deep breath; the air was sweet and musty from the dew making damp the earth and from the greenery in the lane now at its fullest.

Chapter Eighteen

Bill

I poked a knife into the boiling water to see if the hoof was ready to come off; it was, so I chopped the cow heel into four pieces and put it in a pan to simmer for the afternoon. That was tea sorted – I'd got onion, but a bit of parsley would be good. Then I'd have the jelly to add to cabbage soup, or to sweeten by adding a few currants or raspberries for my mother. She had become difficult again. The miracle of the Jubilee had lasted only three weeks and she was now back in her chair complaining of aches and being unable to get about; me and Fanny would have to help her up the stairs or onto the commode. Fanny looked after her while I was at the mill; taking in laundry or doing work for a dressmaker. This kept some extra money coming in, and we now needed every penny. My brother, who could still do no wrong in mother's eyes, had lost his job, or rather had thrown it away through poor time-keeping, ale, or both – or God knows what. Now, having all that time on his hands, he was to be found lounging around on street corners, or in the park, seeking work he called it, rather than helping in the house. Somehow he still managed to scrounge enough money for beer, but as long as he kissed his mother when he got in and spoke kindly, acted sympathetically, it was still: "You are a good boy to your old mother, so you are."

I had only managed to get out a couple of times in the evening; I felt duty-bound to let Fanny escape to meet young Connelly, and, besides, I didn't want to cadge and was not good company right now. This was my punishment. That afternoon after the choir in the park, I had landed my fish, and well worth landing it had seemed at the time, but now I was being made to suffer. John had been so free and easy, not at all like I had anticipated. I had thought it might be difficult or awkward, that I might have to try hard to get what I wanted, but everything had gone my way. John was so sweet, clueless really, but that made it all the better. And now I was stuck, emptying stinking chamber pots and scraping meals together from next to nothing and a potato. Walter had called round. I had half closed the door behind me and almost spoke in whispers to him on the doorstep. He had tried to persuade me to go out, but I really couldn't face it.

'We're trying to sort out another supper party at Tom's. Tha'll have to come to that though, won't tha?'

'I'll have to see Walt. I'd like to.'

The parties at Tom Brown's were not to be missed, but the subs would be at least a shilling, plus extra for beer when that ran out. There was no way: every penny was being spent on the rent, coal and food. Every bloody, sodding penny.

My brother came breezing in the front door, threw his cap on a nail and went over to kiss mother. He took the lid off the cook pot, replaced it then went through to the scullery. I followed him.

'Gi' us summat to eat, our Bill.'

'There's nothing Tom. Just a bit of bread for collops.'

'That'll do, ta.'

'But, Tom…'

'Tha'll find summat else. I'm starving – it's a hungry business tramping round for work. Right, seeing as it's Saturday, I deserve a drink.'

He went back through to the living room and started looking round for the tin. I watched him look on the dresser, the mantelpiece, and in the coal scuttle. He looked around the range, and scowled at me, but I was careful to keep my gaze from where the money was hidden. The tin had been abandoned after the last time and there were now three small caches of coins that only me and Fanny knew of.

He came up to me. I smelt his breath as he leaned in.

'Where the bloody hell is it?'

'We need all of it.'

'Tha can spare a few coppers, tha tight-fisted little sod.'

I stared him out.

'Mother, tell him to let me have a couple of pennies for some beer.'

'Be good to your brother, William,' she said without even turning her head.

I looked into his eyes, staring blankly.

'You little shit!' He grasped my cheeks between his thumb and fingers. I shut my eyes, to shut out Tom's wild eyes, the pain. I was pushed aside and he strode out picking up his cap and slamming the door.

'No need for that sort of behaviour, William,' said the chair.

I got to my feet and went through to the scullery. I sank down onto a stool, head in hands.

Chapter Nineteen

John

I had all on not to break into a trot as I headed down Wellington Road towards the Bradford Road viaduct. I rounded the corner and stopped. Josie wasn't there. What did I expect? That Josie would be stood there every evening just on the off chance I'd turn up? He had said to just wait though. I stood near to where we had met him before and adjusted my new straw hat on my head. A long slow train rumbled overhead. I realised I was stood like I was on point duty and tried to look more casual by leaning against the wall. I watched two trams roll by on their way up to Batley and Birstall, and teamers with their loads of bales making steady progress to the mills up the road. I kept a look out for a familiar figure approaching. I pulled out my watch – half an hour had passed since I'd arrived. From the Dewsbury end I noticed a man walking along in a mackintosh – funny since it was warm – perhaps in anticipation of a thunderstorm. He held a silver topped cane. He looked directly at me as he approached and slowed his stride. The man smiled half a smile and nodded to me. Peculiar fellow. Then he continued past me. Shortly after I saw the same man walk back down on the opposite side of the street. Josie was obviously not around tonight.

Just as I was cursing my foolishness and turning to head to the station, Josie rounded the corner with two other young men and broke into a broad smile on seeing me.

'Been here long?' He nodded to his to companions and walked alongside me.

'No, I was just passing and thought I'd see if you were around and fancied a pint.'

'Yeah, that would be good. Tell thi what, there's a beer shop just round from Tom's. We can call in there on the way.'

I didn't like to ask "on the way to where?" I followed Josie up the road. Josie told me about a man at the mill he worked at who had broken both his legs that day. Whilst pulling a bale in to a teagle opening on the third floor he had slipped and fell. But for landing on some bales of wool he would have been killed. 'Can't see the poor fella working again for sometime, if ever. Might have been better off dead.'

We headed up Mill Road, and, outside the grocer's, Josie said, 'Wait here. Not be a sec.'

He emerged with a couple of quart stone bottles: 'Come on.' He led the way round to Tom Brown's house and let himself in with a key from his pocket. In answer to a look from me, he said: 'Tom and Henry let me use the house when I like.'

A short passage ended in a door but Josie opened another door off to the side which opened into a living room.

'Sit down,' he said indicating some wooden chairs by a kitchen table.

I placed my hat on the table. The table was over to one side and on the other was a horse hair sofa that had seen better days. Josie put the bottles down then took off his cap and sent it spinning onto the sofa, then ran his hands through his mop of rather long hair and scratched his scalp. He had nice hair. Then he looked in the dresser and found two pewter mugs which he brought to the table and filled from one of the beer bottles.

'Here's to thi health.'

'Yes, and thine, Josie.'

I looked round. It was a very plain room with a stone flag floor, white-washed walls and grey net curtains hung over the window. A plank door in one wall presumably led to a cellar.

'I'm sorry, I can't make it on Saturday.'

'That's lucky then, because it's off. We're going to do it the following week instead. We couldn't get word round to everyone in time for this week, not to make it worthwhile anyhow. What about the week after?'

'Yeah, I should be able to.'

'That's good.'

I stared at Josie as he spoke. Josie didn't seem to mind, like he enjoyed it.

'Drink up,' he said.

'Why?'

'Come on – with me.' I followed him, heart pounding, along the passage. Josie opened the door. There were stairs at the other side, and Josie took hold of my hand and led me up. The stairs opened straight out into a bedroom containing three beds. Josie stopped at the top of the stairs and faced me – then started to undo buttons.

The rest of the beer was poured at the table and Josie got out a silver cigarette case and handed one to me.

'I said I wasn't little Josie didn't I?'

I looked up from my beer at Josie's beaming face. I suddenly felt very embarrassed and out of place. 'I'd best be going.'

'Which way's tha going?'

'Down to the station.'

'I'll walk with thi.'

I felt better once I was out of the house and walking down the street, doing something normal. I realised I had not paid for my share of the beer.

'What do I owe thi by the way?'

'Normally it's four bob.'

'How much?'

'Four bob, and eight pence for the beer, but that was a free one.'

Suddenly the railway arch and the other people I'd seen there became clear. How could I have been so naïve; and me a copper too? I felt like running, but that would make me look even more foolish.

'Don't come the innocent. Tha knew what tha was letting thissen in for. Can't kid me. Ever since tha clapped eyes on me. But I wanted to; not for any other reason; not for the money. And the beer's on me an' all. I like thi, John – simple as that, don't look so surprised.'

'No, no. I'm not. That's fine.'

'Look, let's meet up again next week. What is the matter with thi? Not gone off me all of a sudden?'

'No, no.'

'Good, I should hope not. Tuesday then, about seven?'

'I can't, I don't finish till ten.'

'Well, meet me in the Railway after that then.'

I hurried off feeling embarrassed and a bloody fool. I had wanted to appear cool and in the know but I must have come across like some daft puppy.'

That feeling faded with the distance as the train made its way up the Spen Valley. By the time I put on my uniform, walking out into the dark, becoming PC 188, it seemed little more than a dream.

*

I sat with Annie by the window in our room after breakfast on Sunday. I was reading *The Police Review*, a small pile of them was on the floor by the window. I looked up at her staring out, she caught my eye and smiled at me, I went back to reading. I knew she was wanting to chatter on about nothing, but I was more interested in reading about the campaign for one day in seven. Really that was only right. Even common workmen got Sundays off, so it was only fair.

'John – '

I looked up.

'– would you like to go for a walk?'

'We'll go for a walk when we go to church in a bit.'

'I just thought…'

An advertisement for a shoulder brace for round shoulders caught my eye. Perhaps I ought to get one – made in America – three shillings and nine – seemed a lot, but if it worked?'

'Do you think I have round shoulders?'

'Round shoulders? What on earth are you talking about? I thought you were studying police stuff.'

'I am. It doesn't matter.'

Annie picked up a paper from the pile and started flicking through. That didn't feel right somehow. Like she was interfering with police property.

'Look, it says here that you should get someone to read this out to you so that you can write it down. It's a sergeant's exam thing. Get a pencil and paper. Go on. It'll be fun.'

I reluctantly did as she suggested. After all, it was one of the things I had to get better at.

'It says you're allowed no more than three errors or you fail. I am supposed to dictate it at a fairly sharp rate. Ready? "Look closely at the word passion. We sometimes regard a passionate man as a person of strong will, and of real though ungoverned energy. But passion teaches us quite another lesson; for it – as a very solemn use of it declares – means properly "suffering," and a passionate man is not a man doing something; but one suffering something to be done unto him. When then a man or child is "in a passion," this is no coming out in him of a strong will of real energy but rather the proof that for the time at least he is altogether wanting in these: he is suffering, not doing, suffering his angry, or what other evil temper it may be–" '

I scraped my pencil over my writing and scrunched up the paper. I'm just not in the mood.' I had already made many more than three mistakes.

'John, whatever is the matter? You'll have to get better at this if you are to ever have a chance of becoming sergeant.'

She picked up the ball of paper and gave a little snort.

'Anyone looking at you would think you were a passionate man. It's a good job I know you better.'

I stood up and looked out across the field at the houses beyond.

*

On the Tuesday, after work, I rushed home and changed. I told Annie that I had some plain clothes work I was needed on.

'Oh, how exciting. They must think highly of you. What is it?'

'I can't talk about it.'

'Of course.'

'It's nothing special. Don't wait up for me.'

I ran to the station and just made it onto the platform as the whistle blew. I sank onto a seat in the carriage, my chest heaving, and got my handkerchief out to wipe my brow.

'She's a lucky lady,' said an elderly gentleman in a shabby, tweed suit, eyeing me up and down.

'I beg your pardon?'

'A lucky lady. Who's worth all the rush and getting in a lather over.'

'Oh, I see. No, it's not that.' I was irritated. I wasn't going to be drawn into a conversation with the impudent little man.

I stared out into the dark. I wanted to see Josie again. I had tried half-heartedly to ignore it, but it was never far from my thoughts. I wanted to see if it really had been a dream; it wasn't enough, I wanted more. If it was a sin it was a beautiful one, and, if it was, I was already too far in; it was too late. What drove me could not be a sin. All flames burn pure as Josiah liked to say.

Josie was at the pub with the two Walters. The wretched train had stood outside the station for a ridiculous time, though it was probably only minutes, and I was only just in time to buy a round before last orders was rung. I pushed a small stack of ha'pennies for four pints across the bar and downed the first before the potman had finished pouring the last.

I sat listening to them talk, not really saying much; late into the conversation I was not part of it and they were talking about Yorkshire having lost to Sussex and being out of the hunt for the title – I could think of nothing worth saying as it bandied quickly back and forth, fuelled by beer and merriment. Then the landlord was shouting "beer off gentleman please" and we were getting to our feet.

Outside, Big Walter said, 'We're going to go and see if we can't find a lock-in. You fellas coming?'

'No,' said Josie, 'I've had enough. See you Saturday if not before.' He patted his jacket pocket. 'I've got both of you in my book.'

I crossed over the road with Josie. I'd had no opportunity to talk to him. At the corner of Halifax Road, I stopped.

'What now?' asked Josie.

'Heading back, I suppose,' I said pointing up the hill. 'I've missed the last train now.'

'Where's tha heading for?'

'Liversedge.'

'Don't be daft, tha can't walk that far.'

'It'll only take an hour or so.'

'Come and stop over at mine.'

I couldn't believe what I had just heard. I looked down at my boots.

'I've got four shillings for thi this time.'

Josie slapped me on the shoulder. 'No need, keep it.'

'But…'

'Mention it again and tha'll insult me. Come on.'

*

On Thursday morning I got an early train to Dewsbury and went straight to Josie's house, a single two-roomed dwelling, crammed with others into a courtyard off George Street. Children were already playing in the dirt with a couple of scraggy-looking chickens. Josie invited me in. I kissed him on the cheek.

'I'm due at the mill in a bit, I can't…'

'No, I know. I'll not stop. I've come to go for a swim and thought I'd see if I could catch thi in. I just wanted to give thi summat.' I pulled a paper bag from my pocket. Josie pulled out the green silk necktie.

'It's to say thank you for… for thi kindness.'

'It's lovely. Just my colour. I'll not put it on now.' He laughed as he looked down at his corduroys and adjusted a shabby looking neckcloth. 'Not exactly dapper togs.'

'No, but still beautiful to me.'

'Don't, tha'll make me blush.'

'Good. It makes thi look sweet.'

'I'll wear it on Saturday.'

'Oh, I've still not paid my subs. I meant to the other night but…'

'Tha was distracted?'

'Something like that.' Now it was my turn to feel the colour rise to my cheeks. I fished in my pocket and shuffled coins round on my palm.

'Damn, I've not got enough – I need that for swimming and the train back. I can give thi eleven pence though.' I handed over a sixpence and some coppers.

'Tha can owe me the penny.'

'What time does it start?'

'Any time after half seven. I'll be there from then, anyhow. I'd offer thi a drink but…'

'No I'll get off.'

'I'll walk with thi as far as the baths then.'

Chapter Twenty

Annie

I was thinking that John seemed much happier now. Some days he's got a real spring in his step; it's good to see. But on other days the anger that is still there seems to burst out. I am still a little worried about him. He took it very badly. I wonder if in a way, experiencing it: it happening to me, actually made it easier to bear mentally. I was part of it, I wasn't suddenly presented with the fact like he was. To him there was no physical sense to it all, whereas I could feel something going wrong inside. It is not, after all, uncommon. It is part of the mystery of God's creation. A test.

My faith has helped me through it; God has spoken to me. I mustn't presume to try to understand his scheme. When it is meant to be, it will happen.

John cannot see that; doesn't feel that. He needs to open his heart to God, not rail against the world. It is a slow process but I think he's coming round. We had a lovely afternoon on the bank holiday, and a nice picnic despite the cloud of flies hanging round our heads. It felt very much as if things were returning to normal. I look forward to those moments when I have his undivided attention.

It is hard to talk to him – and I don't want to intrude on him by telling him how *I* feel – that will not exactly help. So I put on my brave face for him and try to get him to give himself over to our Lord. I will soon be ready to try again as well, I know that is what he wants.

Mrs Shaw has been like a mother to me – in fact I would go as far as saying she has been better even than that, may I be forgiven for even thinking it. But she has been mother, friend and older sister all rolled into one. And she knows what it's like – she has lost children herself.

Then to cap it all, poor John got kicked by a drunk. He wouldn't show me the bruise, but it must have been quite nasty, the way it made him limp. I do worry about him when he's out there on the beat, there are some nasty people around. But at the same time I am so very proud of what he does, protecting people and helping them. In many ways he is doing God's work – in a very real sense; not just talking about it, but making it happen. For that I can only admire him and be grateful.

Chapter Twenty-one

Murdoch Campbell, Chief Inspector Murdoch Campbell, looked down on the town of Dewsbury. He lived on Clarke Street which he said was in Westborough, not Dewsbury. From the bottom of his street there was a significant five hundred yards of fields separating him from The Flatts in Dewsbury. From his terraced house, that he called "a villa," he was raised up above the back-to-backs of The Flatts, and the filthy courtyards of the old town which bred villainy and created conditions ripe for disease. He looked down on the mills and the stinking river, the rooftops, chimneys and smoke. Up on his hill, amongst decent people, his wife cultivated fragrant roses in the small front garden, and in the back garden he grew marrows, leeks and potatoes that would win prizes were it not inappropriate for a member of the constabulary to enter such things and risk the whiff of compromise or favour.

Murdoch Campbell, with his magnificent side whiskers, at nigh on six feet tall looked down on the residents of the borough. They were stunted, weak, and had sallow complexions. Up in Inverness-shire they were forged of better stuff. His childhood memories of Kingussie were of wholesome vittles, clean water and fresh air. He had roamed from the age of five with the other boys all over Badenoch; up to Ruthven castle, to Creag Bheag and over to Loch Ganach, where in the summer they swam or where they heard snipe calling over its cold grey waters. He saw deer break out of the woods or wild geese flying and urging each other to stay in formation overhead. Down by Ballochbai Island the waters teemed with salmon. Aye, that bred men. Men with sturdy frames, sturdy minds; upright men in every sense.

Murdoch Campbell also looked down on the people of Dewsbury in a less literal sense. In truth they were little more than beasts, such was their depravity. They delighted in every sin – they swore, they drank – not that there was anything wrong with whisky in moderation; he had been brought up to respect drink, his father ran the Star Inn after all, but these people showed no constraint; it went beyond companionship and conviviality. They drank with the sole purpose of getting drunk and misbehaving. It was fortunate that his good wife, Sarah, didn't know what went on.

Their depravity was at it's greatest when it came to fornication. They were indiscriminate and despite their poor nutrition and apparent lack of desire to raise children they still multiplied like vermin, and these unwanted offspring roamed the streets and turned inevitably to crime, despoiling the town, and they sold their bodies and souls on street corners for a few pence. But, being a policeman, it was a burden he bore to have to face these things.

He had gone south to get far away from something that had happened out on the hills, and joined the Dewsbury Borough Force at the age of seventeen. He was a sergeant at twenty-one, a bright young man with a superior Scots education and intellect. Then he found that merit was no longer sufficient to get on. Despite being the best and most dedicated he found himself pipped to the post of inspector by lesser men, by men with connections and backgrounds, men who were not foreigners, who spoke highly of themselves and who convinced others of their merits. Men who subscribed to that Sherlock Holmes dictum, he liked to quote to his Skye terrier: "what you do in this world is a matter of no consequence − the question is what can you make people believe that you have done." But he had had age on his side and you can't keep a good man down, so at thirty-four he was appointed one of three inspectors in the force.

He had considered himself married to the job, a bachelor for life, until he met Miss Mislian, a fine woman of thirty, a dressmaker, clearly not a local girl, at a civic function. She reflected his view of the world back to him, she was up to the job, a satisfactory arrangement all round. Much to his anger, they had never had children. It was inexplicable, and made him all the angrier when he saw unwanted street urchins being removed from the streets to be placed in industrial schools.

He had been promoted to Chief Inspector last year and knew he had reached as high as he could ever hope to go. It was clear to all that the post of Chief Constable was not for the likes of him. No one wanted someone with experience and long practicable police service. Everyone appointed outsiders. Ex-army or navy types, men from Oxford or Cambridge whose knowledge of human behaviour was far superior to his own, having been derived from a study of the Ancient Greeks or Roman poets − or from rowing in boats. Still, on forty-eight shillings, he was comfortable, had kept a respectable house, and all those years as a lodger meant a nice little nest egg had built up. A few more years and he would retire and take his wife to live at the seaside, somewhere refined − like Blackpool.

It was Saturday the fourteenth of August and he was at his desk early, compiling notes for the Chief Constable's monthly report to the Watch Committee. It was going to be a big day. A day when some of the vilest felons would be swept from the streets of the town; it was a stain on the Borough that unfortunately had to be revealed before it could be wiped clean.

He had made arrangements for a special briefing that morning. This was not something to be left to others. Two years they had been after this gang. Now, all that careful work was about to pay off − he knew something big was going down that evening.

There was a knock at the door.

'Come in. Yes, Sergeant?'

'Visitor for you, sir. From Wakefield.'

'Yes, come in. Harris, is it?' A rather shabby looking man in a greasy cap and a tattered blue serge suit stood before him. 'Good to see you're suitably attired.'

'Yes, sir. Hope it's not over-doing it, sir.'

'No, Harris, you look every bit the common navvy, just the ticket. Now, you come highly recommended by your Chief Constable, Captain Russell. He has kindly agreed to let you come and work with us on this one. We needed a man from outside who would not be recognised when keeping watch over the house for the day, someone inconspicuous. How much do you know?'

'Not much, sir.'

'Well, we've had this house under suspicion for a while. Lots of complaints and that sort of thing from neighbours. Young men coming and going, drinking, noise. Look, I'm terribly sorry, Harris, but there's no pleasant way of phrasing this, it is a beastly business, I'm afraid. We believe the house is used for… unmentionable acts…' He hoped he wasn't going to have to elaborate, but Harris looked blank. 'For sodomitic practices.' Harris had still not twigged. 'For buggery, Harris.' His own sense of repulsion at the word was mirrored in Harris' repressed expression. 'I'm sorry, Harris, it would be a less unpleasant business all round if it had been a good old-fashioned rape or murder, but there it is.'

'I see, sir.'

'Don't worry, Harris. Your job is just to keep watch – there's only one way in through the front door. You've got your notebook, good. The house is Brick Row, number twenty three, at the bottom of Lidgate Lane in Batley Carr. You know Batley Carr? Here's a map showing the location of the house.'

'Very good, sir.'

'The house is occupied by a Thomas Brown, a man of about fifty; he runs a sweet shop just round the corner. Also living there is a retired painter called Henry Crosse, sickly-looking fellow. We've had complaints about both of them and the way they carry on with young men – boys really. We want you to carefully note all the comings and goings, discreetly into your book – we have a detective called Crawshaw to whom I'll introduce you shortly. He will make contact with you at intervals and you can pass on any intelligence to him. Stay well back, out of sight – do whatever it takes not to get spotted.'

'I shall do my utmost, sir.'

'We expect there to be some sort of gathering there tonight, an orgy; we shall launch a raid. We may rely heavily on you for the timing of that. Note any movements you see in the house; especially lights on upstairs, curtains drawn etcetera. Understood?'

'Yes, sir. How do we know it's going on tonight, sir, may I ask?'

'We have intelligence, Harris. We've leaned on a young lad who was in with them, so to speak. Lives on the next street. Only seventeen if you can believe it, Harris. Sometimes makes you glad not to have children of your own. You got children, Harris? Good God, how far we have fallen. Anyway, they invited him, but because of our, shall we say… influence, he did the sensible thing and told us instead. Right, I'll introduce you to Crawshaw and you can get into position. Good luck, Harris.'

Campbell decided to go for an early luncheon and arranged for a cab to take him home. There he sat in the dining room and ate a civilised meal with his wife, fortifying himself for what was to come. He did not feel like talking beyond commenting on the smoked haddock being a bit overdone, and the egg custard being a little on the soft side, and the good woman had the sense not to answer back or bother him with trivialities. He retired to what he called the drawing room, overlooking the front garden and got out his briar. He smoked for a while. Yes, he had it all covered. He had seventeen men, including two sergeants and an inspector. Even his Chief Constable, Mr Henry Mansfield Shore himself, wanted to be in on this one; to steal the glory if there was any to be stolen. He had the town clerk and justices on standby for the Sunday morning; he would get a photographer to take pictures and a chap from the borough surveyor's office to do a full survey of the house and produce a plan. He rested his eyes; he should rest, it could be a long evening.

He received reports from Detective Crawshaw when he arrived back at the Town Hall. The only comings and goings had been Brown and Crosse, a delivery boy from the grocers, a large quantity of beer bottles had arrived and a butcher's boy had delivered a basket. Good, very good. That looked promising.

Mr Shore summoned him to make him run through his plan once more. He thanked him for his lame suggestions. Of course we didn't want uniforms everywhere. Naturally, he had considered the need for refreshments for his men.

'Thank you for your helpful suggestions, sir, I'll make sure the men are fully briefed.'

'Terrible business, Campbell. Wish it wasn't happening here. Won't reflect well on the borough you know. One can only pray that we get them and put a stop to it.'

'Yes, sir. We shall do our utmost to reassure all good people that such evil will be hunted out and crushed.'

'Quite right. Good Christian folk will feel reassured once they're locked away. That our sons are safe. Thank you, Campbell. I'll see you at parade.'

He could sense the excitement amongst the men as he entered the room. He knew what that sense of anticipation was like. It was one thing stumbling across a crime being committed when out on the beat, but a planned raid brought all the build up, the chatter, hands twitching on staffs, the thoughts of what you were going to do: the sense of that moment when you caught a criminal red-handed and the fear in his eyes was followed by the realisation that the game was up. The men were like clockwork toys being slowly wound up since they had reported for duty, not knowing quite why their normal shift patterns were being disrupted or why some had been told to report in plain clothes. Inspector Warwick and Sergeant Kendall had already outlined the plan.

'Those of you in uniform will be travelling in a van which will be positioned at the Mill. There you will remain until the signal is given, then the van will bring you up to the house and you will join the raid. Those of you in plain clothes will make your way in ones and twos to the Sunday School on Upper Road. Let's not make it obvious that there is a gathering of burly men – some of you go up Halifax Road, some up Bradford Road and Mill Lane, the lucky ones can get the tram up to Town Street. You will remain at the Sunday school until told. Then you will again leave in ones and twos and take up position near the house. There is a shop on the corner opposite, marked on the map. You will all have a line of sight to that. I shall place myself there under a street lamp and signal by raising my hat twice – thus – then we shall enter the premises – we have a good idea of the layout – Inspector Warwick will give you details of which of you are to go upstairs, which to stay down. Everyone inside will be restrained and brought down to the station where the cells await them. These are of course heinous crimes. I think you should prepare yourselves for seeing some of the most unpleasant things of your careers. We believe that we may find evidence of the gravest of crimes... unmentionable acts.' His men looked uneasy and glanced at each other. They understood, he needn't go on.

'We shall arrange to take a photographer there to assist with the collection of evidence.' This was the bit he was dreading. He looked at a spot on the wall at the back of the room. 'For a conviction for the abominable vice there has to be proof of penetration, and of the emission of seed. Of course you are not expected... well... just take careful note of what you observe, that's all. Any medical business will be dealt with by the surgeon when they are brought back here. However, under section eleven of the Criminal Law Amendment Act of Eighty-Five, we only need evidence of commission, or attempting to procure the commission, of any acts of gross indecency. We'll arrest the lot, however – irrespective of whether we eventually charge them with felonies or misdemeanours. No jury would question that we had reasonable grounds, unless of course we all burst in to find them sat drinking tea and eating lemon sponge whilst reading texts.' The men laughed at his joke. Good to lighten the air. 'Very good. Fall out.'

He had some tea brought to his office and went through his plan once more. Then at about seven o' clock made his way up to the Sunday school with the Chief and the Inspector in a four-wheeler. Soon it would be getting dark, then he would feel more comfortable.

The van was in place and the men had been provided with tea and were now playing cards or reading the papers. No doubt those same presses would be working flat out next Friday bringing the week's news to satisfy the rabble's taste for gossip. He regretted that it couldn't all be dealt with in secret.

Detective Crawshaw brought the latest report from PC Harris. Brown and Crosse had been busy all afternoon – smoke had been seen coming from the chimney all day. Crosse had now left, but two slim men around five feet six, in their early twenties, arrived at just gone seven. Then at around seven forty-five a tall man in his late twenties arrived; then six others since then.

So far so good. He paced from one end of the wooden floor to the other. Funny how Sunday schools always smelt the same, he thought – a smell that takes you right back to being in short trousers. He read the texts on the walls, he knew many of them by heart. One of his earliest memories was of standing by the fire, everyone gathered round: old people, aunts, uncles, grannies – perhaps at Hogmanay or Easter, and he was reciting Psalm twenty three from memory. The world turned round him then. He could have been no older than four or five. How proud they were of him.

From somewhere some beer arrived; he suspected the Chief had sent someone on an errand. Still, a small bottle each would do no harm.

At just after nine, Crawshaw returned. 'Looks like they are sat down at the table sir – only the downstairs light is on and there's not much movement. There would appear to be twelve of them, sir.'

'Thank you, Crawshaw. I particularly want to know if a light goes on upstairs, remember.'

He was beckoned over by Chief Constable Shore, to where he sat, stiff in his chair like a monarch in court.

'What are we waiting for, Campbell?'

'Activity upstairs, sir.' He was immediately embarrassed by the way he had phrased it. 'I mean we might expect the light to go on upstairs sir, if anyone goes up.'

'Quite right, when the light goes on upstairs, that's when we should act.'

'Yes. Good point, sir.'

Crawshaw was back again soon after. 'A light went on briefly upstairs, sir, could have just been a lamp as someone went up. Another one's arrived at the house too. Now there's music downstairs.'

'Music?'

'Yes, sir, sounds like an accordion, sir. The curtains are drawn, there are also sounds of merriment.'

'Such as?'

'Laughter, shouting, carrying on, sir.'

'Carrying on?'

'Well, you know like you'd hear coming from any pub, sir.'

'Let's get the van brought up into position.'

'Right you are, sir.'

He felt sorry for the men in the van – being stuck in the dark with half a dozen men and their stink. They will be keen once they're out.

He picked up a paper and flicked to the court reports: some good arrests they'd made recently. A thirteen-year-old stealing turnips – at least he had shown contrition. He's done nothing but "bluther and roar" his father had said. Educative the law. And the arrest of the man with the bulky clothes was there: concealed were: two tins of salmon, ninety tins of metal polish, twelve cakes of fancy soap, twenty-four packets of black lead and a plate: he would have liked to have seen that arrest.

Time dragged by – surely something would be happening soon. It was gone eleven after all. What was keeping them? Perhaps his plan was flawed. Perhaps they didn't retire to bed to commit their felonies. He had just imagined that is how it would be – as if somehow they mimicked behaviour of normal people.

Some of the men in the school room were now getting restless, although some sat with their eyes closed. One or two were wandering about. One of them in his perambulations had climbed up onto the raised platform at one end, like he was about to address them.

'Go on, sing us a song, Dick,' someone shouted. He looked embarrassed. 'One of your jokes then.'

'Go on then – I say, I say, I say, have you a mother-in-law? No, but I've a father in gaol.'

'Boo. Gerroff!'

'Suit yourselves. What about this then. The other night when I was up at Crackenedge, I stopped a vagrant. Instead of arresting him I gave him a shilling. Why? do I hear you say?'

'Why you idiot!'

'I'll tell you why. I shone my lantern on him and he says, "Please sir, would you be so awfully kind as to 'elp a poor man what's down on 'is luck? Besides this 'ere bludgeon loaded with lead I've nothing in the whole wide world to call my own.'

Boos now issued all round, followed by hoots of laughter.

Towards midnight, Harris came in. Looked like he'd been running.

'One man left a minute ago sir, Crawshaw's following him. A light went on upstairs. It was bright to start with, but now it's gone dim, sir.'

'Right, quick lads, into place, some go via Mill Lane, some down Smith Road – not all at once – do you want to give the game away?'

He put on his hat, on old felt one he used for gardening. Only the Chief was dressed like he was on his way to church.

'May I suggest that you bring up the rear, sir, to make sure everything's in place.'

'Just what I was thinking, Campbell.'

'If you approach from the other side of the street, sir, then follow everyone else in you can keep a vital overview.'

His heart pounded, he resisted the urge to run. He could see his men spreading out ahead, some were already sat on walls or hanging about, trying to look casual. He reached the corner shop. The upstairs was indeed lit – only a dim light. Downstairs the lamps still shone brightly. He looked around, he sensed everyone focussing on him. Just round the corner he could see the van and just made out the horse in front with its head in a nosebag. The front door to the house opened and two men came out. One of them looked up into the street and went back inside. He raised his hat twice and the chase was on. Blue uniforms poured out of the van and headed for the door. The man still outside was grabbed. At the door they struggled to get in, there were so many of them. There were shouts and screams as the occupants felt the force of the law. He jostled with the others and pushed his way in to the living room. Those inside tried to shove their way out in the chaos. Two men ducked under his arm and scrabbled past the constables queuing to get in.

'It's the police. You are all under arrest.'

One of the men inside collapsed to the floor. Men were grabbed and their arms forced up their backs. Oh, the looks on their faces! Some had un-tucked shirts, others were hastily doing up buttons on their trousers. Such vile corruption and sin! One of the old ones was sat on a sofa, staring fish-mouthed. There were curses and complaints of "Ow that hurts" as his men applied hand cuffs.

'What shall I do with this one, sir?' He looked down at the young man with the boyish face – every bit the pouf – totally clean shaven, girly big eyes and long lashes. Then he saw he was wearing a skirt.

'And this one's got a bloody apron on, sir.'

Get yourselves dressed properly for God's sake. We can't have you out in the street like that.'

'Take these… these… items of clothing as evidence.'

Harris came down from upstairs. 'No one upstairs, sir, except this one – found him under the bed – he's been doing something, sir, clothes all in disarray.'

Campbell looked at him, not much more than a boy.

'Get these perverts lined up and marched down to the station. Who's got the chain to fasten them together?'

As they assembled outside a man was being escorted back.

'The one who made his escape, sir. Didn't get far.'

'Good work, PC Clachrie. Can always count on you.' Fine chap, fellow countryman.

'Inspector Warwick, please place a guard on the house and await further orders.'

Chapter Twenty-two

John

I was very drunk; I had gone outside feeling sick, and one of the others had come out with me. I just happened to glance up into the street. Even in my drunken state I knew something was wrong. I saw men, big men – the recognition was instant. No mistaking a copper. In a panic I went back in and tried to shout 'police' but it caught in my throat, but still I heard the word echoed upstairs. Then I realised I was trapped, I should have just leapt the wall and run straightaway. I went back out but it was too late they were on me. I was thrust against the house wall by two of them and felt the snips round my wrists. I was feeling sick before, but now threw up in the yard.

'Dirty bastard,' said one of them, dodging to avoid splatter on his boots.

Oh Christ! What had I done? I had supped with the devil and now my life was over. If I could have dashed my brains out on the wall I would have. I had seen people try it, and all they ended up with was a headache and blood everywhere which made them feel even worse.

I was manhandled up the steps and forced into a squatting position on the kerb at the edge of the pavement.

'Don't bloody do that again, you filthy bugger.' I slumped forward, my head between my knees, hiding my face. When I was a child asleep in bed I sometimes knew when I was in the middle of a nightmare, when witches were after me; then, if I squeezed myself tight into a ball I could force myself out of the nightmare. If only I could do it now.

There was movement around me. They were being brought up the steps: Bill, Josie, Walt, Big Walt, Henry, Tom and the others. By now the street was filling up – people had got wind of something exciting and were coming out of houses and gathering in chattering huddles to watch the scene unfolding. I tried hide my face. The chatter over the road built. Someone shouted 'fucking poufs,' and someone else 'string 'em up the bastards.' We were lined up and a chain was passed through our handcuffs and padlocked. We were ordered to move. A loathsome woman came up close, one of those with a face twice her real age: features bequeathed by her lifestyle: grey, haggard and toothless at thirty, face contorted and full of hate. She unleashed a mouthful of phlegm. I managed to avoid it. 'Rot in hell!' she screeched. I had to think, and fast. I was sobering rapidly. Being sick had helped. No one spoke, except for the odd 'don't worry, we'll be all right, they've got nothing.' Whistling in a bloody gale!

The party was not what I had expected. I was not prepared for such indiscretion. In the pub, nothing was said about what made them different, but those rules no longer applied inside Tom Brown's. Several remarks were made, suggestions of things I would rather not acknowledge even happened – things that should be kept between two people and never mentioned. During supper the conversation was mingled with bawdy comments: things like the size of the sausages, and I was shocked by the suggestions some people made and the performances they put on when eating them. Fear and shame welled up in me: I had wondered about leaving. And yet at the same time I could not deny my own arousal. Repulsed and attracted – I was in a state of paralysis. Someone said "pass us the salt little Walt" and Walt had said, "I'm sick of little Walt this, little Walt that." He stood up and quickly unbuttoned his trousers – and to hoots of laughter and table slapping proudly announced "is that little Walt?" "littler than me" said the other Walter." "Prove it," someone said. "Later – some of us have table manners and don't put even our elbows on the table" – which brought roars of laughter.

It had soon become clear to me that Josie held no special place for me, in fact for no one it seemed. Josie was free and easy with everyone. I had been disgusted by the lack of sense of privacy or discretion. In fact people seemed to revel in that.

No, I had to think. There must be a way out of this. What about poor Annie? Oh Christ! what would happen to Annie?

We were walking quickly through the dark streets – everyone wanting to get away from the rabble, some of whom had decided to follow us, to keep up the haranguing. Some of the rabble fell back as we reached Bradford Road, but then as we approached town more people came out to stare at us and hurl abuse: somehow news of what these men were seemed to have swept before them. Something struck my face: horse-muck! The town hall rose up before me, a dark mausoleum.

Bill

They were going to make me go in there! The blue lamp over the door.

'No, I'm not going in!' I struggled and pulled. I nearly toppled two on either side of me as I lurched like a dog at the end of its chain.

'It's all right, Bill. Don't worry, everything will be all right,' someone said.

I turned and pulled, then felt the pain of a copper's staff in my side, winding me. I doubled over, stumbled as a blow landed on the back of my legs and was kicked in through the door by a shiny black boot.

I wasn't going to go – I couldn't afford the shilling, but they'd had a whip round for me, my mates. They were good mates – said I deserved to go. I knew how much fun these parties were: beer, food, laughs and no inhibitions. I was shaking now, trembling. Had been since the raid. Like I'd got palsy. My trousers were wet – I hadn't been able to help it – please sir, may I be excused? – not very likely. Bloody coppers. Now they'd got me. We were lined up at the desk. The chief copper with the big whiskers, the Jock, now back in uniform behind the wooden counter glowering down at me; I looked down to avoid his eyes. One by one they were asked their names, addresses and ages – the scratch-scratching in the book.

'Name!'

'You – what's your bloody name!' I got a kick on the shin from one of the coppers. I looked up.

'Bill.'

'Your Sunday name.'

'William Kilroy.'

'Address.'

'Twenty-seven High Street, Daw Green.'

'Age.'

'Twenty-nine.'

Above the chief copper, a lamp, which dimly lit the room, seemed to sway. It threw just enough light onto the wall behind. A picture of the Imperial Frog, scowling at me, smirking at me. 'Got you now you little bastard.'

'Name!'

'I object to being charged.' I knew the voice. 'My name is John Higgins. I am a constable in the West Riding Constabulary. I entered the house of Tom Brown last night at a quarter to eight and, between that time and half past twelve this morning, I saw an offence committed between Tom Brown and Richard Hemingway, and also between Waterhouse and Johnson. I also saw others indecently behaving with one another.'

Everything went black.

When I realised where I was, it all became clear to me. She had had coppers out looking for me: for the one who killed her Albert. And *he* had been sent to seek me out and catch me, to lure me in and drop the cage over me, snare me. Oh, but she was clever! The only way to get to me and she and her German spies had found it.

John

It had been creeping closer to me as the Chief Inspector went down the line; like in school before the headmaster. I was there, a policeman in a police station, on parade. I was on home ground. I stood taller as it came to my turn. Evidence. What did they have? What were they after? The stakes were high. It had to be big. What was it they wanted most? Then it had come to me. It seemed obvious: it was my way out. The only way. I had something they needed. A powerful bargaining chip. The chief inspector didn't know what to say when I spoke out. He just stood there; you could almost see the wheels of his mind turning it over.

'Inspector, take over,' the Chief Inspector had said. 'Come with me.'

I was put in an office with a constable watching over me, while the chief inspector went away. He returned shortly afterwards.

'Mr Shore has departed for the evening,' he said to the constable. He turned to me. 'You say you have evidence against Brown, Hemingway, Waterhouse and Johnson?'

'Yes, sir.'

'Of what exactly?'

'I saw them in bed, engaged in certain acts, sir.'

'Yes?'

'Of the worst kind, sir.'

'And are you prepared to testify?'

'Yes, sir.'

'Put him in a cell until morning, constable. Until I can speak to Mr Shore. It could be all nonsense.'

'It is the truth, sir.'

'Then we shall see what to do with you in the morning.'

'What are you holding me for, sir?'

'Do you wish that I charge you?'

'No, sir.'

'Then hold your tongue. It has been a long night and your impudence is trying my patience. Be a good fellow and do as you are told.'

I found myself in a cell, not unlike the ones I had placed others in. The only light coming from the corridor through a small window. It smelt of carbolic, only vaguely covering up other smells. The stone floor was damp; glazed brick walls closed me in. I made my way over to the plank bed and lowered my head onto the wooden block that served as a pillow. My head on the block! I had to think. I went over the words I would say many times before they merged into fitful dreams and restless sleep.

*

Not far away a man sat on his haunches, sobbing and shaking. Prisoner William Kilroy had been given yet another kick as he was delivered to this place. He was covered in bruises, around his wrists, on his legs, in his side where he was struck by the copper with the cudgel.

The chief copper had charged him with something or other and he had been escorted to see a man in spectacles. His hands were still bound. He had been told by the man to drop his trousers. He had refused and been struck again by the copper who guarded him. He now did as he was told. The man in spectacles told him to bend over and place his hands flat on the floor. He looked at the copper who only had to raise his cudgel. As he bent he felt cold hands part his buttocks and a finger poke at him. Then he was marched down some stone steps into a corridor and thrown into here — this hole underground. He heard voices somewhere in the dark telling him be quiet, to calm down.

*

Chief Inspector Campbell had a lot to do that Sunday. He would have to go to church in the evening if he could. He had thirteen men in custody, and evidence against only five of them. Somehow when they had entered the premises they didn't find much. Untucked shirts and unbuttoned trousers, but that's not enough to convict someone, no matter how guilty you know them to be. If the man Higgins was to be believed, what he had to say may contribute to a charge of sodomy. He awaited the report of the surgeon who had examined the prisoners. Then, the youngest of them, Pyrah, had made a statement also naming one other, Kilroy, for indecency.

He would speak to Mr Shore; see what was to be done about Higgins. How the bloody hell had a West Riding constable been in on it? Someone had been round to the County Office — it was true! He didn't believe a word of it — he was one of them — guilty as hell like the rest. He knew the sort, could tell. To think that inverts like him could be policemen too. Unless he was somehow involved in a West Riding job, but how? And, if so, why didn't the wretch speak up earlier — no, it couldn't be — it had happened on his patch not theirs.

Evidence. Evidence. The bloody law got in the way of justice sometimes with its obsession with evidence and corroboration. He needed something for the justices later — he had to get them all remanded until the Police Court on Tuesday. He had to protect people from them. He may have to settle for what Higgins had to offer as the best evidence he could get — let one go to catch the rest. Make the best of what he'd got. Unless he could get one of them to confess.

He was waiting outside Mr Shore's office when he arrived.
'Sir, do you know anything about a West Riding constable involved in this?'
'What are you talking about, Campbell.'
'One of the men arrested last night, the big chap, is a constable from the County force.'
'Well I'm…!'
Campbell explained the situation. Mr Shore looked grave.
'Leave me for a while please, chief inspector.'

I awoke when I heard hatches on metal doors being opened for breakfast. Black tea and coarse bread, but welcome nonetheless. A little more light was filtering into the cell from the so-called window – high up and barred: designed by some fiend so that no matter how you craned your neck you could never see God's sky.

My door was unlocked soon after, and I was taken to empty my bucket and then told I was wanted upstairs.

'Who are we going to see?'

'Shut up, you'll see.'

The constable knocked on a door and showed me in.

'Prisoner Higgins, sir.'

'You may stand,' said the man. 'I am Chief Constable Shore. I have no doubts as to your position, Higgins, and, let me be clear, you disgust me. However, we must retrieve what we can from this situation. We cannot have the good name of the Police sullied. What is said will remain between you, me and Captain Russell. You will give evidence on everything you saw. We will say you have been working undercover on my personal instructions. I don't know what you've been up to and I don't want to know either, but you had better learn from this and avoid such things in the future. Whether Captain Russell later seeks your resignation on some spurious grounds is a matter for him. I know I would. Get treatment for whatever sickness or evil it is. Next time you will not be so lucky. You will write me a report on what you saw and will give evidence to the magistrates at the remand hearing later on today. You also need to know that one of your colleagues, PC Harris, from Wakefield, was involved last night. And for God's sake smarten yourself. Get that report on my desk as soon as you can; then report for the Magistrates' hearing later on.'

'Yes, sir.'

'You may go.' I didn't move.

'I said you may go.'

'Sir, if I may, I have a suggestion.'

The chief constable took a deep breath and narrowed his eyes. 'Go on.'

'If you have need for corroboration, one of the prisoners, Kilroy, may be able to provide it. I didn't see him commit any offences.'

'You are in no position to make such presumptions Higgins. You are in no position to make requests. We owe you nothing. You may go.'

'Sir.'

That was the best I could do. Josiah had left before the raid took place. He might get away unscathed. The others would have to answer for themselves. I couldn't lie for Walter; I had seen too much and I would jeopardise my own position. Also Josie I could do nothing for – he had been after one thing only last night; flouncing around in a skirt, and when I had rejected his advances he had moved on to others. What I had felt for him – well, it wasn't principally his character I had felt drawn to.

Campbell was called back to Mr Shore's office.

'Right, Campbell. I have spoken to Higgins. And I have raised Captain Russell on the telephone. This is how it is. I had instructed him, just as I had PC Harris. He was working to my orders and because of the sensitive nature of his mission no one else knew about it – utmost secrecy was essential, if he was to infiltrate this gang. The good name of the Police is to be upheld, Campbell. Understood?'

'Yes, sir.'

That level of machination had not occurred to him, perhaps Shore was not quite so green as cabbage looking, after all.

He then went up to the house with the photographer and the surveyor. The beds were photographed. The sheets were peculiarly soiled. Later he received the report written by Higgins. They also brought in the man whose luck it was to have left the house early that night and slipped the net: Hinchcliffe. He had been given little option but to provide corroboration for Higgins's evidence. He now had enough to remand them all in spite of the surgeon not giving him anything at all to go on. Blast the man! Descriptions of arses he didn't want to read. But nothing of any evidential use.

Chapter Twenty-three

John

I had been made to appear briefly before the magistrates to give evidence along with the chief inspector. A few magistrates had been rounded up from their Sunday leisure to remand the prisoners in custody. It was all very cursory. They clearly regarded being dragged to their duty as an irritation, something to be disposed of as quickly as possible.

I then had to wait to see the chief constable again. Everything would be squared with my inspector, including my absence without leave that morning. I was to report back to Dewsbury Police Court on Tuesday morning. I was dismissed.

I stepped out into the fresh air of the Market Place. I took a deep breath and was taken aback by sobs coming from my own chest. I had survived. What had seemed hopeless the night before had suddenly swung around – I still had several hurdles to overcome but I wasn't heading back to the cell. I had somehow clawed my way back to being on the right side, the side without reproach. I choked down the sobs and strode across the square in search of a drink.

It was dark when I reached Liversedge. I yawned as I headed down Station Lane, turning into Barker Street as I made my last few steps home. I was exhausted; survival instinct kicked in to keep me going and now I had used up every last bit of energy. I turned the corner into Mark Street. How good it would be to be sat in my chair with a beer and a full belly. A dark shape leapt up from where it crouched by the wall. I heard a startled yelp – my own – then felt a grip round my neck tighten, a punch in my ribs, followed by another. I hooked my leg round looking for my assailant and toppled him over, landing on him. The grip was released and I struck out wildly. The man beneath me stilled. I looked down to see the man's face in what thin light was shed by a gas lamp some way off.

'You bastard,' said the man.

'Josiah?'

'How could you betray us like that. We trusted you.'

'What? No, I didn't.' I got up off the ground and put out an arm to help Josiah up.

'Get off me.' Josiah got to his feet.

'Josiah, I didn't do anything.'

'You've set us all up. And I let you in. When you told me you were a copper I should have known – told you to get stuffed.'

'No, why would I have told you in the first place if that were true. I'd have kept it secret wouldn't I?'

Josiah felt at his nose, there were dark patches on his face and hand – blood. I took out my handkerchief. 'Here let me.' I dabbed gently at Josiah's face.

'Thanks.'

'Come on, let's move away from the houses.'

I went back up the way I'd come, back up to Barker Street, to where empty spaces stood on either side of the road, where houses had not yet been built.

'I was arrested with everyone. I had to talk my way out of it. I could only do that by naming others. I'll have to give evidence.'

'Me too. They arrested me this morning.'

'What did you say?'

'What could I? I'm on oath before God. I tell the truth and condemn my friends or condemn myself for an eternity. Luckily, I chose not to see too much. Bloody hell! What are we going to do, John? I've let them down. I should've seen this coming.'

'The police had a spy watching over the house.' I saw Josiah's dark face raised to mine. 'I knew nothing about it.'

'Someone must have squealed.'

'Well, not me. It could just have well have been you. You left just before the raid didn't you?'

'I'm sorry for jumping out on you.'

'It's forgotten. Sorry for making your nose bleed.'

'So, what do we do now?'

'There's not much we can do. They're going to prison – all we can do is save ourselves, by bargaining with them – they didn't get as much from the raid as they wanted. The lad Pyrah has been leaned on and given them evidence. Whatever we say won't make it any better or worse. I tried to do what I could for Bill but – he won't speak to them – and Pyrah's named him anyway.'

'What about Walt?'

'I think he's in too deep – you saw him at the table.'

'That was just a joke.'

'But a misdemeanour in the eyes of the law that can carry up to two years. Then, everyone will have been examined for traces of… acts.'

'But what if someone speaks out against us two. Makes allegations?'

'They can't give evidence under oath: they are the accused. And they will only implicate themselves further by trying to throw dirt in cross-examination. No one would say anything against you and you've done nothing wrong in the eyes of the law, have you? And who are the jury to believe, a prisoner or a police constable?'

'I don't know what I'm going to do. What a bloody awful mess. Good-night, John.'

'Yes, good-night.'

Then he was gone, swallowed up into the darkness.

*

Annie was at the supper table with the Shaws when I pushed open the front door. She rushed out to me and put her arms around me.

'Oh, you're safe. I was so worried, John.'

'You knew that special case was going on.'

'I know, but that doesn't stop me worrying. Especially when you don't come home for the night.'

'Well, it's over now. It's over.'

'You look terrible. Come and get some supper with us.'

'No, can you bring something up for me. I've a headache and just want to sit quiet.'

Annie brought me up some shepherds' pie and a glass of stout and sat watching me as I ate in silence. Afterwards, she passed me my pipe and I immersed myself in its comfort and aroma.

'Annie, I'm going to have to tell you a little about this undercover work.'

'I've been dying to hear about it. Is it like in the *Illustrated Police News*? Did you arrest any villains?'

I looked at her and tried to suppress my contempt for her light-heartedness, for her attempt to lighten the mood. 'It's not a pleasant business, but you will probably hear about it. It's best to be prepared.'

'Are you all right though, John?'

'Yes. I was unharmed.' I puffed; the bowl of the pipe glowed and I released the smoke in a cloud. 'It involved a group of men who were behaving in a rather unpleasant manner. I don't want to speak about it, but I had to get on the inside of the gang.'

'Oh, John. Poor you. How horrid.'

'Yes, it was rather. But it's all part of the job. Unpleasant, but necessary to protect society: that sort of thing. There will be court cases and publicity. It will all be a bit embarrassing for a time, but hopefully people will be grateful for the hard work the police put in to root it out.'

'I'm sure they will, John.' She reached out for my hand. I squeezed it back. 'I think you are awfully brave.' I tried to smile at her. 'How can people behave in such a sinful way?'

'I don't know.'

There was only one topic of conversation as we assembled for parade in the morning. The raid in Dewsbury had created great excitement, especially the intrigue involving one of their own. PC Love deliberately let himself be

150

overheard when he said: 'Well, pretty boy's just the sort you'd want for a job like that – would fit right in.' I chose to ignore it. I apologised to the sergeant when I got chance for not having been able to tell him about it beforehand.

'That's understood, Higgins. Special orders from the Chief. You should be proud to serve.'

'Yes, sir?'

'Couldn't have been nice for you, though.'

'No, sir.'

'Unfortunate business.'

'Yes, sir.'

'Wonder how the Chief knew you were the man for the job though? You must have impressed somewhere along the way. Wonder why I wasn't in the loop?'

'I don't know, sir.'

Chapter Twenty-four

He thought he had spent two or three nights in the underground place from which he was never going to escape when the metal door opened.

'Get to your feet.'

He was made to stand outside. Other doors were opened. Twelve of them all together. Twelve – like the apostles. He saw Walter emerge and give a half smile. 'Chin up, Bill.' 'No talking,' one of the Queen's men said.

They were herded along a corridor and told to wait.

Indecency he had said, the whiskered Jock. He had said he was being held on suspicion of committing the offence. He was to be careful how he replied because it may be used as evidence against him. Best not speak.

There was noise of people, of talking, banging overhead. They were told to climb some steps and he emerged blinking into a room – his eyes experiencing proper light for the first time since Saturday. There was a clatter all round and a voice said, 'Clear the court of ladies and young persons. Order, please.' He looked around. The voice came from the front where nine men sat in a row, a lion and unicorn above their heads. It was like being in church, all wood and brass and high windows. Outside there was noise, like there were lots of people. He heard a noise behind, an insult. He turned and saw above his head a balcony packed with men, like this was a music hall. The whole room was full of men in beards and whiskers. And coppers. A man stood up and started speaking.

He placed his hands on the polished brass rail penning them in – like sheep at auction they were. He studied his hands.

'There is a distinction made by the prosecution between four of the prisoners: Thomas Brown, Richard Hemingway, Walter Johnson and Ernest Waterhouse. These four are charged with the most serious of offences, of a grave character, namely sodomy; the other eight are charged with gross indecency.'

Someone else said, 'I understand that the Town Clerk is only going to call sufficient evidence to justify a remand your worships.'

A man half got to his feet, but sat down again.

'I do apologise, who else do we have?'

'Mr Blakeley, sir. I appear on behalf of the prisoners Hemingway, Ripley, Longley and Johnson.'

'Mr Dwyer?'

'I appear on behalf of Arthur Senior, sir.'

'Mr Lee.'

'Your worships, I appear for the prosecution. I am sure you will appreciate that so little time has elapsed since the prisoners were arrested that I am not in a position to place the whole of the facts before you today. I am instructed to ask for a remand until next Tuesday. I shall call sufficient evidence to justify your doing this.'

There was a silence and the man in the middle at the front, a man with a big beard, nodded from side to side. He didn't speak, just nodded. He was in charge.

'If I may call the first witness. PC John Higgins.' John who he'd had – but who all along had really had him. He was not dressed like a copper – it was all part of the trick.

'I swear by Almighty God, that the evidence I shall give, shall be the truth the whole truth and nothing but the truth.'

'On Saturday last, you visited a house in Lidgate Lane, Dewsbury?'

'I did.'

'That house was occupied by?'

'Thomas Brown.'

'One of the prisoners?'

'Yes.'

'Did you see the prisoners there?'

'I did.'

'Did you see any offence committed?'

There was a pause.

'Yes, PC Higgins?'

'I saw sodomy committed between Thomas Brown and Richard Hemingway.' A hissing noise from above.

'These two?' The man was pointing.

'Yes, sir. And between Walter Johnson and Ernest Waterhouse.'

'With regard to the other prisoners?'

'I saw the other prisoners indecently abuse themselves – abuse one another.'

'After that I need not ask further questions today.'

'Mr Blakeley, Mr Dwyer, do you have any questions for the witness?'

'No, sir.'

'No, sir.'

'Do any of the prisoners wish to put any questions to the witness?'

'Yes, you. Stand forward. Your name?'

'Brown.'

'Go on.'

'I don't have anything to ask, but I would very much like to see two of my neighbours if I may: Mrs Lockwood and Mrs Perry – they will speak up for me.'

'You may not. You, no, not you man. You in the white shirt.'

'Waterhouse, sir. I want to know why he brought us here?'

The man at the front with the big beard spoke: 'You have heard the evidence.'

'He has not spoken the truth.'

'You – yes the elderly one.'

'I am Henry Crosse, sir. I wish to refute the accusation that he saw all of the prisoners abuse themselves. I did nothing wrong, I was only sitting in a chair.'

'Yes. Name?'

'Wilson.'

'Yes?'

'I want to know why I have been brought here. I was outside the door at the time of the raid – as well he knows.'

'You boy.'

'My client, sir: Pyrah. May I have a quick word with him? There was some whispering between Pyrah and a man in front, then Pyrah spoke: 'I'll wait until next week, ta.'

'What about the others? Hirst is it? Kilroy?' Mustn't speak. No. Opening his mouth letting evil in.

'Yes, Mr Lee?'

'If we could call Chief Inspector Campbell, please.'

There was some more swearing by Almighty God and the chief copper stood there like sculpted stone.

'Did you arrest the prisoners on Saturday?'

'I did, sir.'

'All of them?'

'Yes, sir.'

'Did you charge them?'

'I did, sir.'

'What with?'

'Brown, Hemingway, Johnson and Waterhouse with committing sodomy at the house of the prisoner Brown between the fourteenth and the fifteenth of August. Before doing so, I cautioned them all and Brown replied…' He consulted a book. "I did not commit it." Waterhouse said, " I had no sex with that man" and Crosse said "I did not do what you say I did."

'I then cautioned the remaining prisoners and charged them with having committed acts of gross indecency at the house of Thomas Brown between the fourteenth and the fifteenth of August.'

'Your worships, that is as far as I propose to go today. I ask that the prisoners be remanded for a week.'

'Have you anything to say as to why you should not be remanded until Tuesday?'

'Sir, may I ask that the prisoners be remanded to Wakefield. There is not accommodation for them here.' Men bobbing up and down.

'Yes, Mr Blakeley?'

'I suppose I cannot object to the application by Mr Lee, but would this be a convenient time to ask your worships to grant bail to my clients? Of course I am aware of the seriousness of the charges but so far as my clients are concerned I am able to say that they have hitherto borne irreproachable characters and there is no question of doubt that they would answer bail. If they were sent to Wakefield it would inconvenience to a considerable extent the preparation of their defences. They are all of limited means. Your worships this is a strong point which I would urge in applying for bail. Although my fees are being kept to a minimum, the additional expenses in crossing the County will severely stretch their resources. It is not an unreasonable request; I trust that your worships will see your way to granting it.'

'Yes, Mr Dwyer.'

'On behalf of the prisoner Senior sir, I would make a similar request to allow bail. There is a distinction to be made between the two charges before the court. The major charge is indeed a very grave matter, the minor one with which my client is charged is not so serious – a misdemeanour. Mr Senior does not deny being at the house that night, but it was the first time he had been there and your worships will see that he might – of course it is not for me to say what might be proved – that he might have gone there innocently and without any knowledge of what might have been going on. He has been in the employ of the Cleveland Dairy Company for five years and prior to that in the employ of Messrs William Blakeley and Co. He has a certificate of character from both of these firms and from the Reverend TM Audley. Whatever he might be now, he had, you will see, hitherto borne an irreproachable character.'

'That is the matter as it stands today. At the adjourned hearing it is quite possible that all of the men may be indicted for the more serious offence.'

'But your worships, for the present, at any rate, my client is only charged with a misdemeanour and next week it might equally be the case that he could not be committed for trial. I do not know whether the Town Clerk opposes bail but even if he does I must say I have never known a man who had been admitted to bail not surrendering to it. My client is a householder of hitherto irreproachable character. I have forborne to ask the witnesses any questions but if my instructions are correct my client is as innocent of this misdemeanour as I am. I do think you might discriminate in this matter, your worships.'

'I am bound to oppose most strongly the application. It has rightly been said that the offences were most serious, and on the night of the arrests several of the prisoners attempted to escape –'

'My client didn't.'

'– on that account and for other reasons I cannot state, I must oppose the application.'

'You won't discriminate at all?'

There was a brief silence, then murmurs came from behind. The man in charge with the beard muttered from side to side – heads shook and nodded in turn. Then for the first time he spoke. His eyes. Voice. Harsh. Mean.

'Prisoners at the bar. The bench has decided to grant the request of the Town Clerk and remand you all until this day week. We refuse bail, and remand you to Wakefield.'

Then a clatter and voices, excited voices, vicious words from overhead.

'C'mon you lot, down you go,' a copper said.

The greasy soup with its chewy gristle was at least warm. It quelled the shivers for a while. Shivering in August, underground. Where had his jacket gone? He'd had it on earlier. Someone singing a hymn to themselves: "amidst th'encircling gloom, lead Thou me on. The night is dark, and I am far from home, lead Thou me on! Keep Thou my feet; I do not ask to see the distant scene; one step enough for me." He heard his mother singing it to him, at night time; when he was loved. No point in stupid tears. He was going to Wakefield. Been to Ossett once on a delivery wagon. Further than that, no.

'Get up, tha's going on a week's holiday! Shame it's not Scarborough, but I'm sure tha'll enjoy thisen in Wakey with the muggers and rapists. Don't forget thi suitcase. Never mind, tha'll not need one.'

Back out in the corridor with the others.

'We'll take 'em up to the Railway Street entrance. It's calmed down a bit out there now – if not as much as I'd hoped. Get the van brought round.'

Led out and lined up. Handcuffed and chained in threes. Something going on outside. A bang on the door and a shout: "bring 'em out 'ere – we'll show 'em justice." The door opened and a noise started up, a commotion, like a football crowd.

'Good God, sergeant, there must be thousands of them. We'll need more men. Shut the door again.' It was the chief – the jock.

More coppers arrived.

'Right sergeant, clear a path to the van, form a cordon.'

The door opened again to another roar. Horrible noise. Bright light. Boo! Hang 'em! Rot in Hell! Oscar Wilde! Laughter. Watch 'em: could get up to owt in there! More laughter.

'In yer get quick! Two compartments, some in the front, some in the back. Dark in there. Banging on the side. Starts to move. Wheels rumble on the stones. Drowns out some of the noise outside. 'You all right Bill?'

'No talking!' the copper says.

Stopped again. More shouts and booing. Loud shouts, whistles. 'Clear the way there!' Starts again. Shapes in the dark of men hunched, leaning on each other. Purgatory. The end. Starts and stops, then moves again. More bangs on the side, more shouts.

'How far are we going in this. I can't breathe. I'm not well.' It's Henry's voice.

'Only as far as the Great Northern Railway station. No more talking.'

Door opens. A line of coppers holding back – a mob!

'Devils! Evil bastards!' Coppers link arms. Noise gets louder. Unbearable. The line breaks. 'Crosse you fat pouf! What did tha do to my boy?' Grabs at him. Henry scared.

'Get back you! Keep 'em coming. Let us do our jobs!'

'Oscar Wilde! Wakefield's too bloody good for 'em!'

'Get back! Draw your staff men! Don't use it except on my orders! Keep moving. Get back or you'll get hurt. Let us do our jobs, sir. Don't interfere! Get back I say!'

*

The station was full, like Batley station when the locomotive decked out in cerise and faun jerseys brought their Challenge Cup heroes home. Never before had there been such an interest in catching the 4.16 train to Wakefield: some dedicated travellers buying returns all the way, others single tickets to Earlsheaton, some not travellers at all: just buying tickets with no intention of boarding just so that they could enter the station. They wanted to give them a send off to remember. The train pulled away to boos, banging on the windows and streaks of gob. At Earlsheaton the scene was repeated, people waiting to see the monsters up close through the windows if possible and pass on heartfelt messages to them. At Wakefield they were greeted by a crowd not quite as large as that which sent them off. They were marched the short distance from Parliament Street to the prison, again accompanied by vociferous well-wishers, hooting until the prison gates closed behind them.

Chapter Twenty-five

John

I had avoided eye contact with anyone at the back of the court at that first hearing. I faced the bench and looked sideways on at the Town Clerk when questioned. I had to be PC 188 of the West Riding Constabulary. I had a job to do and the opinion or thoughts of John Higgins were not relevant. I had been asked to identify the prisoners I had mentioned by name but just turned my head and replied yes without really looking. I escaped without being cross-examined. No one said anything that merited a reply. I would have preferred to have been in uniform but when it came to leaving the court I was glad that I was in ordinary clothes. I nonetheless was full of fear that I would be recognised as one of those arrested, and set upon. They would not understand the subtleties of undercover work. The mob did not see me give evidence. However, I slipped out of a back entrance and melted into the crowd, no one noticing me – they were all watching the main entrance. The jeering mob of Saturday night had become thousands strong and full of bile for the prisoners – for what they believed they had done. I, PC 188, hurried home. In a week's time it would have to be done again – the prisoners were to be committed to Leeds Assizes.

I had the rest of the day off. I ate lunch at Zillah Law's dining rooms where I was served by my wife; then I bought a friendly bottle of whisky to take home, to help the afternoon pass.

On the Friday I picked up a copy of *The Reporter* and read the account of Tuesday's hearing. I warned Annie that it would be best to avoid reading it and avoid discussion of the matter with others. She said she would be advised by me, and did not give me reason thereafter to question that.

'You mustn't add to your worries with concerns for me, John. I shall be here whenever you need me. Why don't you go out for a drink with your friends and try to relax. It would do you good.' I turned away from her and looked out of the window into the distance. I might at least find some comfort from seeing Josiah.

'I might do that. Perhaps before work tomorrow night.'

Annie smiled at me and squeezed my hand.

I walked over to Batley after tea on Saturday. It was a typical August evening: full of promise of brightness that never materialised. Then, just past Healey, a dark cloud welled up and released the sort of August rain that panics people into running in an ungainly fashion for cover, where drops bounce back up off hard surfaces and rapidly form puddles. I looked around for a tree or somewhere to run to, but there was nowhere, and within a minute it was too late to bother anyway.

I arrived in the yard outside Josiah's, wet to the skin. I climbed the steps looking forward to a hot coffee and getting dry. I knocked, but there was no reply. I tried again. I turned to go down the steps. At the bottom an old man, unshaven, wearing slippers and an old overcoat peered up.

'I thought I heard someone. He's not there.'

'Never mind. I'll call another time.'

'No, I mean he's not there. Does he owe you money?'

'No. He's a friend. What do you mean?'

'He's gone. Left. Flitted. I saw a cart taking his things away the other day.'

'Did he say where he was going?'

'No, I didn't see him. Just saw his things going. Not been back all week.'

'He works in a mill near here – do you know which one?'

'Wheatcroft, I think he said, just up the road.'

'Thanks.'

I asked at the mill office. Hinchcliffe had left they said. Suddenly. Not giving them notice – most irregular. Left them in the lurch. No, he hadn't left a forwarding address – why would he?

I headed back as another shower passed over. The rain dripped off my hat and trickled down my collar.

I was excused nightshift the night before the adjourned hearing. I went through the notes I had made of my evidence – I knew what I was going to be asked – and went to bed at the same time as Annie, curling up against her warmth. I slept for the early part of the night but woke early, even before first light.

Arriving early at the Town Hall, I sat in the corridor outside, for what seemed an age, going through my evidence in my mind, trying to find the right words, before the court usher arrived to unlock the room.

This time I was in uniform. PC 188.

'Terrible business this,' said the usher. 'Were you involved in the arrests?'

'Yes, sort of.' I went to sit in the court on a bench behind the witness box for a change of scenery. Already the seats in the public gallery were starting to fill. Gradually the room came to life with anticipation: newspaper reporters with rows of sharpened pencils in breast pockets, solicitors, the Town Clerk, the Magistrates Clerk, the Chief Inspector and others. The public gallery was as full as it could possibly be with all the seats taken and several men standing. Only the dock and the bench remained empty. There was a rap on the door at the back.

'All rise!'

I counted the magistrates: none of them wanted to miss out on this. Everyone claims to be shocked but they all want to hear every detail. There weren't enough chairs and two extra had to be brought through, everyone having to step over each other and shuffle along in an attempt to assert some kind of pecking order: Aldermen getting better seats than plain old misters.

One or two women had tried to make themselves inconspicuous in the gallery and were asked to leave.

The case was then announced and there followed a lengthy wait while footsteps were heard from below and one by one the sorry looking heads appeared above the brass and wood enclosure of the dock. The charges were read out – charges of conspiracy and aiding and abetting had been added. Every page of the book being thrown at them had been weighed carefully.

Introductions were made. The Town Clerk Mr Trevelyan Lee again prosecuted on behalf of the Public Prosecutor who had undertaken the case, and Mr Blakeley had gained two more clients, two more fees, since last time, scraped together from mere subsistence. A Mr Welch now appeared on behalf of Wilson and Waterhouse. Only Pyrah and Kilroy weren't represented. Bill wouldn't have been able to afford a week's wages to pay for a solicitor.

Dwyer, the solicitor for Arthur Senior got to his feet. I had spoken to Senior at the party – he had seemed an ordinary enough man – he had not behaved as outrageously as the others – he seemed happy enough just to be there, getting drunk and watching everything that went on. Just before the raid he had gone outside with me for some fresh air and to cadge some tobacco.

'I don't know whether the witnesses are out of court. I should like them to be.'

The clerk replied, 'Do you want them all out while the opening statement is made?'

'Yes please, sir.'

'Could all witnesses please leave the court until called. You must not leave the building, however, without permission.'

I left the courtroom along with several others. Being one of the last out, there was nowhere left to sit; I found a place to stand by the window. The sun through the glass caught the back of my head. I was hot in my tunic. Added to that my nerves were making me sweat. I wished they'd hurry up. I took out my handkerchief and mopped my brow. Then I noticed a man on one of the benches looking at me. I hadn't spotted him before – it was Josiah. I hadn't spotted him because something about him made him unfamiliar. He sat hunched forward, not erect and in control like Josiah. He looked tired and his cheek bones were prominent. I caught his eye. He did not smile, but then nor did I – what was there to smile about. Josiah's eyes flashed at me, a brief look of recognition, then he looked down at his feet. I couldn't stop looking at him. I wanted to go and sit with him, reassure him, put my arm around him, find out where he had gone, what he had been up to, how he was faring.

The usher came out of the court.

'Police Constable Higgins, please.'

Josiah lifted his head and our eyes made contact one last time before I went in and climbed onto the stand. I was addressed by the Town Clerk.

'You are John Higgins, I believe. Could you state your position.'

'I am a police constable in the West Riding Constabulary, stationed at Liversedge.'

'Did you by instruction of the Borough Police come to Dewsbury on the thirtieth of July last?'

'I did.'

'Whom did you meet?'

'Josiah Hinchcliffe, one of the witnesses for the prosecution.'

'Did you subsequently meet any of the other prisoners?'

'Yes. On the third of August.'

'Who?'

'Josiah Longley, Walter Ripley and Walter Johnson.'

'Did Longley say anything to you?'

'He spoke to Hinchcliffe about a supper which was to take place on the Saturday night.'

'Saturday the seventh?'

'Yes.'

'Where was it to be held?'

'At the house of Tom Brown, Lidgate Lane.'

'Did he invite you to be present?'

'Yes. Hinchcliffe, who was with me, asked if he might bring a friend.'

'What was the answer?'

'Yes.'

The Magistrates' clerk spoke: 'Could you speak up PC Higgins? You're quite softly spoken – if you could project your voice. What was the answer?'

'Yes.'

The Town Clerk gave a small bow to the front.

'Was there any question of payment?'

'Yes.'

'What?'

'One shilling for the supper. Longley entered it in a book.'

'Did you meet Longley again?'

'Yes, on the fifth, by the Bradford Road.'

'Was there any further conversation about the supper?'

'Yes, he told me that it had been postponed until the fourteenth.'

'Was he alone?'

'There were two others with him.'

'Did you meet any of the prisoners again before the supper?'

'Yes, on the ninth I met Ripley, Johnson and Longley at the same place.'

'Those were all you saw?'

'Yes, sir.'

'Did you see any of them again?'

'Yes, on the twelfth of the month I saw Longley who was by himself. I walked with him as far as the public baths.'

'Did you give him anything?'

'Yes, eleven pence on account. I told him I had brought a shilling but I had spent a penny of it. I told him I would give him the other penny on the night.'

'Did any of the prisoners say anything that led you to understand that sodomitic practices may take place?'

'Yes.'

'Did you go to the supper?'

'Yes.'

'What time did you go?'

'Seven forty-five.'

The Magistrates' Clerk again spoke: 'What house?'

'That of Thomas Brown, Lidgate Lane.'

The Town Clerk resumed: 'Was anyone else present?'

'Yes, there were three persons present: Tom Brown, Josiah Longley and Walter Ripley.'

'Did anyone else come in?'

'Yes. Jesse Hirst, Henry Crosse, Josiah Hinchcliffe, John Edward Pyrah, William Kilroy and Arthur Senior.'

'Did they all come together?'

'No, at various times before the supper took place.'

'What sort of cottage is this?'

'A two-roomed cottage. There is the living room on the ground floor, rather below the roadway. There is a passage leading from the doorway into an entrance to the stairs and a doorway leading from that passage into the living room.'

'The stairs lead up to a bedroom?'

'Yes.'

'What sort of steps are they?'

'Stone.'

'Is there a cellar to the house?'

'Yes, there is.'

'Is there a door at the top of the stairs?'

'No, but there is one at the bottom.'

'What time did you have supper?'

'Between nine fifteen and nine thirty.'

'Did you have anything to drink at supper?'

'There was a subscription for beer.'

'Did you see anything improper during supper?'

'Yes, I did.' I looked at the brass rail around the stand. 'I saw one of the prisoners expose his person whilst stood at the table.' Whispers came from the public gallery accompanied by the sounds of shuffling.

'Was more beer sent for?'

'Yes. Brown went for it.'

'How was it paid for?'

'By subscription.'

'What took place after supper?'

'The floor was cleared. One of the tables was taken upstairs and the other things were moved to one side. Dancing then commenced.'

'Was there any music?'

'Yes, an accordion played by Pyrah.'

'What kind of dancing was it?'

'They were simply jumping about.' Someone chortled in the gallery.

'Did any of the prisoners wear anything in addition to their ordinary clothes?' The court fell silent in expectation of the answer.

'Yes, at that time Brown was wearing an apron. Female clothing was also worn by Brown who had a striped skirt. Longley also wore a skirt.'

'Did anything else happen.'

'Longley exposed his person. He wore nothing under the skirt and lifted it as he danced. Brown lifted his skirt to expose his behind.'

'Did you see anything of Crosse?'

'Yes. I took part in the dancing for a quarter of an hour. I then went and sat on the sofa and Crosse sat next to me. In a few seconds he put his arm round my waist. He then put his hand on my thigh and tried to touch me. I got up saying I needed a drink.'

'Did anyone else come in?'

'Yes, after supper Hemingway came in.'

'What became of Crosse?'

'He went upstairs, and I went and sat on the sofa again. After being there a few minutes, Hemingway came and sat on my knee.'

'What happened then?'

'Wilson also sat down and they both made lewd suggestions. They suggested all three of us should go upstairs, that they had things they wanted to show me. And another thing, several of the prisoners addressed each other using female names. Longley they called the "Young Widow."'

'Go on.'

'Several of the prisoners went up to the bedroom. I followed them up the staircase. At the top I saw Crosse in bed, Longley was there too with his skirt off. I saw Hemingway and Brown in bed together writhing about. I also saw Waterhouse and Johnson in bed together. I went downstairs and took some ipechuana wine on the way down in order to make myself sick. It didn't work so I went into the kitchen. I saw others on the sofa in compromising positions: Hirst and Senior; and Wilson and Pyrah. I then asked for some water and Crosse got me a pint pot. I put some salt in it and drank it. I then went outside and Senior came with me.'

'What did you do when you got outside?'

'I gave warning to one of the West Riding policemen who was dressed as a navvy. Then I went back into the house and soon after the police made their raid. I saw one of the men escape and run off. The others were moved into the kitchen and Chief Constable Shore said that everyone was under arrest. All the prisoners, including myself were taken to the Town Hall in handcuffs.'

'What then?'

'At the Town Hall Chief Inspector Campbell said they would all be charged but I refused to be charged. I told Chief Inspector Campbell what had taken place.'

'That's all from this witness sir.'

'Then would it be a good time to adjourn for luncheon, your worships?' There were nods down the line.

'We shall adjourn for luncheon.'

'All rise.'

I got down off the stand. What should I do? I was not hungry: I felt a little nauseous. I didn't want to go outside and face anyone there, look anyone in the eye. The courtroom emptied.

The Town Clerk spoke to the solicitors, 'Are you intending to put any of the prisoners on the stand – where the Act allows?' my ears pricked up.

'I haven't decided yet. It remains an option. Of course there's the risk of opening the door to cross-examination.'

'That is true.'

'And if I put them on the stand would you look to restrict your cross-examination to matters pertinent to the lesser offences only?'

'I may not be able to.'

'Very well. That may well decide matters. Where are you lunching? Mind if I join you?'

I was left alone. I was dazed – I had thought they couldn't give evidence – but it seemed that they could under some of the charges. The law was complicated. If they were to take to the stand what might they say under oath? I took a drink of water from one of the glasses at the front – how dry my throat was – and then sat on a bench, closed my eyes and tried to imagine being somewhere else – in a garden with white chrysanthemums and rows of leeks starting to fatten, runner beans hanging crisply in the sun; soft, brown, welcoming earth.

'All rise.'

'Do any of the solicitors engaged for the prisoners wish to cross-examine Police Constable Higgins? Mr Blakeley?'

'Your worships, after hearing the evidence it would be idle to suppose that you will not commit to trial. That being the case, I reserve my cross-examination.'

'Mr Welch?'

'Similarly, sir, I shall reserve my cross-examination.'

'Mr Dwyer?'

'I would like to ask some questions on behalf of my client as it is unlikely that he will be able to have legal assistance at another place.'

'Very well. Do any of the other prisoners have any questions for the witness?'

Pyrah raised his hand like he was in a classroom.

'Yes, Mr Pyrah?'

'What have I done wrong?'

'You have heard the charge, Mr Pyrah and the evidence. Do you have a question for the witness?' The Magistrates' Clerk was harsh and unsympathetic. Pyrah went red in the face. He looked very young, confused, like he had just been told off by a schoolmaster. He looked down and gathered himself then looked at me with doleful eyes that wove a knot in my chest.

'What did you see me do?'

I swallowed, my throat was dry as dust. I looked away from the boy; summoned up my feelings of shame and disgust.

'I saw you letting yourself be abused.'

'Where did you see that?'

'Either downstairs or up in the bedroom.'

'But I didn't let anyone do that to me. Didn't you see me trying to get away.'

'I saw what I saw. I am sure of it.'

'Mr Dwyer?'

'Was this the first time you have seen Senior at the house? I am assuming you have been before?'

'Yes. Only once inside.'

'You say inside?'

'Yes.'

'Does that mean anything?' I felt my ears go hot, a wave of nausea. People leaned forward in their seats sensing the tension; silence. Dwyer looked straight at me, intense. What should I say? 'Have you been watching it outside?'

'No, sir.'

'Very well, I won't press you.' The danger had passed, the room almost exhaled quietly with me. 'You have never in your recollection seen him before that night?'

'Not to my knowledge.'

'Now, we will come to that eventful night. Did you see him dance.'

'Yes, sir.'

'Whom with.'

'They danced with one another.'

'How many were there?'

'Thirteen in the house.'

'Do you wish us to understand that you recollect all that took place that night?'

'I recollect what I have stated.'

'I put it to you that he never moved out of the chair.'

'Oh yes, he did. He was dancing.'

'What kind of dancing?'

'I don't call it dancing. They jumped about.'

'It was a very small room to accommodate thirteen persons.'

'It was a large cottage room.'

'Can you say on oath that you saw Senior dancing?'

'Yes, sir.'

'Don't you think you could have made a mistake in saying that you saw him on the sofa?'

'I have stated my evidence.'

'Did Senior go upstairs?'

'He may have done.'

'Speak of what you know. Did you see him go upstairs?'

'No.'

'I have no further questions.'

'The witness may stand down.'

I went to sit on the end of a bench. I had to see this out. I had survived the worst, I needed to make sure that nothing else was said about me to drag me down; I would rather know than let my mind fill in the gaps.

'If I could call the next witness: Hinchcliffe, your worships.'

Josiah took the bible in his hand and spoke clearly and with conviction before kissing it.

'I am a gigger and I live at Ward's Hill in Batley.' It was his old address he had given. 'I knew Kilroy and Ripley before this night. Ripley invited me to go to Brown's house on this night. He said they were going to have a supper and he wanted to know if I would give something towards paying for it.'

'Did he say what else they were going to do that night?'

'Yes. There would be dancing and people having a good time. Kilroy took me to the house. I saw Higgins when I got there.' I looked up at the mention of my name, but no eye contact was possible.

'And what then?'

'At supper I sat between Brown and Ripley.'

'And what else happened?'

'Brown attempted to touch me inappropriately.'

'Anything else?'

'I saw indecent conduct between Longley and Hirst – they exposed themselves. Johnson also attempted to touch me inappropriately.'

'Any questions for the witness?'

'Yes, Mr Pyrah?'

'Did you see me do anything wrong?'

'No.'

There was a pause. I looked up. Josiah was looking towards the dock, his brow furrowed, like he was on the brink of tears, his eyes soft, his lips mouthed something. Then I heard Bill's voice, cracked and dry. 'What about me?' he said; pleaded.

'I did not see you do anything. Money was begged for the payment of your supper, and I contributed towards it.' Silence again fell.

'Yes, Mr Welch?'

'You are how old Mr Hinchcliffe?'

'Thirty two years old.'

'At what time did you go to the house?'

'At nine o'clock, and I left after twelve.'

'And what were you doing there yourself?'

'I went there to enjoy company.'

'And was that not what my clients Mr Wilson and Mr Waterhouse were doing also? Just enjoying company?'

'I can't object to that account of things.' There was a snigger, and the hawk-like gaze of the clerk sought out the perpetrator over the top of his spectacles.

'Mr Dwyer?'

'Did you see my client dance?'

'I wasn't paying attention to who was dancing. I didn't dance myself.'

'Could I call the next witness: Chief Inspector Campbell.'

Campbell took the oath then surveyed the scene; searching, scrutinising every face in the room. He was relaxed. He was in control. He was asked a single question: "Can you describe the events of the night of the fourteenth?" He then delivered a monologue:

'On the fifteenth I went to twenty-three, Lidgate Lane, Batley Carr, the house of Brown. I was accompanied by the Chief Constable and several members of the Borough Police Force. When I got there I found Constable Higgins outside the door in plain clothes. Prisoner Senior was standing by his side. On going to the door I found it partly open, and on entering the house I found all the prisoners there. Almost directly after we got inside there was a rush for the door, and the prisoner Hemingway and several of the others tried to escape. Wilson succeeded in making his escape but was brought to the house soon after by Constable Clachrie. Some of the prisoners were found to have their shirts unbuttoned and untucked and unbuttoned trousers. I took possession of a skirt.'

'This is the exhibit your worships.' A patterned skirt was held up. This produced merriment in the public gallery and Campbell had to wait for the court to quieten down before resuming his evidence.

'As we entered the kitchen, Johnson fainted, and later all the prisoners were removed to the Town Hall by order of the Chief Constable. On arrival at the Town Hall, I told them all I was going to charge them with various offences, and cautioned them. The witness Higgins then stepped to the front and said, "I object to being charged." He then said, "I am a constable in the West Riding Constabulary. I entered the house of Tom Brown last night at a quarter to eight o'clock, and between that time and half past twelve this morning I saw an offence committed between Tom Brown and Richard Hemingway, also between Waterhouse and Johnson. I saw all the others indecently behaving with one another." I charged Brown, Waterhouse, Hemingway and Johnson with having committed an unnatural offence at the house of the prisoner Brown between the fourteenth and fifteenth August. Brown replied, "Who did I commit it with?" Waterhouse denied familiarity with "that man," pointing to the prisoner Johnson. I then charged all the other prisoners on warrant with having committed acts of gross indecency to a male person. Crosse replied, "I have not committed the offence." The other prisoners made no reply. A few minutes after, while Pyrah was being booked, he said to me, "I want to make a statement to you sir." I said "What about?" He said, "About Johnson, Hemingway and Kilroy." I had the three prisoners brought into his presence, and he said, "That's them." He then said – '

'Your worships, I object to this statement being included in the evidence – it is not first-hand testimony.'

The clerk replied, 'I cannot exclude the statement Mr Blakeley. Do continue Chief Inspector.'

'He then said, "I was taken upstairs by them and they made me remove my trousers and proceeded to touch me before I managed to escape."

'I later accompanied Mr John Blackburn, the assistant Borough Surveyor to the house of Brown for the purpose of making a survey. The furniture was in the same position and condition as when the raid was made.'

'Thank you, Chief Inspector.'

'Any questions for the witness? Mr Welch?'

'Was my client known to you before that night?'

'No.'

'Mr Dwyer?'

'Did Mr Senior make any attempt to escape?'

'He did not.'

The next witness was PC Harris from Wakefield and an inspector who showed photographs of the beds in disarray and dirtied.

As the photographs were being passed around there was a clatter from the dock. I looked up to see Walter, insensible, being pulled back to his feet by a constable and slapped on the cheek to revive him. He was then taken down the stairs to the cells. The court was adjourned. Most people in the public gallery stayed where they were, guarding their seats. Those in the main body of the court left. I went out to look around for Josiah. He was nowhere to be found.

Walter was restored to the dock conscious but looking pale. There followed a procession of witnesses: sergeants, detectives, constables. Shopkeepers testified to supplying beer, the assistant borough surveyor, the photographer, a local snooper who painted colour onto previous factual accounts and saw "all sorts of comings and goingses," always young men, usually on Saturday nights. A young man by the name of Mitchell said he knew Longley from the mill. He had been invited to the supper but declined. Longley had said: "It's not because you haven't got the money because you have been working all week. I have got your name down in my book. There is a young man called James Wilson coming from Huddersfield: if you don't come you'll miss a treat."

The prosecution case was concluded by the Town Clerk and all defences were reserved.

'The prosecution would like to withdraw the more serious charge against Ripley: that has not been adduced in evidence. The remaining charges stand.'

'Prisoners in the dock, Brown, Hemingway, Johnson and Waterhouse, you are all charged with committing the offence of sodomy. The other prisoners with aiding and abetting in the commission of the offence. Having heard the evidence do you wish to say anything in answer to the charges? You are not obliged to say anything unless you desire to do so, but whatever you do say will be taken down in writing and may be given in evidence against you on your trial. You have nothing to hope for from any promise of favour, and nothing to fear from any threat that may have been held out or made to induce you to do so. You are entitled to a copy of the depositions upon payment of the requisite fee.'

There was silence.

The magistrates conferred and the chairman, the Mayor of the Town, committed them for trial at the next assizes in Leeds. 'The magistrates wish to express our regret that such an occurrence has happened in the town. We have listened to the very painful revelations and felt that a great stigma has been put upon the town by the actions of the prisoners.'

'Yes, Mr Blakeley?'

'Sir, may I ask for bail on behalf of my clients? At present they are innocent in the eyes of the law and it is necessary that they be offered opportunities to prepare their defence. The next assizes will not be held until November and it would be unfortunate, if any of the prisoners were found not guilty, to have been in gaol for three months for nothing. All of my clients have hitherto borne good characters.'

The other two solicitors made similar appeals.

The Town Clerk then added that the Reverend Audley objected to the production of the character reference by Senior. It was given some time ago when the prisoner was out of work.

The mayor responded: 'We do not feel disposed to take the responsibility of letting the prisoners out on bail. The charge is one of the gravest known in the land and we feel that it would be taking too great a responsibility. If the solicitors engaged disagree with that they have their remedy. That concludes our business, Mr Ridgeway?'

'Indeed, your worship. All rise.'

Chapter Twenty-six

It darkened in this underground hole. Dark and quiet. "What about me?" The words echoed round his head. They had come together and formed somewhere as he had looked into Josiah's eyes. Why could Josiah not save him? His mother needed him. Why had she sent him here? How had that copper managed to bring him down? Where had it gone wrong? Where was he going next? He had been on his own so much with these words going round and round in his head.

He had seen the others in that other place, a train-ride away, some of them in front of the cross in the mornings when they were led out of their holes. Then later as well, walking round, going round in circles: "Halt! Step off by the left. March!" He was always in the outside circle, walking fast, sometimes past a familiar face walking slower in the middle ring. Afterwards, being led back into the citadel, Walt had spoken to him quietly, "It's not for long, Bill. Keep your spirits up." "Who's talking there! It's the cat for you if we catch you, smart arse! Or a week on bread and water!" Or he would hear words hidden amongst the songs they sang before the cross.

So much time alone. So many sounds even in the dead of night. Sounds outside the walls, of feet, of a horse, the sobbing or shrieks from within, the hourly chimes of the night. Then the ugly clanging bell at six, the sounds of movement, of cells being scrubbed; then breakfast tins arriving. Breakfast tins with bread and skilly. Tins with messages scratched on. "Tell Hancock I'm after him." "Remember Skinner you owe me." " Oh for a pork pie." "Tell Martha to wait for me. Big Cass." Then the tramp, tramp, tramping begins, overhead, all round, like blood pounding round the skull. The tins come back at midday with new messages. Potato or brown suet pudding like putty that claws inside, or broth and a few flecks of meat. Everything brown or grey. Everything.

Here, in this place, it goes black. Who is it that sings? Then, eventually, from black to grey again. Another day dawning. Bread and cold tea here. No tins. No messages here.

'On thi feet. Let's get thi back to Wakey – tha's been here too long for my liking. Hold out thi arms.' The cold metal is back around his wrists. 'Get out there with thi chums.'

'How long are we going to Wakefield for?' someone says.

'Could be quite some time. The Assizes only take place a few times a year. Blakeley said it could be November didn't he?'

'Not sure I can survive that long.'

'How's tha feeling today, Walt? That's what prison food does to thi.'

'What about thi, Bill? Tha all right?'

'That's enough talking, you lot.'

'Aren't you taking us through the back to avoid people, like on the way here yesterday? Through the goods yard?'

'Terribly sorry, sir – I'll have your brougham made ready, shall I? Any other requests, sir? No? Then piss off out of here and do as tha's told, tha little shit.'

A large crowd had again gathered to watch the prisoners on to the nine forty-six, anger now replaced by less vocal contempt and by the curiosity of the freak-show: wanting to see what such men, such beasts, looked like – whether they bore their sin on their countenances.

*

John

I had survived another battle. I sought comfort where I could, sat alone in the window with my friendly bottle. I shuddered as I recalled the question: "You have been inside before? Does that mean anything?" It meant everything. It had meant everything in that other world; it had meant losing my soul, my being, in Josie's eyes, in the mystery and hard power of that body where fear and hope had mingled. I knocked back another glass, without water. I was disgusting.

I also sought comfort in Annie. I leaned on her, and wept drunken tears; she held me, she kissed away the lines on my brow, she led me to church. She was pleased to have me back; she understood: "this difficult case coming at the time of grief for a child – grief takes time – like a thorn in the flesh – it can get worse and fester until it can be drawn, but everything will be all right now, John, you'll see."

We bought cutlery and linen which was left wrapped under the bed. I suggested that we might move from Liversedge if I could get a transfer – that would give us a better chance of finding the right house at the right price. I would speak to my sergeant. One with a garden would be nice. "Oh, yes John, you really must have a garden," she had said.

I made arrests on Saturday nights following a match; like when, after a twenty to nil defeat to Huddersfield, the Liversedge supporters had drowned their sorrows only to spill out onto pavements at closing time using obscene language and jostling passers-by, unsympathetic to the depth of their sorrows, refusing to desist when told. I administered emetics to downtrodden women found next to bottles of laudanum. I made enquiries about places in industrial schools for young beggars and found a place at St Joseph's House, run by Roman Catholics, not far from where I grew up. In Flush I noticed a local "ne'er do well" loitering with, I thought, intent, and followed him to the Market Place where I watched him standing behind ladies and try to get his hand in their pockets. I had gone in hot pursuit but the felon had thrown his takings away before I caught him down past Pannett's pawn shop. The result was that the complacent magistrates gave him the benefit of the doubt.

I found it was best not to think too much, not to feel; to deny the heart and brain. I had no other course to steer, so, anything other than that was fruitless; unnecessary. All emotion was to be suppressed. It was a weakness.

In place of thought I sought to impose a structure. On passing a stationers, I stopped, seeing a picture in the window of a father sat in a chair by the fire with children at his feet and a wife stood in the background looking on. Surely scenes such as this must be real – perhaps not all those drawn curtains hid battles between men and their families, perhaps not all obscured felonious intent and misdemeanours. I took it home for Annie who was delighted with it. I wanted this place where I could live untroubled, somewhere solid, a reference point to return to, where I knew where I was, where my manhood would be reaffirmed, restored. It only required resolve, backbone.

Chapter Twenty-seven

The warm stuffy air that remand prisoner B.2.38 breathed that late summer turned colder and damper as the solid stone walls started to suck in warmth and exude moisture as if they were undergoing some metamorphosis as winter approached.

The night passes slowly when unrelieved by prolonged sleep – only it can deliver freedom to the spirit – when once again your feet can step on cool grass, or there is companionship, though the beer is never tasted or swallowed, the tobacco never soothes. The hour before dawn is the closest it ever comes to peacefulness. Then gradually the blackness in this cell, three steps wide and six short steps long is diluted. The black iron door can now be distinguished from the whitewashed walls. The shrouded shape of B.2.38 lies on what looks like a bench. There is a shelf on the wall next to the door with four books, a slate and pencil, a small greasy brush and comb still bearing the residues of several previous occupants, a wooden salt cellar, a piece of soap no bigger than a domino, and a wooden spoon: the only eating implement allowed. From two wooden pegs above the prone figure hang printed cards: the prison rules and morning and evening prayers should you find yourself short of inspiration for seeking divine intervention. The morning prayer urges the occupant, with no sense of irony, to: "Bless the Lord for my creation, preservation and all the blessings of this life; for my health, food, raiment, and all other comforts afforded to me."

Then at six o'clock the prison is rudely jerked awake by the discordant clanging bell – a special bell cast for Her Majesty's prisons with any hint of beauty of note specially removed from it by some demonic foundry process. B.2.38, like an Egyptian mummy, unwound himself: he had found a way of making one sheet and two blankets go as far as possible in providing warmth at night. He made use of the waste bucket then got dressed in the clothes that, rather than hanging up the night before, he had arranged on the plank bed to try to relieve the sores on his back from the constant pressure of lying or sitting on solid wood. Unknown to him, prisoners on remand were allowed a thin mattress, a long sack stuffed with coir, but for some reason this had been overlooked in his case. Instead he had just an off-cut of carpet to lie on like the convicts. He had been given prison clothes to wear: not the snuff coloured garments of shame, decorated with broad arrows of the hard labour men but a coarse blue serge suit, so that his own clothes would be fit to wear in court. The others still wore their own clothes; unlike him they had an occasional visit which brought clothes, small comforts and food; for them solicitors' visits meant rules not getting so easily overlooked. He rolled up his bedclothes and taking the bottom half of the bed placed it over the top half to make the table. He poured some water from the can into the small blue papier mâché bowl and used it to wash the sleep away from his eyes. He scrubbed the cell floor. He then stood twitching by the door waiting for it to be opened and to place his bucket and water can outside to be removed by one of the favoured prisoners who got to do tasks, in return for perks, rather than staying locked up. He picked up the prayer book and placed it on the Bible and hymn book. He walked the length of the room until the interlude of breakfast; then resumed his perambulation once more, now clutching the pile of three books. At eight-thirty the door was unlocked to a call of: "chapel" and he quickly fell into line outside. Two yards apart, hands by sides – he had learnt that to place your hand on the rail brought swift retribution from a warder, particularly the one with white, side whiskers and the red face, suggestive of an underlying illness. The warder who always stood stiff, like his spine was a rod, and with a voice that was loud and harsh, pale grey eyes that leered.

At chapel, B.2.12 – who used to be known as Walt – stood by him and sang.

"Rock of Ages…Don't worry Bill,
Let me…we'll get through it;
Let the… we'll meet up in the Anchor again;
From thy… just you see,
Be of sin the double cure
Save from wrath and make me pure."
At the end of the verse Bill dared to look up, Walter gave a half smile.
"Not the labour… My solicitor says,
Can fulfil… a few more weeks
Could my zeal.. to the assizes,
Could my… he says we've
All for… a good case.
Thou must save… Stay strong Bill"

The chaplain rattles off the prayer and liturgy like he's on piece rate then they march back to the cells.

At nine thirty the bell rings again. This time B.2.38 is marched out to the yard and the door is locked behind them. No mulberry bush here to go round. Not a blade of grass nor a single weed grows outside. All is brown and grey. Even the sky today. Never any birds. Even they know these few acres of earth are forsaken, the domain of the dead and dying. Three concentric circular paths trodden by so many familiar heavy feet are marked by small flags in the ground. He goes to the outer ring and awaits the "Off sharp by the left, march!" His ring moves fast almost at a half trot, always anti-clockwise, always two yards apart, to avoid the wrath of the white-buttoned warders with their beaked hats, like some sentinel birds of prey. No talking is allowed but occasional words are heard though no one's lips are ever seen to move: ventriloquism being one of the old lag's arts. The inner circle moves slowly. Henry Crosse will be there with the old, feeble and crippled. Over by the wall one man trudges painfully on his own: he is too slow and broken even for the inner ring. Round they go like some bizarre, novelty timepiece until thirty-five minutes later they stop and their vile presence is removed from the sight of heaven.

Lying down on the bed is forbidden during the day so he alternates between the small wooden stool and pacing the room. The books remain untouched. He had heard Josiah's voice and had picked up the bible; he had slowly traced the words with his finger, words that reminded him of happy times, words that now taunted him. Then there was a religious tract called "Christ the saviour of the poor" that required great effort to try to understand. It told the story of a starving, unemployed labourer who had sold or pawned everything he had to try to feed his wife and children. In despair he had decided to drown himself but on his way down to the river was drawn to a group of people entering a large building. He followed them in and there a speaker said: "When the poor and needy seek water and there is none, and their tongue faileth for thirst, I the Lord will hear them; I the God of Israel will not forsake them." The preacher pressed upon the congregation the question: "Have you put the God of Jacob to the test? The poor and desperate, the sinner, I urge you to go down on your knees and remember your own evil ways, and your doings that were not good. Loathe yourselves in your own sight for your iniquities and for your abominations. Put the god of Jacob to the test." The poor labourer didn't go down to the river, instead he went back to his miserable cellar gathered his family round and prayed. Next morning the postman brought a letter from a fellow workman informing him of a firm in want of men and enclosing one pound as a loan.

B.2.38 tried to do as it advised and went down on his knees and begged for salvation, he sobbed and his body convulsed, confessing his sinfulness. "The poor, the wretched, the blind, the naked, the burdened, the heavy-laden, the hardened sinner, the aged sinner, the daring sinner, the dying sinner, may come and obtain through Jesus Christ forgiveness and eternal salvation, everlasting life and happiness. The poorest and most stammering penitent will be heard, received and divinely blessed for Jesus has said, "him that cometh to me I will in no wise cast him out."

Afterwards he felt no comfort; he felt no different; he felt no hope.

In case he had missed something he went back to the book. He read: "I may say to the poorest of the poor – I should like to know, what happiness can those of you have who are born into poverty, live in poverty, work hard, have scanty needs, and sometimes even without the bare necessaries of life.

But the rich cannot be truly happy, we know from our own experience and from the experience of others that there is no happiness out of God! I have no doubt some of you are tempted to envy the wealth of the rich whilst you yourselves are starving in your cellars or garrets. But if you have the love of God in your hearts, and the rich have only their hundreds of thousands to look at, you are infinitely more to be envied than they are." This recalled words of Josiah's in distant happier days. The book continued: "The suffering you now endure from your privations and hard labour would be supreme happiness in comparison to the misery that you have to endure were the socialists to become the dominant power, and cause property to change hands by spoliation and robbery: one vast spoliation that would be the greatest calamity that ever fell on our country, more horrible than can be imagined. There would be millions of human beings crowded in a narrow space, deprived of all those resources which alone had made it possible for them to exist in such a narrow space. Trade gone, manufacturers gone, credit gone. They would tear themselves to pieces till famine and pestilence, following in the train of famine, came to turn that terrible commotion into a more terrible repose!"

B.2.38 spat on the book and threw it onto his shelf. He was left with a much deeper despair. He was utterly abandoned.

He was seated on the stool, elbows on the table, head in hands, when the door was unlocked to the bark of "inspection." He leapt to his feet, as he had learnt to do. Framed in the doorway was a tall, well-dressed man with a steel grey moustache, skin like tanned leather and rounded off by a hat covered in felt of the same hue. The governor, military by background, nature and outlook, over-layered by a fervent evangelism and a belief that he was doing God's work, was the beating heart of the prison; the embodiment of the institution's soul. B.2.38 saluted, as he knew he must – one of the most important rules – and tried to control his shaking and fear. Without wanting to enter into the unpleasant air the governor leaned forward, a nasal snort was as far as his Christianity would stretch by way of communication before the door closed again.

Dinner was brought at midday and the removal of the tins and their messages marked the beginning of the long stretch until tea was brought at six. The door rarely opened of an afternoon. There might be the fortnightly bath in two inches of tepid water in a bath smeared with greasy scum floated off the ones who went before. Or they might be paraded out once a week for the barber to scrape a blade of sorts across their chins. Or the door was thrown open to a shout of "attention;" in order that the chaplain, hands wringing, could enter a single step to deliver his monthly dose of spiritual consolation.

'Let me see who we have here, Kilroy isn't it?' The only time his name was used. 'Yes, on remand aren't you? Do you have long to wait for your trial?

Don't you know? Ah, that is bad. Hope you found comfort in chapel this morning. Good day to you.'

Later the door had opened. 'Out tha gets. Got a treat for thi.' It was the nasty, red-faced warden.

He fell out into line with some others.

'March.' He did as he was told. They were led down the iron stairway, past the wire netting preventing desperate men from putting an end to the monotony, and down to a large hall. Down the side was a low gallery – steps leading up to it. Up they went to where there were a number of narrow compartments each containing a small flight of steps. The others climbed up the steps, each of which he now saw was a section of a huge mill wheel that started to turn slowly.

'Go on then, off tha goes! Tha'll soon get the hang of it.'

He entered a free compartment and climbed up like the others had in order to grasp the bar running across the top wall. The steps descended and he started his march ever upwards. Soon his breathing quickened and he felt his heart pounding. He coughed and tried to not fall back off in the process. He soon got a pace going: the trick was not to work too hard – to let the wheel sink by itself, not to try and drive it down. By the end of a quarter of an hour he was told to get off and rest. He was warm. Warmer than he had been in a long time. It felt good. Some of the others, older, sicker, less fit were clearly suffering. So this was the treadmill. A punishment! It was the best he had felt since he had arrived in this place.

'Back on again!'

This continued for several hours in ten minute or quarter of an hour bursts with rests between. An old man fell and was told to stop shirking, before collapsing again in exhaustion and being led back to his cell for a doctor to see him. B.2.38 started to tire – a few months earlier and he could have kept this going, but he was not that same person: he put it down to the food. Not enough to sustain a body. By the time he was trooped back to his cell he was relieved it was over: he couldn't have done much more.

'What have you got him for? He's on remand. Look: blue uniform.' It was the deputy governor.

'Is he, sir? There's been a mistake. I'm colour blind see, sir,' the warder said.

'Make sure it doesn't happen again. Rules must be followed.' He saw the warder smirk as he turned away. But the red-faced brute's attempt to punish him hadn't worked. He had been glad to get out to do something, however futile. He devoured his tea with more enthusiasm and that night he slept better, thanks to the harsh treatment meted out to him.

Another afternoon was broken by a visit from a visiting justice who asked, "Everything all right? No complaints?" while the warder stood behind scowling, his body language making it clear how complaints would be viewed.

The peep-hole in the door was in constant use to act as a check against acts indicating a further slide into moral degeneracy and madness.

For B.2.38 it was the nights that were the worst time. Then, thoughts mixed with sounds and voices, when after a vivid dream in which he was somewhere else in someone's company, sharing desires, he'd jerk awake again to find himself in the dark alone.

Mornings arrived when the clanking bell would sound and it was still pitch black and every task had to be carried out in darkness. By the time of breakfast enough of the daylight had strained to get through to at least make out the shape of the tin. Not without good reason would the gas jets outside the cells be lit.

On one such morning after breakfast his cell was unlocked and he was told to get out. It was not time for chapel. He recognised the others with whom he fell into line, though he no longer really knew them. Their names were called out: Ripley, Hirst, Johnson, Kilroy… and there were others – strangers. They were marched in Indian file. B.2.38 was given a bundle containing his own clothes, then locked into a tiny room to change. His own clothes no longer felt like his, they no longer seemed to fit him as well as he remembered. They were then searched and the chief warder checked off all their names on a list.

A gust of wind whipped the rain into his face. Several coppers were waiting for them outside the gate. It was scary outside – noisy, busy. There were vehicles, and horses and people, some of whom stopped to watch them pass: handcuffed and chained in threes. Like they would for the passing of a hearse but with contempt replacing respect. Some of the others lifted their heads and looked around like savages seeing civilisation for the first time. They whispered words to each other, free from the prison rules. 'Armley.' 'Assizes.' 'Next week.' 'Sixteenth of December.' 'Have courage.' 'Let's hope, eh?'

Hope! They were ensnared. He would be punished, no hope for him. The copper had been sent to get him. The German queen would throw him in the Tower or cut off his head and stick it on a spike. They tried to talk to him. But what was the use?

Chapter Twenty-eight

John

As the day of the trial approached, dark figures again started to appear at the window of my cosy fireside scene, making me tetchy and short with Annie without apparent reason. I was unkind and unchivalrous, and the knowledge thereof made me feel worse. I was lucky to have her beside me. I told her it was the forthcoming Assizes that was getting to me and she seemed to understand. She had a woman's strength, I should try to draw on that. To bolster the protective shield of hearth and home I had bought a Christmas tree and stood it by the fire. It looked lovely after Annie decorated it with ribbons. She was very pleased with it.

Annie had again sought intimacy and I had convinced myself that there was a deeper connection, that it was not just something physical. Perhaps we would be blessed, and a respectable family life could be constructed. Once this was over, once winter was passed we could move out and I would be able to return to normal.

As I crossed the Market Place the low sun lit up unique vapour clouds over man and horse in the Market Place. I was on my way to Dewsbury Town Hall to meet the Town Clerk, Mr Trevelyan Lee. During these calm daylight hours, so well did I believe I had banished that person I had, in my weakness, let myself become, that I regarded that other man with what I felt amounted to disgust. I was the respectable Dr Jekyll. No, I was better than that. Stronger. I might have succumbed to the evil in myself, to sin, abandoned self-restraint. But I was in control now. It was not possible to have two identities. It would only lead to ruin, as Jekyll found out. I had come so close to utter disaster, to seeing what could come of secretly indulging my appetites.

It occurred to me that I might see Josiah. It was likely that he would be a witness again and it was in anticipation that I looked around to see if anyone else was waiting to meet the Town Clerk. There was no one. It was four months since I had last seen him – stood there in the witness box, eyes full of pity, of compassion.

I had to go through those events again with the clerk and a barrister. I was forced to re-call things I had worked hard to forget and I had to recall the version of events that justice wanted to hear. I was starting to question in my own mind which version was which.

'What other witnesses will there be, sir?'

'You don't need to concern yourself with that.'

'Of course, I just wondered how much was down to me.'

'Well, there is corroboration but the case largely swings around your evidence.'

'Corroboration?'

'Yes, from the Chief Inspector, photographs, and there's Pyrah too.'

'What about... what was he called... Hinchcliffe?'

'No, blasted man's disappeared. Confound him. Still we'll manage without. You're clear what you have to say?'

'Yes.'

'We'll see you next week then at Leeds Town Hall. Be there for nine thirty. And dress in plain clothes, something very sober. It will make you more believable.'

I looked out over the Market Place. I knew somehow I would never see Josiah again. He was somewhere else, in the company of others. Perhaps gone abroad. To Capri, to walk amongst girls winnowing corn in the warm sun. To hell with him! Good riddance. It was his fault this had happened. His fault my guard had dropped. Yes, I would be glad to never have to see him again.

But Bill I would see again. Images of being in the pool, of Bill ducking me, and of picking up his body, going limp in my arms like a child. I didn't want to see him again. I cleared my throat and strode back across the Market Place.

*

His feet were sore: the skin on his toes red and cracked; now he was on the ground floor, the cell felt even colder, even damper, and his feet never warmed up – the donated boots and socks letting in the cold more than his own ones had done, before they fell apart and he was given these.

They know in here; they all know his sin. In the yard going round and round – now in the middle ring, his feet are so sore – they look at him with cold eyes with hatred; even murderers, who may yet hang, regard him as many steps closer to hell; though he can only imagine who has committed what deed in here.

The voices start up again. In the night. Tha'll rot in hell, ha ha." Was there a shuffle of slippered feet outside? He puts his hands over his ears and tries to sleep. "Thought tha might get some sleep did tha? Tha don't deserve to sleep."

A man comes. Says he is here to help. A doctor. Croaker: that's what they call them. He wears colour: silk, pinned at the collar with gold. It is so bright, so vivid. Makes him want to touch it. It almost hurts to look at it, the only colour in the grey and brown. He asks questions about the people outside the cell, the threats. He asks where he believes he is and why. He expresses interest in the German Queen. Perhaps he knows about it too; he has a kind face. A soft voice.

Another day comes and goes and comes again. He paces up and down. Six shorts steps from door to wall and six steps back.

'Please make them go away!

'I didn't know I was doing wrong.

'I couldn't help myself.

'Please, mother.

'When will father be home?'

"Get up you foul beast. Justice awaits."

Chapter Twenty-nine

Annie

That wretched Christmas tree! I've just bumped into it again, bringing down another shower of needles all over the floor. And they're really quite sharp when you tread on one in stockinged feet. It takes up half the room. Why he couldn't have bought a smaller one I'll never know; but that's my John for you. Not thinking things through and every now and then a surge of exuberance breaks through and the result is excess. I did my best to decorate it and try to appear appreciative. I have to be very considerate towards him right now, helping him through his difficulties. This court case is really troubling him and I'm not surprised. He was asked to do a job that no one should ever have to do – a worse thing than most policeman will ever come across in their whole careers.

But he's such a good man, such a willing volunteer – that's probably why they chose him in the first place – and I suspect they thought that natural trustworthiness he seems to display to the world would make it easier for him to infiltrate the gang. I am not supposed to know anything about what happened really. He tried to protect me and told me not to read the papers, but of course I had to. Not only are they left lying around at Zillah Law's but I also had to, in order that I could understand what he felt and help him through it. It is not good for him, all the whisky he is drinking. I have to do my duty as a wife and stop him just resorting to the bottle. But I can understand his desire to forget. All those horrible things he must have seen. At times I think it was wrong of the police to make John do that, but then someone has to try to stop such things from happening, and why should it be someone else and not John.

What I don't understand is why they had to leave me worrying so. I had all of that Sunday worrying about him, from when I awoke in an empty bed until supper time. Not a word from anyone. I thought he was dead. Even at the police office they didn't know where he was. Typical of the police not to think of how it might affect the wives – so tied up with the crime before them that they don't think any wider. I suppose events moved fast and they were all busy. I have never been so relieved in my life when he walked through the door.

Hopefully, John's heroism will reflect well on him and he will become a sergeant before long.

He is like a child at times, he comes in drunk and sits at my feet and weeps into my lap. It is good that he can let it out with me. I do not mind it even when he gets cross; I want to take my share of his pain. I am doing what I can for him and providing what physical comfort I can, to reassure him of what is normal. It is almost as if this episode has made him fall deeper in love with me – to trust me more than ever. For that I praise God; his ways are indeed mysterious.

He is already talking of getting our own house in the New Year, possibly even moving to another neighbourhood. I think that will be very good for us. And, oh! if he could have a garden again, that would do him so much good. His desire to build a home is really strong now. It fills me with great hope.

Chapter Thirty

The courtroom in Leeds Town Hall is like a theatre where stories are told by a cast of characters you get to know over the period of the telling: some in long wigs and scarlet, some in black with short wigs, either well kept or moth-eaten, others in their Sunday best, and others stood in rags: the recipients of justice, sometimes proud and defiant, sometimes shame-faced with heads hanging down. Heads! Heads that may soon hang in other ways, eh? A theatre! An amphitheatre! Where duals are fought for people's lives, where good and evil clash. Where those who may think of challenge or assault upon the respectable order of things must be shown how the law acts as a deterrent, and so that the law-abiding in their comfortable homes can read every Friday of how their taxes are used for their protection and thus draw satisfaction knowing how those learned gentlemen deal harshly with the vilest in society. And what a place of entertainment! To come and sit and while away a few idle hours listening to these stories and having the comfort of knowing you are somewhat above the proceedings unfolding before you.

And here is an interesting one: anticipated for some time. A scandal of the first order in Batley Carr. Rightly so, that ladies should be spared such detail – as it is hoped will be given. The room is full and awaiting the arrival of the monsters ascending from the hell that must be the cells below. Several of them have barristers to defend them. Four of them do not, it appears – probably couldn't afford to pay a guinea for a dock brief. His lordship, Mr Justice Phillimore, presides, resplendent in his robes. Up they come, two of them, looking around, as well they might, surprising how ordinary they look – just two ordinary lads. Not what you'd expect. You would have hoped you could spot them just by the way they looked.

Mr Mellor opens the prosecution case against them: Johnson and Waterhouse: 'Gentlemen of the jury and others present. I regret that it is unavoidable that some detail of a rather revolting nature has to be entered into and for this I apologise, but it is necessary that we do our duty. The offences the prisoners are charged with are the gravest and most serious known in the English law.

'For some time before the commission of the alleged offences, a certain house on Lidgate Lane in Batley Carr had been watched by the police. On the fourteenth of August last, the authorities learnt that a supper party was to be held there. As the jury would easily understand, to secure a conviction in a case of this kind was an extremely difficult task. Therefore it was considered advisable by the authorities to throw the accused off their guard by some sort of ruse. A police constable named Higgins, of the West Riding Constabulary, stationed at Liversedge, undertook the disagreeable duty of investigating the matter. He made the acquaintance of some of the frequenters of the house before the supper on the fourteenth of August, and towards eight o'clock visited the house in private clothes. Fortunately the company appeared to be unaware that they were entertaining an officer of the law. After the policeman had obtained what he thought to be sufficient evidence of the offences charged, he feigned sickness and managed by that means to leave the house, and give the alarm to a large force of police outside. The latter entered the house and the two prisoners, along with others, who were charged in connection with the same affair, were taken into custody and handcuffed.'

The layout of the house is then described in considerable detail and how the raid was carried out.

'I am afraid I have to detail the evidence required to prove the case. The law says that to prove a case of sodomy there has to be evidence of penetration and of emission of seed – it is of course difficult to secure evidence to prove the actual commission of the offence: it is for this reason I would ask the jury to regard the case as an attempt to commit the offence although the grave offence is open to you as a verdict should you believe the evidence supports that.'

A photographer and a surveyor are called and their various photographs and plans are then passed round the front of the court. It would be interesting to see those photographs; it is suggested that they are of evidential value in that they show the state of the beds!

Then Police Constable Higgins is placed on the stand. Just the sort of chap you'd want out on the street at night, while you sleep soundly in your bed, safe in the knowledge that fine fellows like him are there to keep a sharp look-out for ne'er do wells. He is in plain clothes: a somewhat dated-looking grey suit and a winged collar shirt. He relates what he saw at the house, his voice calm and his tone measured, despite the things he saw. He occasionally clears his throat but never once turns his head from where the judge sits.

'And you were then apprehended along with the rest of the prisoners?'

'Yes, sir.'

'And at Dewsbury Police Station you proclaimed yourself a policeman, and in the presence of the Chief Constable of Dewsbury made charges against the two prisoners, Waterhouse and Johnson?'

'Yes, sir.'

'And they offered no reply to that accusation?'

'They did not.'

One of the prisoners sobs in the dock – such an unseemly lack of self-control, but at least it shows some sense of contrition, of penitence for his hideous crime.

The defending barristers then have their turn. They ask him to trace his movements. He admits to having only gone upstairs once and then very briefly as far as the top of the stairs, but he does not doubt what he saw.

Then there followed the Chief Inspector, another fine figure – just the man to have in charge – takes the job seriously, would let nothing stand in his way in suppressing villainy. So good a chap, in fact, that neither defence barrister dare cross-examine him.

A young lad, Pyrah, one of the prisoners, is placed on the witness stand next, but the prosecutor asks him no questions. The defence barrister then shoots himself in the foot. Never ask a question you don't know the answer to they say:

'Is it not true that you were downstairs and didn't see the offence that it is alleged that Waterhouse and Johnson committed?'

'No, sir, I did go upstairs. I saw them together, sir.'

More sobs from the dock.

The prosecutor, Mellor, then addresses the jury.

'Gentlemen, the key question is whether you can rely on the testimony of the officer, Higgins. If the answer to that is "yes," then his evidence is as good as that of twenty witnesses. And, if I may venture to do so, I think that never has a constable been in so unpleasant a position, or had a more disagreeable duty to perform, and never was a story told with greater propriety or contradicted in so small a degree by my learned friends for the defence. I would urge you, in conclusion, that whilst it is open for you to find the prisoners guilty of the charge of sodomy, the attempt to commit the offence had been amply proved.'

The first defence barrister rises to his feet, almost wearily. 'Gentlemen jurors, I am quite aware that in cases of a horrible nature such as this, it is almost impossible for any human being to escape having a strong feeling of repulsion and disgust towards anyone so charged. I know it is extremely difficult for anyone to dispassionately consider the question – which in other cases is more easy to do – as to whether or not the particular offence with which the prisoners are charged has been proved. I would however appeal to you to consider the case dispassionately and to proceed to review the evidence for the prosecution. There is an element of a doubt whether the officer Higgins actually had had an opportunity of seeing what he alleged he had seen.'

The second defence barrister takes his turn on the stage.

'On behalf of Mr Waterhouse, I would contend that the evidence you have heard only proves that gross indecency has taken place between the prisoners. There is not sufficient evidence to justify you as a jury in convicting on the most serious charge or of attempting to commit it. I would ask you for the sake of common humanity not to convict if you can see your way to avoid doing so.'

His Lordship addresses the jury.

'Before I sum up, may I remark that learned counsel have done their duty in this very disagreeable case and it now remains for the jury to do theirs. In coming to your decision on the question of whether the most serious offence was committed, or whether there was an attempt to do so, I must again point out that there is no medical evidence to support those elements of the actual commission of the act. I will now review the evidence for you…'

Excitement builds and all around everyone had their own verdict. A hush falls when the jury return theirs: guilty of the attempt.

'Thank you gentlemen. Sentencing shall be deferred.' They are led away.

After lunch there is a repeat performance for Brown and Hemingway. Somehow even more revolting, given that there must be an age gap of some thirty years, but no, that implies that physical appearance has some link to the character of the offence!

Brown, it turns out, is deaf and so the witnesses have to stand by the dock so that he can hear. Hemingway's barrister, Mr Compston, offers to defend Brown pro bono. Jolly decent of him. This time the police constable doesn't look so self-assured. It seems that he doesn't like to stand so close to the dock, but who can blame him for that?

He is cross-examined.

'Police Constable Higgins. You say that you made the accusation against my clients in the presence of Mr Shore, the Chief Constable, whereas, if I am not mistaken, when you made your statement at Dewsbury Borough Court you said that you made this statement to Chief Inspector Campbell. If you were mistaken on this point, could you not be mistaken on other points of accuracy? When it comes to identification for example?'

'They might both have been there.'

'Might they? You also said you feigned sickness in order to leave the house, is that correct?'

'Yes.'

'But at the Borough Court you said you made yourself physically sick by drinking something. Again perhaps your recollection is not always clear?'

'I took some salt water, but also had to feign illness.'

'How long have you been in the police force?'

'About two years.'

'And what was it you did before?'

'I was in the employ of a solicitor.'

This barrister is sharp as a razor. His closing remarks are pure theatre. He paused for effect, he chose and weighted his words with precision. He played to his audience. He would have to go into some unpleasant details.

'There is a clear and distinct difference between this case and the last one of such a character that it is necessary for me to go into matters which I would rather not enter into. But I will not shirk my duties, nor, I am sure will you gentlemen on the jury shirk from yours. There is a perverse practice that is an act of gross indecency referred to by medical men as "coitus intra crura" which is an act which suffice it to say stops short of actual penetration: no more than that took place.'

Some jurors nod as if they can conceive of what is meant by that.

'The method of detecting this alleged offence was one which Englishmen do not like, never had liked and never will like. That a man should purposely set to play the traitor in order to detect crime was the last resort of all to which the police of this country should apply themselves. There are other methods of detecting crime, however grave and hidden, but it is not for me to suggest them. In this case, an officer had been sent by his superiors to live a lie week after week, in order to worm his way into the confidence of those on whom he was going to "round." I put it to the jury that this officer with only eighteen months experience as a policeman and possibly with rosy views of promotion, which would follow upon his display of intelligence and cuteness, would see a good deal of what he desired to see.'

Despite that, the jury finds these two guilty of "attempting," as well. They thank Mr Compston for waiving his fee to defend Brown.

More drama when all of the remaining prisoners, except for someone called Kilroy are brought up to the dock, up the stairs from below – more ordinary looking men, anxious and shame-faced. All the prisoners are then charged with conspiracy to commit the offence of sodomy and of feloniously aiding and abetting in the commission of acts of gross indecency. But before they get to enter their pleas there follows a confusing discussion in legalese which even us regulars in the gallery struggle with. The men in wigs argue over indictments and admissibility and amendments and count this and that, and the twelfth section of Fourteen Victoria, and that is most people's cue to head to the pub: no proper business will get done today, not now the judge had his mind on his beef and his claret.

The next day they resume where they must have left off, whilst the prisoners take their time to digest their breakfasts in the luxurious accommodation down below. Mr Mellor interrupts by suggesting they could expedite one of the cases promptly. The prisoner Pyrah is brought to the dock. He looks up. Your mother's not here, kid. No women allowed. He is formally charged with aiding and abetting the offence. He pleads not guilty. But then as the theatre behoves, there is a surprise. Prosecution counsel rose: 'Considering his youth, and circumstances which transpired in the course of yesterday's evidence, we call no evidence against the defendant your honour.'

The jury are therefore directed to return a "not guilty verdict," which they duly do, and Pyrah walks free, evidently confused as to what has just happened. Just keep running and don't look back in case they change their minds, kid.

Indictments were amended, counts were quashed, others which had been quashed perhaps shouldn't have been. Where they were bad for "uncertainty" – in not specifying the names of those that acts were committed with – some names were added; others were made to read "with persons unknown." There was more bickering between wigs, and names of various Justices invoked, before his Lordship lost patience and put his foot down: he would state a case if applied for. The kids stopped their bickering.

It then became clear why the prisoner Kilroy had not been charged. The surgeon at Armley prison was being called to give evidence. An adjournment for early lunch was called to allow him to attend.

At twenty-to-one the prisoner Kilroy appears in the court room. Only the back of his head is seen. He sits slumped and when ordered to stand hangs his head and doesn't move.

'Gentlemen of the jury, your task is now to decide whether the prisoner Kilroy is fit to stand trial, whether he is sufficiently sound of mind to plead. Mr Bartley Moynihan please.' The gentleman entered the court. The prisoner doesn't move.

'You are Mr Moynihan, the prison surgeon at Armley?'

'Yes.'

'Has the prisoner been under your care during the last few days?'

'Yes, he was remitted from Wakefield prison.'

'Have you examined him with a view to forming a judgment whether he is in a fit state to understand the charge?'

'I have.'

'In your opinion is he in a fit state to appreciate and understand the charge prepared against him?'

'He is insane undoubtedly.'

The judge spoke: 'Is he fit to give instructions for his defence?'

'No, my lord.'

The prosecution resumed: 'Is the insanity temporary and likely to pass away?'

'Yes in time, I think. At present he is subject to delusions and hallucinations and imagines people are speaking to him from outside his cell and he does not recognise the voices. He is also decidedly melancholy.'

'Is he capable of appreciating right and wrong?'

'I would say he is quite capable of appreciating the difference, yes. He is, however, in a state one would have no difficulty in certifying as insane.'

The judge looks down on the prisoner: 'Mr Kilroy, have you heard what has been said about you?'

The dark head, with long tangled hair rose slowly to see where the voice was coming from.

'Yes,' replies the cracked voice.

'Do you understand it?'

'No, sir.'

'You do not understand what has been said?'

'No, sir.'

'Gentlemen jurors, you have heard the medical evidence which has been put before you to guide your consideration of the prisoner's state of mind. This has showed that he is sensible enough to do some things and not others, that he is able to tell the difference between right and wrong, yet incapable of giving instructions for his defence. If you think that the prisoner is to that extent insane, you must say so.'

The jury conferred and the spokesman said that the jury found him to be insane and unfit to plead.

'Mr Kilroy, you have been found unfit to plead and therefore no case can be brought against you. You shall be detained during Her Majesty's pleasure.'

A noise came from the dock, an animal noise, something between a whelp and a growl; then he was led away.

The main act for the afternoon then commences. Ten prisoners were brought up and the trial against them resumed on the remaining charges of committing acts of gross indecency under the Criminal Law Amendment Act. This time they enter "not guilty" pleas.

The ten are then reduced to six as no evidence is brought against the ones found guilty yesterday and they are acquitted and led back down – for now at least. Only Longley is not represented, but when asked he says he would like to be tried alongside the others.

Police constable Higgins is called again. There are whispers around the public gallery as we wait for him to enter. Then the poor devil is made to go through his ordeal all over again, and then every detail is raked over yet again in cross-examination. Was he really where he said he was? Could he not have been mistaken in what he says he saw? A lesser man may have got muddled and started gibbering but not our fine Bobby; though at one point he does wobble:

'And you stated yesterday that you were a solicitor's clerk prior to joining the West Riding Constabulary?'

'No, sir.'

'I beg your pardon?'

'No, sir, not as a clerk.'

'What then was your employment before you became a policeman?'

'I was employed by a solicitor, sir, but –'

'In what capacity were you employed by a solicitor?'

'As a head gardener.' The ponderous music hall policemen, bending at the knees, with the yokel accent, suddenly came to the front of the stage and there is laughter all around the court, glad at the opportunity of a little light relief. Higgins looks temporarily irritated and his cheeks redden.

The Chief Inspector then stands imperiously on the witness stand and gives another virtuoso performance.

Mr Waddy then takes the opportunity to place his client, Senior, in the box. Senior denies everything. He is a married man, upstanding, if we are to believe him, a milk salesman for four years. He had gone to the house at eight o' clock and drunk a good deal of beer. That was in fact all he had done, sat and drunk beer.

The prosecutor got to his feet: the risk they take putting him up.

'Mr Senior, this was not your first time at this house on Lidgate Lane?' The way he delivers the second "this" says so much – no ordinary house "this," a notorious house, a den of iniquity, of moral corruption, vileness, of sin, "this."

'No, I had been there once before, and that was to arrange about the supper.'

'Indeed.' Again such weight in a word.

'I never went upstairs, I never saw anything indecent. I was drinking beer.'

'How *well* did you know the other prisoners?'

'I was only slightly acquainted with them.'

'I believe a man named Stephen Mitchell alleges that you once importuned him in the streets of Dewsbury and that you committed an indecent assault on him.'

'That is a lie.'

His barrister then tries to claw things back: 'Gentlemen jurors, you have heard only the scantiest of evidence against Mr Senior, who just happened to find himself in the wrong place at the wrong time, having gone round for a drink with slight acquaintances, totally unawares of the situation. You will undoubtedly have the greatest difficulty in keeping your minds un-prejudiced by everything you have read in the newspapers or anything you have heard. He is a man of previous good character. Whilst at the house he sat and had a few drinks, a few too many perhaps, but that is his only sin. He did not see anything untoward; then was outside when the police arrived. Police constable Higgins was overcome, as surely he must have been, by the revolting spectacle he had witnessed in the chamber of the house. It is not, therefore, unlikely that he was able to know or describe accurately what he saw in the living room. Of all the prisoners only Mr Senior has dared to go into the witness box to deny the offence. Do you think he would have done so if he was a guilty man?' He sat down.

One of the prisoners, an old man, then spoke.

'Your worship, may I say something in my defence?'

'Crosse, you have been represented by Counsel. But go on, let us hear what you have to say.' Total silence fell. What would the old Marjorie say?

'I do not believe I have been properly represented. Where is he now?' It was true, the barrister had left the court some time before. 'I have just been a lodger at Tom Brown's house – I never took part in this thing. I had nothing to do with anyone who came to the house. I don't see how I have come to be accused of anything. Twelve years ago I had an operation for haemorrhage of the lungs, I was a painter, see, and have been a weakly man ever since. I was in fact bleeding from the lungs at the time of the raid. I had gone upstairs to lie down to get away from the noise of the dancing. I have been under the doctor at Wakefield prison. All of these facts ought to have been made by my barrister.'

Longley was asked if he wished to say anything to the jury; he shook his head.

'On behalf of Mr Wilson, I would like to ask the jurors to find that what happened that night was nothing more than an orgy of drunkenness. The police constable went to the house to see something and what he actually saw was a rough crew of men – ' (a stifled snigger is emitted from somewhere in the gallery) '– excited by beer, enjoying themselves in their rough way, which he, with his previous experience of a gentleman's servant, did not appreciate, and which he had, later, a wrong and extreme view of. That was the whole story; nothing more.'

Mr Justice Phillimore sums up the case: 'If you believe the evidence of Police Constable Higgins, then you will not have much doubt as to the acts of which they are accused under statute, being of a grossly indecent character, but if you think that the constable had in some particular case, or in all the cases put an unfavourable construction upon the matter, that will form an element in your deliberations when you decide your verdict.'

He then goes over the evidence against each prisoner. On mention of his name, the old man Crosse cries out: 'I have not committed the offence.'

'Crosse, you must be silent now. You have had two opportunities, one by Counsel. I will hear you again presently.'

He says the evidence against Ripley and Senior is not so strong.

At a quarter to four the jury retire and the courtroom again reaches its own verdict in their absence, and wagers are laid. No one risks losing their seat: it remains full except for the jury benches. Half an hour passes and they file in to a hushed court. It is as expected by some: Ripley and Senior "not guilty," the rest "guilty." Money surreptitiously changes hands.

Just four left standing in the dock. Then they are joined by the other four guilty men.

Now the Chief Constable appears and is sworn in. He says that he believes Brown and Crosse to be the two principals of the school. 'I have received several complaints as to Crosse's conduct with boys in the street and elsewhere. We have been watching Brown's house for two years on and off.' The Chief Constable is dignified and self-assured. He is the law of England personified. He is thanked by the judge. The first person the judge has shown any deference toward.

His honour says, 'Does anyone wish to make a statement before I deliver sentence?'

The old man speaks again. He doesn't know when to hold his tongue, when to admit defeat: 'I would appeal to you for mercy your worship. My health is poor. I am an honest man – as honest as nearly everyone I meet.'

A barrister stands: 'Only to remind your lordship that the prisoners have already served four months in prison.'

'Before I deliver sentence, could Police Constable Higgins be recalled please.'

The Bobby enters and stands looking round to see who is still here. He looks a little shaken now.

'Police Constable Higgins, I just wanted to say that I think your conduct has been most admirable throughout the whole of these difficult and delicate proceedings, and your evidence was extremely well and fairly given and I hope these remarks will be brought to the notice of your superiors.

'Thank you, my lord.'

No one would be surprised to see him get to be sergeant soon on the back of that.

'Brown, you are the eldest of the prisoners and I regard you as the worst, being the keeper of the house and the institutor of this filthy orgy – you will be sentenced to six years penal servitude.

'Hemingway, you are a younger man, much younger, fortunately for you, and taking that into account, I sentence you to three years penal servitude.

'Johnson, not only were you one of the actors in this horrible thing along with Waterhouse, but you also attempted to corrupt the boy Pyrah. You are sentenced to four years penal servitude.

'Waterhouse, you will serve the same as Hemingway: three years penal servitude.' He is led from the dock emitting a load groan.

'The remainder of the prisoners are only convicted of acts of indecency, the maximum punishment for which is two years hard labour.

'Hirst, I do not know that you did much harm, the sentence will be eight months.'

'Thank you, sir.'

'Crosse, I consider you to be the next worst to Brown. You will be imprisoned for twenty months and the prison surgeon will see that you do not do more work than you are fit for.

'Longley, you are very young, but you had a great deal to do with organising this disgusting business so I must give you twelve months.

'Wilson, you are older than Hirst and I must give you nine months hard labour.'

They are removed from sight. Everyone feels satisfied that an example has been set, that the conclusion was satisfactory and that it furnished enough material for several pints worth of analysis and numerous pipes' worth of supposition.

Chapter Thirty-one

John

I walked back to the railway station alone. I was exhausted and my head ached. Two days I had spent in this place – waiting, worrying, being questioned and cross-questioned. Always on my guard, trying to watch out for traps, for pitfalls. Even when I thought my ordeal was over, I had been recalled by the judge. I thought some discovery had been made, that perhaps I had been exposed. But it was over with. That was the end. Thank God that England had no court of appeal.

I would move on now, and yet there was still so much going round in my head. Things I needed affirming or denying by someone; someone who would tell me I had done the right thing, someone to understand. I had been called a traitor in there. Was I? That I had been sent to live a lie week after week.

I had not wanted to live a lie: that was the point, but what else could I have done? And where was Bill? Had he been acquitted? – it looked like Pyrah had been, and, as I waited outside, I saw Walter walking free. Omitting certain things from my evidence that no one questioned me on, and that no one else had mentioned, had worked in Walter's favour. I would have done the same for Bill if I had had the chance.

I had not managed to avoid looking at them in the dock. And the day before I had had to stand so close to Brown and Hemingway that I could smell the prison on them.

If I could just talk to someone and explain.

It was dark and cold outside the train, just a few lights of houses and mills somewhere up past Morley.

I alighted at Dewsbury. I couldn't go back home yet, not until I had cleared my head. I bought some fried fish and then looked for a public house. I found myself near the baths and wandered down Wheelwright Street past the corner where I had first met them with Josiah. Where had he gone? – perhaps he would meet up with Walter and Bill. Bill must have been acquitted too – otherwise he would have been there in the dock. I was not far from the Anchor – perhaps they would meet up there. I could explain; admit my mistakes; then we could all move on.

It was all so familiar but at the same time different, like I had been away to sea and returned to find things the same and yet not: faces changed, objects displaced, colours faded. I ordered a pint and sat in the corner by myself. I was quickly on my feet ordering another. Then I went round to the Crow

Nest. I bought another pint. No one there either. Another pint. I was alone; no one was coming. I was just a fool.

I went down Webster's Hill and found myself by the river where I stood on the bridge. The water was dark and chill beneath, just the odd reflection on its surface to reveal its depth and flow. The judge had said my conduct had been admirable. Some day the others would end their sentence. I knew I never would. I pulled my coat tighter round me.

How many had stood here and thought that they had come to the end, thought it time to sleep, to rest, devoid of love. Had I ever loved? Was it denied me? What was it I had felt for Josiah? For Bill? For Edward? For Annie? It was always tinged with guilt, with shame. And poor sweet Annie! I was not good enough for her, that much was clear. But perhaps I could still make her happy, if I tried. Perhaps, if I tried, I could find in her, steady ground?

Epilogue

Bill Kilroy's life is steady. He has routine. He eats reasonably well and gets fresh air when he needs it, outside in the garden or at the airing court when the weather is poor. He plays bowls with the others in the summer and takes part in football matches in the winter. He has one or two people who he calls his friends, people who he is happy to sit with and share a smoke. Others he avoids; though generally people are kind to him. He is placid and well-mannered and is one of the ones that can be trusted. He puts his skills as a cook to great use; he is a valuable person to have in the kitchen and he enjoys it too: enjoys being useful and being appreciated for his hard work. He still gets upset sometimes but that usually passes without the need for a dose of bromide from the surgeon. He usually sleeps through the night these days and no longer disturbs the others in adjacent beds by waking up and shouting in the middle of the night. In fact, on the whole, after those first few years, his troubles have eased – since sometime around the time of the Coronation party in the summer of 1902 that was held here at Stanley Royd. That party, with bunting and cakes for everyone, that Bill helped make, and the dancing in the evening for the residents, was almost something of a release for him. His delusions are now mild and he has largely lost his distrust of the attendants these days. It seems unlikely that he will ever be able to go home – partly because there is nowhere for him to call home. He has no family that he talks of or who have ever been in touch. He is not capable of surviving outside these grounds; and besides he is too useful.

He is in the kitchen now, rolling out dough for scones for everyone's tea.
An attendant calls him over; he smiles at him.
'Bill, put that down for now, someone else will take over.'
'Why's that?'
'There's someone to see you. A visitor. Says he's an old friend.'

Dear reader

If you enjoyed reading *Boy in Blue*, I would really appreciate it if you'd write a review on Amazon or Goodreads or whichever online sites you use: just a line or two would be great. Word of mouth is so important when you've not got a marketing department and financial backing behind you. Thanks!

More information is at: 1889books.co.uk/boy-in-blue

Acknowledgements

Those closest to me for tolerating this madness that is writing a novel. Jodi for her incisive comments into an earlier draft. West Yorkshire Archive Service, Kirklees – libraries are so valuable to communities and should be cherished. The staff at Dewsbury Town Hall for showing me round the court room and former police cells. All the good folks on *YouWriteOn.com* who gave me feedback and encouragement on my first chapters. The car park attendant at St Vincents who gave me a tour of the tragically derelict interior. The lovely folks at the National Emergency Services Museum in Sheffield for digging out the period police cape for the cover photo and letting me see contempoary police notebooks.